THE GUILD CODEX: UNVEILED / THREE

THE TWICE-SCORNED LADY OF SHADOW

ANNETTE MARIE

dark owl
fantasy

The Twice-Scorned Lady of Shadow
The Guild Codex: Unveiled / Book Three

Copyright © 2022 by Annette Marie
www.annettemarie.ca

Dark Owl Fantasy Inc.
PO Box 88106, Rabbit Hill Post Office
Edmonton, AB, Canada T6R 0M5
www.darkowlfantasy.com

Cover Copyright © 2021 by Annette Marie

Editing by Elizabeth Darkley
arrowheadediting.wordpress.com

ISBN 978-1-988153-66-7

BOOKS IN THE GUILD CODEX

UNVEILED

The One and Only Crystal Druid
The Long-Forgotten Winter King
The Twice-Scorned Lady of Shadow
The Unbreakable Bladesong Druid

SPELLBOUND

Three Mages and a Margarita
Dark Arts and a Daiquiri
Two Witches and a Whiskey
Demon Magic and a Martini
The Alchemist and an Amaretto
Druid Vices and a Vodka
Lost Talismans and a Tequila
Damned Souls and a Sangria

DEMONIZED

Taming Demons for Beginners
Slaying Monsters for the Feeble
Hunting Fiends for the Ill-Equipped
Delivering Evil for Experts

WARPED
with Rob Jacobsen

Warping Minds & Other Misdemeanors
Hellbound Guilds & Other Misdirections
Rogue Ghosts & Other Miscreants

MORE BOOKS BY ANNETTE MARIE

STEEL & STONE UNIVERSE

Steel & Stone Series

Chase the Dark
Bind the Soul
Yield the Night
Reap the Shadows
Unleash the Storm
Steel & Stone

Spell Weaver Trilogy

The Night Realm
The Shadow Weave
The Blood Curse

OTHER WORKS

Red Winter Trilogy

Red Winter
Dark Tempest
Immortal Fire

THE GUILD CODEX

CLASSES OF MAGIC

Spiritalis
Psychica
Arcana
Demonica
Elementaria

MYTHIC

A person with magical ability

MPD / MAGIPOL

The organization that regulates mythics and their activities

ROGUE

A mythic living in violation of MPD laws

THE TWICE-SCORNED
LADY OF SHADOW

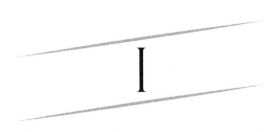

I

♠ ZAK ♠
TEN YEARS AGO

"IT'S IMPOSSIBLE, *isn't it?"*

Sitting against the brick wall beside me, the girl clenched her hands into fists. The dim light from a streetlamp barely reached us in the dark alley, and her face was half in shadow, but I could still see the worried crease between her eyebrows.

"She's gonna sell me to Bane," she continued, sounding hopeless. I didn't like it. I preferred it when she sounded brazen or sarcastic, or when she sometimes got that soft, sort of breathy note in her voice. "And he's going to … what?"

"Feed you to a fae, probably," I guessed.

She didn't flinch. Instead, she studied me as though puzzling something out. I liked her eyes. Her blue-gray irises were so pale it was like I could see through them, but at the same time, they had this intensity that made it hard to hold her gaze. Her eyes suited her much better than her blond hair.

Faint sounds of conversation leaked from the building behind us. Inside, the girl's aunt was probably cashing in. I'd overheard enough from Bane and the other regulars to know that Ruth sold expensive, rare poisons. Bane had complained more than once about her prices, even for raw ingredients.

Poisoning her wouldn't be easy, but it seemed like the best option. And death by poison for an alchemist was nicely ironic.

"What if ..." I hesitated, then threw out the question. "What if I could get you a poison with no antidote?"

The girl wrinkled her nose. "Where would you get that?"

Fear spiked in my chest at the plan I was proposing. "It's one Bane doses himself with for his mithridatic training. I could steal it."

Hope brightened the girl's eyes. "Really?"

Could I steal from Bane? Accessing his poisons wasn't a problem. Getting away with it was the issue.

Bane had trained me in everything I needed to become an evil bastard as unstoppable as he was. He'd hired the best dark-arts sorcery and alchemy tutors money could buy, and the rest he'd taught me himself: druidry skills, different forms of combat with and without weapons and magic, fae customs and culture, negotiation, manipulation, deception, and a hundred ways to kill.

I'd mastered everything he'd taught, but I was still no match for him. He had me beat in every druidry skill, and he knew almost as much about poisons as a master alchemist. Plus, he had a pack of vicious familiars at his beck and call. But the way he somehow knew what I was thinking or planning—that was what really scared me. He was always twenty steps ahead of me. I never caught him off guard. I never got away with anything.

I glanced at the girl. All that training, but I was completely out of my depth having a conversation with a girl my age. Not that this counted as a normal conversation. Either way, it was fucked up.

"What will happen to you if your aunt dies?" I asked.

She twitched her shoulders dismissively. "My parents are dead, and if I have other relatives, I don't know them."

So she was as alone as I was.

"Bane might try to take you anyway," I warned her, "depending on how bad he wants you."

Why he wanted her, I wasn't sure. Grenior had told me she had faint spiritual energy, meaning she was probably a witch. It wouldn't be the first time Bane had bartered a live witch to a dark fae as part of a deal, but I didn't understand why he was so determined to get his hands on her. There had to be easier, cheaper options.

"So we have to kill them both."

My attention snapped back to her.

She met my eyes, her gaze sharp. "Especially if you're going to steal from him."

We were back to that: killing Bane and whether I could do it. I let out a slow breath. Killing Ruth was barely a challenge—unless I was badly underestimating the alchemist. Bane, on the other hand …

Stealing from him scared me. The thought of trying to kill him stirred panic in my chest.

As though reading my mind, she asked, "What's the biggest thing stopping you from killing him?"

My nerves twanged with paranoia. "His fae. They're always there. Always watching my every move. He knows I'd murder him in a heartbeat, so he always has one shadowing me."

She stiffened. "Even right now?"

"Not now. My familiars are keeping his away, but that won't work if he's nearby. He'd notice right away."

I almost reached telepathically for Grenior but stopped myself. If Bane's vargs had been close enough to hear our conversation, Grenior would have warned me.

The girl's gaze drifted across the dark, damp alley. She tugged absently at the collar of her jacket. "If you could get past his fae without them noticing you, could you kill him?"

"Yeah," I replied, even though "maybe" was a more realistic answer. "But it's impossible to sneak past those fae."

She pulled at her collar again. "Actually, you can. With the right magic."

"What magic?"

"I have a … an artifact." Her intense blue-gray eyes locked on mine. "It hides the person wearing it from fae senses. I could lend it to you."

"Something like that exists?" Impossible. If it did, I'd have discovered it already. I'd been searching for ways to escape from or kill Bane for years. I hesitated, then asked, "You'd let me use it?"

"Borrow it," she corrected me, emphasizing the word. "It was a gift from my parents. It's the only thing of theirs I have left."

"Borrow," I repeated hastily, my mind racing ahead, already planning. "For one night. Just long enough to …" Doubts cut through my exhilarated strategizing. "Are you sure that's how it works? It will hide me from any fae?"

"My parents said it doesn't matter what kind of fae or how powerful. As long as I'm wearing it, no fae will notice me."

"That's … that's unbelievable." Was it too good to be true? I dragged my hand absently through my hair, knocking my hood back. "I could test it with my familiars, figure out exactly how it works …"

I trailed off, thinking it through. I'd have to confirm the artifact worked as she said, and if I combined it with other potions and spells … but what if that wasn't enough? Bane was always prepared, and he expected me to try to kill him. The training he'd put me through—the grueling, never-ending hours of physical drilling, book studies, psychological conditioning, mental games, and underhanded tests—he'd done it all to turn me into a copy of him.

And when the "copy" was complete and I surpassed him in power, I would kill him. That was the deal.

Until then, I was at his mercy in every way. He already punished me for my failures, big or small. If killing him was my ultimate "test," then the punishment would be worse than anything he'd ever done to me before.

But if I didn't try, I'd have to keep going as his apprentice until I was strong enough to be one hundred percent certain I wouldn't fail. I'd have to let him train me and test me and twist me until I was just like him. He was recreating himself in me, and if I stayed, I might become him.

I'd rather try, fail, and die than turn into Bane.

I forced my gaze back to hers. "If the spell does what you say it does, I can do it."

"You can kill him?"

I nodded, even though I felt nowhere near confident. "He relies on his fae to watch me. I can slip away using your artifact, and while they're searching for me, I can kill him."

"And I can kill my aunt with your poison." A grin flashed over her face, but the expression quickly faded. She glanced away, ducking her head. "And after they're dead, we could …"

I waited a moment. "We could what?"

"We could … band together?" She abruptly straightened, forcing a nonchalant expression, even though she was still blushing. "Better than going at it alone, right? I mean … if you want to."

"Like … long-term?" I asked uncertainly.

She tried to meet my eyes, couldn't hold them, and looked away.

Band together with this girl? She was tough enough to endure her aunt's abuse and brave enough to plan a double murder, but she wasn't like me. I doubted she had any useful survival skills.

"I …" *My shoulders flexed. I'd have to protect her, but was that so bad? Like she'd said, it was better than being alone. And I'd been alone for a long time.* "I like that idea."

"You do?"

Doubts flickered, then quieted. "Yeah."

The flush in her cheeks deepened, and she abruptly grabbed my wrist. "How's the cut?"

Her voice had gone high with embarrassment, and she hid her face as she examined the scar between my ring and middle fingers where she'd cut me.

She grimaced with obvious guilt. "Sorry."

Her remorse was so over-the-top it was funny. You'd think she'd gutted me, not nicked me with a tiny knife, and I couldn't hold back a short chuckle. "A memento, I guess."

"You don't need a memento of me." *She arched an eyebrow.* "We're going to stick together, right?"

"Right."

"We are … aren't we?"

It sounded like she really wanted this. She wanted to be with me—and I liked that. "Yeah. Together."

Her cheeks flushed again and she gripped my hand tightly. "Then I guess we should, you know, introduce ourselves. My name is—"

"Wait." *I pressed my fingertips to her lips as a strange, nervous anticipation spread through my chest.* "Not yet."

"Then … when?"

Her lips were so soft under my fingers.

"After they're dead," *I whispered.* "A reward."

Bane controlled my entire life, and as long as he lived, I had no future. I wanted the moment I learned her name, the moment she became a real part of my life, to be the same moment that my future began.

My fingertips slid across her silky lips. "I need something to look forward to."

Understanding softened her expression. My touch drifted from the corner of her mouth to her cheek, and she tilted her face toward mine in invitation.

I leaned down. Our lips touched. Soft. Warm. Inviting. With my hand cupping her cheek, I fitted our mouths together. Her breath hitched. For a second, she didn't respond, then she copied me, each press of soft skin sending a thrill through me.

Everything outside of this moment vanished from my head, and I kissed her harder, my fingers digging into her cheek. A small, startled noise escaped her.

Zak.

Grenior's deep growl cut through my head, and I pulled back. The girl's blue-gray eyes rose to mine—heated and dazed and questioning. Her tongue ran across her lower lip.

"I have to go," I said reluctantly.

She glanced toward the building, where the rumble of conversation had gone quiet, then nodded.

I slid my hand from her cheek. My fingers had left pink imprints on her fair skin, and I felt a flicker of guilt. I should've been gentler.

"Next time." I pushed to my feet and pulled up my hood. "I'll bring the poison."

At the reminder of our plan, the flush in her cheeks drained away. But she didn't look scared as she nodded and promised, "I'll have my artifact."

I hesitated, unsure what to say. We'd never bothered with goodbyes before, so I turned and walked away. I could feel her watching me.

Grenior's silent voice beckoned me into the next alley. The huge black wolf appeared at the end, a distant silhouette, then slunk out of sight. Gravel crunched under a heavy boot, and I turned.

Bane strode into the alley I'd just entered. The distant streetlamps gleamed off his shaved head, a contrast to his thick black beard. His dark, deep-set eyes cut dismissively across me, cruel and confident, and his leather coat swept out with his long steps. The closer he came, the smaller his powerful bulk made me feel.

As he passed me, I fell into step behind him. I wasn't worthy to walk beside him, and he never let me forget it.

"Nu i kak vse proshlo?" I asked. He preferred his mother tongue, and when my master preferred something, I had no choice but to prefer it too.

"It went well," he answered in Russian. His deep growl of a voice held a mocking note as he patted the front of his coat where he probably had something small, expensive, and deadly hidden in an inner pocket. "And if you're lucky, Zaharia, you'll never learn what these do."

I didn't react to the veiled threat. I hadn't expected him to reveal what he'd bought, but if he thought I was interested in his purchases—and how I might use them against him—then he wouldn't be looking for signs of my real plan.

He knew I would kill him someday, but he didn't think I was ready yet.

I didn't think I was ready either.

But I couldn't wait any longer.

2

"WELCOME to the Crow and Hammer, Miss Orien."

The man on the other side of the desk extended his hand to me, and I reluctantly stretched mine out. He grasped my hand with strong, warm fingers.

"Darius King," he introduced himself in a deep, pleasant voice. "It's a pleasure to meet you."

He was a handsome man in his early fifties with salt-and-pepper hair, a short beard, and a charming, roguish air—and he was triggering all kinds of warning bells. My instincts whispered that he was dangerous, and they were usually right.

My gaze flicked sideways, leaving the older man for only a second to glance at the younger man in the office with us.

Agent Kit Morris was smiling, but there was a slight difference in his body language compared to when we'd first walked into the guild. He wasn't tense or nervous, but he was more alert. Attentive. Focused on the man shaking my hand.

I pulled my fingers free, my cold stare boring into the man's clear gray eyes.

"Saber," Morris whispered. "Stop glaring at your new guild master."

I didn't reply. I didn't stop glaring either. Better not to show weakness in front of the man about to take control of my life.

Darius sank into his chair. "Have a seat, Miss Orien, Agent Morris."

I lowered myself onto the edge of a cushioned chair. Under my jacket, I felt a small tug as Ríkr, in the form of a ferret, adjusted his grip on my shirt.

Morris took the seat beside me. "Saber is a bit prickly," he said as though I wasn't two feet away and listening to every word, "but she's like a lovable cactus. She'll only stab you if you try to hug her."

Darius steepled his fingers together, his wrists resting on his desk. "Prickly is nothing new at this guild. How much do you know about the Crow and Hammer, Miss Orien?"

"The name," I said baldly. "There's a pub downstairs. And this is a shit part of town."

"Loveable cactus," Morris stage-whispered to Darius as though trying to convince him.

Darius's lips twitched in a faint smile. "This location suits our membership quite well. Agent Morris thinks it will suit you, too."

"Because I'm an ex-con?"

"Because you're unimpressed by authority."

How observant of him. I bared my teeth in a smile. "I don't like playing by other people's rules. They always fuck me over."

Morris sighed heavily.

Darius studied me, and I glared back, waiting for his reaction. Waiting to see what kind of guild master he was—and what my next move would be. Would he lash out in anger? Put me in my place? Intimidate me into submissiveness?

"I understand your aversion to rules," he finally said, "but you'll need to follow several to be a member of my guild. Given the potentially deadly magic of a druid, my priority is the safety of my guildeds."

"You think I might hurt other members?"

Again, he assessed me. "The first rule of the Crow and Hammer is 'don't hit first, but always hit back.'"

My eyebrows rose. "Let me guess. That rule won't apply to me."

"It applies to everyone, including you. There is no situation in which a person is not entitled to defend themselves. However, as one of the more powerful mythics in the guild, you have a responsibility to consider the appropriate level of force to use against others."

My fingers slipped into my pocket and curled around my switchblade. I wasn't used to being counted among the powerful. Wasn't I a weak witch with nothing but a switchblade for protection?

"Our third officer, Felix Adams, will supervise your rehabilitation. To start, you'll have twice-weekly meetings with him here at the guild, and monthly meetings with the three of us. You'll also be required to attend the guild's regular monthly meeting."

Twice weekly? I hadn't had to meet with my parole supervisor that frequently since my first two years out of prison.

"Agent Morris indicated that you want to continue living at your current residence near Coquitlam?" Darius asked.

"It's an animal rescue nonprofit," Morris offered. "Saber volunteers almost all her spare time to running the rescue."

"I don't run it," I corrected. "I just help out."

"I have no issues with you continuing to live there on the condition that you attend all your meetings with Felix," Darius said. "As per MPD requirements, however, your residence will be subject to short-notice inspections by your rehabilitation supervisor."

"How short notice?" I asked.

"An hour."

Morris crossed his ankles. "Plenty of time to hide a body."

I shot him a disbelieving look, then refocused on Darius. "Anything else?"

Darius leaned back, his gray stare probing. "Felix will be your rehabilitation supervisor, but every guilded here is also assigned a mentor—an officer they can go to with questions and concerns. Their mentor is also responsible for their mentee's guild responsibilities, training, and discipline."

I bristled at "discipline."

"To keep your guild membership as separate from your rehabilitation as possible, Felix won't double as your mentor. Instead—"

A rap on the office door interrupted him.

"Come in," Darius called.

The door swung open and a man breezed in—tall, athletic, tousled copper-red hair, and a generous sprinkling of freckles across his fair skin. A smile flashed over his face as his blue eyes landed on me.

"Is this the newbie?" He swung around my chair and perched on the edge of the desk in front of me. "Not what I was expecting."

My hackles rose.

"Miss Orien," Darius said, "this is Aaron Sinclair, our fourth officer. He will be your mentor at the Crow and Hammer. He'll help you settle in at the guild."

Aaron grinned again. "On a scale of one to badass, how strong of a druid are you?"

I pressed my lips together—and before I could think of a response, a ripple of shivery-cold power pulsed against my side where Ríkr was hiding. Frigid cold plunged over the room and thick frost formed on every surface, encasing us in bright white. The three men stiffened as the subarctic air sparkled.

Ríkr, I silently admonished.

I will expound on all the ways this charade of justice is an insult when we have the leisure, he replied. *Unless you give me leave to freeze them solid this moment?*

Aaron's shocked exhalation puffed white, his eyes wide. "Whoa."

Morris turned to me and his eyes were even wider, but not with shock. "Saber, there's a kryomage I really need you to crush with fae ice magic. It's my dying wish. Please."

"You're dying?" Aaron asked.

"I'll die of happiness when she turns Agent Park into teeny, little Vincent crystals."

Darius cleared his throat, and when I turned, my instincts flared, that sense of danger returning in a flash.

"Miss Orien, the Crow and Hammer is a guild of second chances. You aren't the first ex-convict to join, and among us you'll find reformed rogues, delinquents, troublemakers, trouble magnets, and more. Many members are rough around the edges." He sat forward in his seat, his attention fixed on me like the unyielding press of a blade. "You won't be the only one who's defensive, aggressive, anti-authority, or provocative."

I met his stare.

"There are mythics here who share similar backgrounds to you. How you respond to them will determine whether they become companions and confidants, or adversaries."

I opened my mouth to retort that how *they* reacted to me would determine that, but I hesitated. Was this more of that "reacting with appropriate force" thing he'd mentioned?

Darius leaned back. "Aaron, why don't you give Miss Orien a quick tour? That will be enough for this evening. We can give her a proper introduction on meeting night."

"Sure." Aaron pushed off the desk. "Come on, Saber."

I rose to my feet, and when my eye level came within inches of my new mentor's, he blinked in surprise, caught off guard by how tall I was. The frost on his shirt had already melted, and a faint hiss of steam emanated from his t-shirt.

With a final glance at Darius, I walked out.

OUTSIDE DARIUS'S OFFICE was a larger room packed with five desks in varying states of disarray. Aaron fell into step with me as we headed for the door at the far end of the room. I could feel his gaze, and when I looked over, I found curious blue eyes scanning me.

"Just so you know," he said, "everyone in the guild loves to talk, meaning they all know we're getting a druid."

My lips thinned. What was I, a collector's card?

"But no one outside of guild leadership knows you're here for rehab," he added.

I stopped. He took another step, then swiveled to face me.

"Are you going to tell them about my criminal record?" I demanded. "Do *you* know what I did?"

"You killed your abusive aunt a decade ago." He arched his eyebrows. "But you're not murdering people these days, right?"

My mind flashed over the past two weeks. "No."

He squinted at me. "Did you just hesitate?"

"No."

"Pretty sure you did."

"Are you giving me a tour or not?"

He pushed the door open, revealing a short hall. "Anyway, it's up to you what you want to share about your past."

That little reveal churned in my head as Aaron led me down a flight of stairs to the second level. He was talking, telling me about the shared workspace that took up most of the floor, but I couldn't focus.

Most mythics here didn't know I was a killer. After my experience at my old coven, I knew there was no way any normal guild would accept a murderer, even if I played nice for years. I'd been prepared to use my reputation and the threat of violence to intimidate my new guildmates into leaving me alone—but without my ex-con status to sabotage me, did I have a chance at being accepted here? If I played "nice Saber," could I fit in?

I was still chewing on the questions as Aaron led me down another flight of stairs. A wash of conversations rolled over me as we entered the pub on the main floor. Dark beams and wood-paneled walls gave it an intimate atmosphere undercut by a general air of shabbiness. I didn't mind it.

But I did mind the way dozens of eyes turned my way, watching my every move with interest. Even more people had shown up since I'd arrived with Morris thirty minutes ago.

Aaron either didn't notice or didn't care that everyone was watching us. He guided me to the long bar that spanned the back of the pub and pulled out a stool.

"Have a seat," he said. "Order a drink. I'll be right back."

I slid onto the stool, aware of the gazes tracking my every move. Adrenaline dumped into my veins. There were over twenty mythics in here, and I didn't like having them behind me. At least there was no bartender in sight, so I didn't have to bother refusing a drink. As if I'd dull my wits right now.

Conversations picked up again, and among the jumble of voices, I caught the word "druid" several times. Clearly, I'd been identified as the new guild member.

With the prick of claws, Ríkr wriggled out of the front of my jacket and hopped onto the bar. Heaving a ferrety sigh, he shook his long, white-furred body, then sat on his haunches and peered around. Everyone was now staring at the ferret instead of my back, but I didn't feel any less tense.

"Is that her familiar?" someone asked, their voice carrying a bit too clearly.

"I thought she was a druid."

"Shouldn't she have *powerful* familiars?"

Ríkr's whiskers twitched. *What is your assessment, dove? Shall I unleash a wintry nightmare upon this guild?*

I propped my elbows on the bar top, tuning out the conversations behind me. *Tempting, but no.*

His immediate disappointment was obvious.

You've shown off enough, I added. *Why the display of power? That's not your usual style.*

He was an ambush predator at heart, always showing his weakest face until the last possible moment.

He fluffed his fur in irritation. *They treat you as a petitioner groveling for leniency, but it is they who should curry mercy with you.*

"It's *your* mercy they need," I corrected in a low murmur. "Not mine."

You are my consort now. In matters of humankind, I am your weapon to wield.

A faint smile curved my lips. Mere hours ago, Ríkr and I had completed the simple but powerful magical ceremony to make me his consort, binding us together for life—well, my life. He was immortal.

Does that mean when it comes to fae, I'm your weapon? I asked.

He smiled, showing his tiny, razor-sharp teeth. *Precisely, dove.*

I drummed my fingers on the bar top, then turned sharply. As my glare swept across the two dozen mythics in the pub, half of them looked away, pretending they hadn't been watching me. The other half continued to stare, unabashed or openly challenging.

Turning back to Ríkr, I drummed my fingers more forcefully. Since these people didn't know about my past, it made sense for me to play "nice Saber." If I acted warm, cheerful, and kind of dumb, they'd lose interest in me. I'd fade into the background, conflicts avoided before they could begin. Even the rarity factor of being a druid would wear off if I was bland enough.

My fingernails clacked rapidly on the wood. *I don't want to be nice to these people.*

Of course not, Ríkr replied. *Why would you?*

"She's pretty hot," a male voice remarked from among the assorted mythics. "Cameron, you should ask her out."

"You think?"

"She's got legs for miles, man. You've gotta—"

I turned around again. I couldn't tell which cluster of men had been discussing my assets, so I slashed my glower across all of them. Fewer people looked away this time. The air of challenge was stronger.

As terse readiness gripped my chest, I realized why I couldn't make myself play nice. By embracing my druid power, I'd given up "nice Saber." She'd been born of insecurity, of the belief that no one would accept who I really was. I'd been afraid to be at odds with the entire world. To be an outcast. To be completely, utterly alone.

But now?

I looked down at Ríkr, and my lips lifted in a faint smile. Before he could react, I patted his furry head affectionately.

His whiskers twitched in confusion. *Dove?*

Thank you, I told him. Before, I'd always been cautious about saying those words to him, but I was his consort now. The ties between us ran far deeper than debts.

I pushed off my stool and swung around. Every pair of eyes snapped to me as I faced the pub.

"If you all keep staring at me, I'll start carving eyeballs out."

Silence weighed down on the room in the wake of my flat, icy declaration.

Then another voice rang out, loud with derision. "You and what knife?"

I didn't see who had spoken, but it didn't matter. My hand drifted toward the pocket where my switchblade was nestled. But the switchblade was a weapon for taking on humans, not mythics.

So I lifted my other hand. The rune on my wrist flared cold, and with a flash of blue light, a four-foot-long ice spear formed in my hand, the crystalline point aimed at the mythics.

"With this."

This time, their silence was from surprise, all eyes locked on the gleaming spear. I stared them down for a moment more, then swung the spear. Everyone flinched as it struck my stool and exploded into a starburst of ice.

Ríkr sprang onto my shoulder. As his weight settled next to my jacket collar, I strode past the jagged ice formation, heading for the door. I was done with this. With them. With all this bullshit. I'd show up for my rehab meetings. I'd attend the monthly guild meeting. But that was it.

Morris had said this place could be a home for me, but I didn't want a home. I had one already.

As I swept toward the door, my skin prickled in warning. My gaze snapped to my left. There, standing almost out of sight on the staircase, one shoulder propped against the wall and arms crossed, was my mentor, Aaron Sinclair.

Had he been waiting there this whole time? Had he left me alone at the bar on purpose, testing my reaction the same way I'd tested Darius in our meeting?

My upper lip curled, and I shoved through the door into the cool night air.

I didn't need a home here. The rescue was my home, and these people and their judgments could burn in hell for all I cared.

3

THE MUSTY ODOR of manure permeated the morning air as I stood at the rust-spotted metal fence. A nonstop chorus of whinnies, grunts, and stamping hooves was occasionally pierced by high-pitched neighs. Distress and despair hung over the endless maze of pens like a miasma. I was choking on it, sick with it, my human and druid senses overwhelmed.

Three horses milled anxiously at the back of the small pen in front of me, and with a quick glance to ensure no one was paying attention, I climbed over the barrier.

The horses pricked their ears toward me, white showing around their eyes. Cooing softly, I approached to within a few feet, then offered a welcoming hand and waited. The nearest, a bay mare, stretched her neck out. I leaned in and blew softly toward her face. Her nostrils worked, and she huffed back at me, stepping closer for a better greeting. I blew on her nose again, a horsey hello, then stroked her bony neck.

A brief examination showed she was malnourished and in desperate need of a hoof trim, but otherwise in decent shape—terrible shape compared to a healthy horse, but decent when measured against many of the horses up for auction.

Rub marks on her belly from a cinch strap revealed she'd been ridden—but how recently? I laid one arm over her back, then the other, watching her head and ears for signs of trouble. She slanted an ear toward me, far calmer than when I'd entered the pen. I shoved up, putting weight on her. She didn't react. I jumped up again, laying across her back for a moment before sliding to the ground.

The second horse, a piebald, was in similar condition but more nervous. When I put weight on his back, he shuffled away but didn't lash out. Good enough.

When I approached the third horse, however, he pinned his ears warningly. I hummed, exuding calmness. Two minutes wasn't much, but it was all I could give him before attempting to approach. He showed me his teeth, ready to bite, and I backed away with my heart sinking.

I was just climbing back over the fence when Dominique reached the pen, a clipboard in hand and a deep furrow between her brows.

"How are they?" she asked, flipping a page.

"The bay and the piebald are good-natured and should be ridable. I don't see any major health concerns." The sinking feeling in my chest deepened. "Not the buckskin."

Her eyes tightened unhappily as she glanced at the third horse before making notes on her clipboard. I exhaled slowly, hating this. Hating that I'd just sentenced that buckskin to death.

He was scared. Maybe he was in pain. He might be the sweetest horse in the world with extra attention. But Hearts & Hooves Animal Rescue relied entirely on donations and fundraising to rescue horses, and our budget for this auction was small. We had to choose animals with good odds of being adopted by a caring new owner.

When the auction began, the best horses would be bought and sold by ranchers, breeders, and enthusiasts. Those animals didn't need any help. But as the auction wore on, the horses would get older, thinner, wilder. The buyer pool would shrink. Most people would leave. They'd be long gone by the time the last of the horses were chased into the show pen and herded around, frightened, limping, bony, and weak.

By then, there were only two kinds of buyers left: charities like Hearts & Hooves, desperate to save lives with their limited funds, and the meat buyers, loaded with cash, their semi-trucks parked in the lot and waiting to be stuffed with animals headed for the slaughterhouse.

Dominique pushed her red-framed glasses up her nose, a sheen of sweat on her skin. "We have thirty-seven candidates, then."

Thirty-seven horses that were in too rough of shape to be bought by a reputable owner but still had a chance of being rescued and rehabilitated—if we bought them instead of the meat buyers.

"How many can we afford?" I asked.

"Depending on how much those soulless bastards drive up the prices …" She bit her lower lip. "Six."

My hands clenched. I hated this. Hated it, hated it, hated it.

"Thank you for coming, Saber," Dominique whispered. "I know it's hard."

I forced my limbs to relax. "I'm glad I can help."

Greta and I took turns. Neither of us could handle back-to-back auctions. I had no idea how Dominique could bear it. Yes, we saved a few equine lives every time, but for every horse we saved, we had to watch a dozen more disappear onto the meat trucks.

Usually, Ríkr came with me, but I'd asked him to stay home this time. Now that I knew he had the power to level this whole operation, bringing him along would've presented too much temptation.

Side by side, Dominique and I headed toward the auction building. I looked at every horse we passed, doing them the courtesy of acknowledging their existence, their precious lives that so many considered worthless.

"Colby is moving to Ontario," Dominique said abruptly.

My head swung toward her. "When?"

"Mid-August. He got accepted at the University of Toronto."

Colby was a frequent volunteer at the rescue. Though he wasn't the most knowledgeable about farm animals, he always worked hard at whatever we assigned him. We had other volunteers, but their hours were sporadic.

"Good for him," I mumbled.

She nodded, forcing a smile. "We'll need someone to make up for his hours."

Easier said than done. Most volunteers showed up all excited to cuddle baby goats and groom horses, only to discover that the jobs we needed help with weren't fun. Mucking stalls and scrubbing floors weren't glamourous and rewarding.

"I was wondering..." Dominique hesitated, peeking sideways at me. "... if Zak might be interested in volunteering?"

Hearing his name out of the blue felt like a punch to the solar plexus—I'd been doing such a good job not thinking about him—but the surprise quickly passed, a frown replacing it. "How do you know his name?"

"Oh." She smiled uncertainly. "Didn't he mention it?"

"Mention what?"

"That day when he was waiting for you to get off work for your hiking date—"

Our *hiking date*? Did she mean when we'd trekked into the mountains to slay the heart-stealing Dullahan before it killed again?

Dominique was still talking. "—introduced himself and asked if he could help with anything. It took me about thirty seconds to realize he knew his way around horses. He's a hard worker."

I almost rubbed my hand over my face, remembering at the last second that my palms were covered in dust. "Why didn't you tell me this sooner?"

"I didn't realize you didn't know. I figured he would have told you about it."

"Did he tell you we're dating?"

"No." She touched my arm. "I'm sorry. I shouldn't have assumed anything."

I understood why she'd made that assumption. She'd stumbled upon me and Zak making out like we were seconds from tearing each other's clothes off, followed by him staying the night, volunteering at the ranch all day, then meeting me for a "hiking date."

She sighed. "But that's really a shame, because he's the hottest stud I've ever seen on my ranch."

I rolled my eyes. "His personality doesn't match."

"Really? He wasn't talkative, but he was excellent with the horses. Gentle and patient."

Having seen him interact with our horses a few times, I couldn't disagree.

Since realizing three days ago that Zak had disappeared without a word, my initial reaction had been a furious desire to track him down and give him a piece of my mind. But with no clue where he'd gone and no way to contact him, I couldn't even try to find him.

Which really, *really* pissed me off.

Since then, I'd been trying hard not to think of him—and I'd been doing a pretty good job until Dominique had brought him up.

I refocused as we neared the auction building. Ahead, two stocky men in stained shirts were laughing together, and my fingers curled, aching to shove my switchblade between their ribs. Meat buyers, the heartless scum.

If killing them would've changed anything, I'd have done it. If leveling the auction building could've saved the horses, I'd have asked Ríkr to turn this whole place into an ice Armageddon. But it wouldn't fix anything. There were a dozen livestock auctions within driving distance. The horses would simply be moved to another one and sold off the same way. Even if I could somehow take every single horse back to the rescue, we didn't have the space, manpower, or money to care for them.

I breathed through a sharp-edged surge of impotence. I might have more power now, but not enough to change the things I really cared about. Although, I might figure out a way to make those meat buyers bleed before the day was over.

As Dominique and I were about to step through the open doors into the auction building, a distant frenzy of panicked whinnies erupted from the far end of the pens. We spun toward the sound.

"What's going on?" she asked.

The commotion was coming from the same direction as the bay mare and the piebald gelding I'd examined.

"I'll check it out," I said. "You go in."

She nodded, and I sprinted back the way we'd come. The farther I ran, the more agitated the trapped horses became—rolling eyes, pinned ears, jostling each other and the metal fencing.

"Who's got a gun?" someone shouted.

"Hurry up and—"

The hoarse bellow of a stallion cut through all other sounds, and I pumped my legs faster.

The maze of fencing and pens ended abruptly, and a barren field stretched toward a line of trees, the forest spilling down from a mountain slope. A group of men, several wearing polo shirts with the auction facility logo, were shouting and waving their arms as though trying to scare something off. Another screaming cry erupted, followed by a resounding metal clang.

I expected to see a horse trying to kick its way out of a pen, so I was shocked to spot a black stallion smashing his way *into* a pen.

Not just any stallion.

His coat was as glossy as polished obsidian, and muscles rippled over every inch of his magnificent body. A mane like silk flowed down his arched neck, and his long tail streamed like a black banner. He had to be twenty hands tall, but he was built like a show jumper rather than a draft horse.

He was gorgeous—and he was *angry*.

Spinning in place, he kicked out with his back legs. His hooves slammed into the pen's gate. It tore free and thudded in the dirt. The stallion charged into the pen, terrifying the five horses inside. He swerved around behind them, and with sharp nips of his teeth, he sent the horses racing out into the field.

He sprang effortlessly over the fence and into the next pen. Another double kick and another gate broke.

As he chased three more horses out into the field, I had the crazy thought that the stallion was *rescuing* the other horses. But no horse was that intelligent.

At least, not a mortal horse.

"That damn stallion is back!" a man shouted. "Kill him this time!"

The crack of a gunshot blasted my eardrums, knocking me out of my trance. A rancher aimed his rifle at the stallion and fired again—right as I grabbed the barrel, shoving it upward so he'd miss. I tore it out of his hands and ran, ignoring the men shouting at me.

With my ears ringing, I vaulted a fence, the rifle in one hand, and raced across the empty pen toward the stallion in the next one. His elegant black head whipped toward me, and his orange eyes blazed like burning coals.

Tossing the rifle aside, I jumped onto the fence and launched myself at the fae stallion's bare back.

I landed across his back with a *whuff* of air leaving my lungs. Only because my sudden leap had surprised him did I have a chance to sit up and clamp my legs around his sides before he let out a bellowing scream and reared. He was even more vexed to have me as a rider than Tilliag had been.

Grabbing his mane, I threw a telepathic thought at him. *You have to get out of here! They're going to shoot you!*

His head dropped, and I leaned back as he bucked violently. *I'm helping you!* I shouted at him. With me on his back, the auction staff wouldn't shoot—hopefully.

He spun in a tight circle, trying to dislodge me, then reared again, throwing his head back to try to smash me in the face. Front hooves kicking, he reared even farther until his back was vertical and I could barely hang on.

Men were running toward us. More guns. The moment the stallion threw me off, they'd fill him with bullets.

I grabbed him around the neck and shoved my face against his mane. Instead of words, I pushed my druidic power toward him, filling it with everything I felt—the desire to help, hatred for these humans who wanted to kill him, urgency, and fear.

The stallion dropped his front hooves to the ground, his sides heaving and both ears slanted toward me. I sat astride his back, breathing just as hard, my hands fisted in his mane.

A dozen feet away, three men had rifles aimed at us, and half a dozen more stood behind them, holding ropes and whips.

You've been causing trouble, haven't you? I murmured. A man had shouted that the stallion was "back." Had he tried to save horses before?

The horse's ears flicked—and a voice brushed across my mind in a jumble of unfamiliar sounds. Another language? Did this fae not speak English?

"You, girl!" a rancher with a gun shouted. "Get off that horse before you break your neck!"

I leaned forward, urging the stallion to move. His ears swiveled again, then he sprang into a canter. I held on tight as he thundered toward the fence. With another easy leap, he cleared the barrier and thumped down on the other side. The open field stretched ahead of us.

Run! I told him, hoping he could feel the meaning of the word.

He took off at a gallop, faster than a Kentucky Derby winner. The eight auction horses he'd freed from their pens scattered fearfully as he sped past them, streaking for the trees at the far end of the field. In seconds, we reached the woods, and I ducked low as branches whipped past.

The stallion slowed to a death-defying canter as he bounded over the uneven ground, swerving around trees and leaping fallen logs. I barely clung on, my limbs burning with the effort.

After a minute that felt like ten, we burst into a small clearing and the stallion slid to a stop. I fell onto his neck before pushing myself upright and hastily sliding off his back. One ride was enough for me.

His head swung toward me, and I was caught off guard by his beauty in the dappled light beneath the trees. Cautiously, I raised my hands and cupped his flat cheeks, his coat silky under my palms.

"You can't do this," I told him, trying to share the meaning of my words. "You can't save those horses. You'll just end up dead."

He pinned his ears.

"I know, but even if you set them free, they won't survive out here. The mountains are no place for domestic horses."

He nudged me hard in the chest with his nose, and a wave of his unfamiliar language rattled through my head. I couldn't understand him, but I could feel his question in the sounds.

"I can't save them either." Pain, fury, and helplessness thickened in my chest, dulling the grind of sharp edges. "You need to take care of yourself, okay? Head that way"—I pointed north—"and keep going until there are no more humans."

A puff of warm breath blew strands of sweat-dampened hair off my forehead. The stallion stepped back, pulling away from my hands. His burning orange eyes gazed into mine, fierce and furious but somehow sad.

An odd, uncomfortable feeling prickled up my spine—then recognition hit me.

Stunned by the realization of where I'd seen this fae before, I didn't react as he turned. His tail swished, raven hair streaming, then he trotted into the trees. The shadows engulfed his dark form, and I lost sight of him.

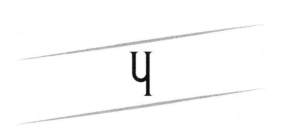

THE DULLAHAN'S STEED? Ríkr repeated disbelievingly.

I nodded as I picked a comb through the tangles in Whicker's mane. The gray gelding was doing much better. He'd gained weight over the past few weeks, and the thrush infection had cleared up.

"When Lallakai knocked the Dullahan to the ground, his horse ran off." I glanced at the white cat sitting on the side of the tack stall. "I didn't give him a second thought, to be honest. I assumed he went back through the crossroads to wherever the Dullahan came from."

That would have been my assumption as well. Ríkr gave a slow, thoughtful blink. *I doubt the stallion served the Dullahan willingly. He may have been unprepared for his sudden freedom.*

"I wonder if that's why he's still hanging around." I smoothed Whicker's mane. "Rescuing auction horses ... I've never seen a fae go up against humans like that."

It is uncommon in this age of deadly human weapons, but not many centuries ago, humans feared us. Ríkr stood and arched his back in a stretch. *Perhaps the stallion was in the Dullahan's power for so long that he is unaware of how humanity has evolved.*

In medieval Europe, a horse with fiery eyes would've terrified villagers. But nowadays? He was lucky he hadn't been riddled with bullets.

"I hope he goes north," I murmured, patting Whicker's neck. "He needs to get away from people."

Indeed. It will be inconvenient if he continues to cause mischief on the doorstep of our territory.

Our territory. It was a strange thought. I'd been his consort for three days and he already had me practicing aura spheres on the hour, every hour. Attuning the land to my power, he'd said.

A memory reared up in my head of the aura sphere I'd created at Luthyr's crossroad. I could feel Zak's hand grasping mine as he'd added his power and aura. For those brief moments, we'd been in perfect harmony. My hands clenched.

Whicker's head turned as he caught my tension, and I hastily reassured him with another pat on the neck. "Ríkr, were you able to find out anything?"

He swished his tail. *I gleaned nothing about Zak's movements. He must have traveled in his vehicle, either to cover more distance or to avoid notice.*

"Or both," I muttered, unclipping the crossties keeping Whicker in place. "Do you think he went back to Hell's Gate?"

I cannot imagine why he would. Ríkr hopped to the ground, following as I led Whicker to his stall. *Zak's thoughts I cannot guess, but whatever drew him and his lady away must have been of great urgency for Lallakai to leave without the power of The Undying.*

Unease twinged in my gut at the reminder that Ríkr had promised to share the unique magic that made him near-impervious to death. I couldn't imagine anything good coming out of Lallakai gaining the same level of invincibility, but Ríkr had agreed, and it was his call whether he wanted to keep his word. At least the deal had been that he "share" his power and not give it away entirely.

What could possibly have drawn them away? And so soon after our return from Hell's Gate? Zak hadn't even stayed the night, though he must have been exhausted. I bit my lower lip, trying to convince myself that I only cared because Zak owed me an explanation for what had happened between us ten years ago.

"I suppose that almost guarantees they'll be back sooner or later," I said as I closed Whicker in his stall. He stuck his head through the opening in the door and I rubbed his forehead. "Lallakai won't forget about your promise."

Maybe she'll perish before she can return, he suggested hopefully. *That would eliminate several inconveniences at once.*

If Lallakai died, Zak would probably suffer the same fate, and I had too much unfinished business with him.

I headed toward the stable doors. "Speaking of inconveniences, I need to leave soon."

For the guild meeting? Ríkr trotted beside me, his feline paws silent on the concrete floor. *The sooner you demonstrate your supremacy, the less time we will waste cowing them.*

I grimaced as I walked into the yard. Clouds hung low in the sky, threatening rain.

"I don't even know how many guild members I'd need to intimidate." I brushed my bangs out of my eyes. "Some of them might not be intimidated at all."

Like Darius King, the guild master, and Aaron Sinclair, my "mentor." Neither seemed like the type to back down from a challenge.

I stewed in my thoughts as I trekked up the stairs and into my small apartment above the tack room. As Ríkr hopped onto the sofa, looking for all the world like a house cat intent on a late afternoon nap, I slid my switchblade from my pocket. The olive-green handle was smooth and polished. It still looked brand new.

I didn't regret skipping my switchblade and summoning an ice spear at my last visit to the Crow and Hammer, but I also felt a bit weird about it. Like it hadn't been the best move.

"I'm not sure intimidating them is what I want to do."

Ríkr lay down on the sofa, paws tucked together. *What do you wish to do?*

"I don't know." I tapped the switchblade against my palm in a nervous rhythm. "But intimidating them seems ... well, it might backfire, for one. And aside from that, it just ..."

It does not seem necessary? Ríkr suggested.

My brow furrowed. "Yeah."

Ah. His ears slanted back, his expression one of satisfaction. *I understand.*

"You do?" Because I didn't.

It is simple, dove. You no longer need intimidation as a defensive maneuver. You are more powerful. If they challenge you, you can meet them on their level.

The simple truth stunned me. For years, I'd brandished weapons to dissuade people from messing with me. I'd been weak, and I'd *known* I was weak. How else was I supposed to stave off confrontations I might lose? But I was a druid now. I wasn't sure how powerful I actually was against other mythics, but I no longer needed to posture and fluff my fur to look—and feel—stronger than I was.

I stood for a moment, then sat on the coffee table facing Ríkr. "What am I supposed to do?"

Pardon?

"How should I behave at the guild?"

You're asking me? He blinked. *Dove, have you forgotten what I am?*

"You understand politics and social hierarchies. A guild and a court can't be *that* different."

I am quite confident they are incomparable.

"You must have some advice. You love giving me advice." I gestured at his small feline body. "If you were joining a new court, how would you behave?"

He chuffed. *I would be ruling the court, not joining it.*

Groaning, I pinched the bridge of my nose. Asking a fae how I, a human, should interact with my peers was pointless, but I was at a complete loss. I was too used to being weak and defensive.

With a frustrated shake of my head, I pushed to my feet. "I guess I'll have to wing it."

Ríkr closed his eyes lazily. *Keep it simple, dove. Ignore them unless they challenge you.*

"And if they challenge me?"

He cracked one eye open, the pale blue iris gleaming. *Then crush them.*

"PLEASE GIVE SABER your warmest welcome to the Crow and Hammer," Darius announced, projecting his voice to the room.

Standing beside the guild master, I gazed across a sea of fifty unfamiliar faces. Everyone was focused on me, their expressions varying from curiosity to suspicion to boredom. The guild's monthly meeting had brought every member, minus a few who were out of town, to the pub. Fifty people wasn't a huge guild, but it was several times larger than the Coquitlam Coven had been.

"Saber, would you like to say anything?" Darius asked in an undertone.

A dozen thoughts spun through my head. I'd arrived minutes before the meeting started, and I still hadn't figured out which face I wanted to present to this guild. Not nice Saber and not hostile Saber, I knew, but those were the two facades I'd perfected.

Ríkr's small ferret paws gripped my shoulder, and I glanced at him.

"I understand I'm the first druid to join this guild. This is my familiar." I pointed at my shoulder. He wasn't technically my familiar anymore, but I didn't want to get into the nuances of the consort relationship—especially when I didn't understand it yet myself. "If you mess with him, I'm not responsible for what he does."

A beefy man in his early thirties laughed. "Are we supposed to be scared of a ferret?"

"Did you rattle your brains loose on our last job, Darren?" a short blond woman barked. "That's a fae, not a rodent."

Darren snorted derisively.

"Are you saying you can't control your familiar?" a woman on the other side of the pub asked.

I swung my gaze around, but I wasn't sure who'd spoken. "Do you 'control' your friends? He's not my pet. If he decides you deserve to be frozen into a solid block of ice, that's his prerogative."

A rustle of what might've been concern ran through the crowd.

"Doesn't this guild have witches?" I fired at Darius. "Have these people never met a fae before?"

"We have six witches, several of whom have familiars, but their fae companions don't usually visit the guild," Darius replied in a low tone for my ears only. "Our membership could learn a lot from regular exposure to a fae."

My eyes narrowed. "Did Morris tell you anything about my familiar?"

"I understand he's more powerful than the average fae."

How delightfully vague, Ríkr remarked in my head.

So did that mean Darius knew Ríkr was an immortal fae king with magic that exponentially outstripped any mythic's, or did he merely know Ríkr was stronger than most familiars? How much did Morris know?

I swiveled back to my guildmates. "Any other questions?"

"Are you single?" someone in the back called.

I flipped him my middle finger.

To my surprise, laughter rang out. Everyone, even the guy who'd asked the question, looked amused instead of appalled.

"Is that a yes?" he asked.

"Thank you, Saber," Darius said, ignoring the second wave of laughter. "Take a seat, and we'll continue with the meeting."

I strode back to my table and dropped into the seat beside a blond man in his mid-thirties. He had a receding hairline, large glasses, and a thin build. Felix Adams, my rehab supervisor.

He'd waved me over as soon as I'd arrived and introduced himself before the meeting began.

The short blond woman who'd spoken up a minute ago reached around Felix to offer me her hand. "I'm Zora, by the way. Felix's wife."

I shook her hand. Her grip was strong.

"Darren and Cameron feed off each other's idiocy," she told me, flashing a grin. "Feel free to smack them up the sides of their dumbass heads if they annoy you."

"Darius told me I'm not allowed to hit first."

She laughed. "That's true, but our second rule is 'Don't get caught.'"

My eyebrows rose.

She glanced at my arms. "I bet you hit pretty hard. Do you work out?"

My navy tank top showed off as much of my arms as Zora's black corset-style top, and we were similarly toned.

"No," I replied. "But my jobs are very physical."

Zora grinned. "So is mine, but I work out too."

Felix cleared his throat and nodded toward Darius, who had begun to speak. His wife straightened in her seat, returning her gaze to the guild master. I leaned back, half listening as Darius talked about guild members' special accomplishments, safety notices, and near-miss reports. It was remarkably similar to a staff meeting at the vet clinic, and I relaxed a bit.

An hour later, the meeting adjourned. Chairs scraped across the wood floor as members swarmed the bar to order drinks and food. Unlike my first visit, several people were hustling behind the bar, taking orders and making drinks.

"Want anything, Saber?" Zora asked with a friendly smile.

"A water would be good."

"Sure."

As she joined the crowd around the bar, someone called for Felix. He hurried away from his chair, and I found myself alone at the table—aside from Ríkr on my shoulder. My gaze moved across the people filling the guild, ranging from young and fresh to old and grizzled, and everything in between. There was a lot of conversation, frequent laughter, and a fair amount of goofing off.

A thought drifted through my head: What would it be like to be part of a group like this? To chat casually, laugh, act a little silly? I couldn't imagine acting silly, but the idea had a daring appeal.

Remembering Morris's warning that this place might eat me alive, I reassessed the room. Some members looked distinctly average, like they could've wandered in from the local shopping mall. But about half of them were athletically built. Some were thick with muscles. Others moved in that smooth, confident way I'd learned to fear when accompanying Ruth to the crime den as a teen.

Pushing my chair back, I rose to my feet. Restlessness vibrated in my leg muscles. I'd done too much sitting lately. I needed to move.

"Oy!"

The shout came a second before something small slid into the side of my shoe. I looked down. A throwing dart?

Turning, I found four people standing near a worn dartboard on the wall. A guy who couldn't be much older than eighteen held a handful of matching darts, his expression guilty. On the scrawny side and with a mop of bleached-blond hair, he was not among the potentially dangerous mythics I'd been assessing.

"Sorry," he called sheepishly.

Picking up the stray dart, I walked over and offered it to him.

A tall, muscled man with a shaved head and thick beard swatted his younger counterpart in the back of the shoulder. "That's what you get for showing off, Liam."

Liam wilted.

"And you call yourself a telekinetic," the third man declared. Shorter than the beefy guy but just as muscular, he offered a smile. "We were about to start a game. Want to join us?"

"I don't know how to play," I answered.

"You've never thrown darts before?" Unfriendly surprise soured the voice of the fourth member of the small group, a woman around my age with long blond hair tied in a ponytail. She reminded me of a cranky mare sizing up unwelcome competition in her herd.

Your first challenger? Ríkr murmured, sounding bored.

"I prefer to throw knives," I told the woman. A slight flinch rippled across her features, but the two older men exchanged grins.

"That works too." The shorter guy dipped his hand under the back of his shirt. His hand reappeared, holding a weapon that resembled a small bowie knife with cutouts in the handle to reduce the weight. "Shall we throw knives, then?"

The tall guy offered his hand to me. "I'm Lyndon, by the way. This is Drew." He canted his head toward the guy with the knife, then nodded at the skinny boy and the blond woman. "That's Liam and Cearra."

"Saber," I said, though they already knew my name.

"Same rules for knives as darts, Drew," Cearra said archly. "No telekinesis."

He smirked.

"You're a telekinetic?" I asked warily.

Liam brushed his hair out of his eyes. "Drew and I are both telekinetics, but we won't cheat. There's no challenge otherwise."

Telekinetics were a type of psychic. I was familiar with the different classes of magic, but aside from my alchemist aunt, I'd had little exposure to mythics beyond witches.

Drew set his feet shoulder-width apart and faced the dartboard from ten feet away. Holding his knife in a blade grip, he took aim.

"So what made you choose the Crow and Hammer?" Lyndon asked me.

Drew flung his knife. It stuck in a black section just above the bullseye.

"I didn't choose it."

He and Liam looked at me in confusion. Cearra appeared to be studying the dartboard, but she was easily within hearing range.

"Then why'd you join?" Liam asked.

I hesitated, unsure how to salvage my thoughtless answer, then threw caution to the wind. "I was assigned here."

"Assigned?" he repeated blankly.

"Oh, you're a parolee?" Lyndon asked. "Same."

"Same?"

"Well, not anymore. But I first joined the Crow and Hammer while I was on parole—or rehab, or whatever the hell their feel-good term for it is now."

"What were you arrested for?" I asked, not caring if the question was rude.

"Possession of illegal magic," he answered with a shrug. "Assault using illegal magic, theft, extortion … My old guild was a bad crowd."

Drew joined us, offering Lyndon a matching knife to the one he'd thrown. "Your throw."

Grinning, Lyndon took the knife and faced the target. He raised the knife using a simple hammer grip. He threw with good power and aim but too much spin, and it hit the target on an angle, bounced off, and stuck point-first into the floor.

"Oops," he muttered, glancing around furtively as though expecting someone to shout at him. He hastily plucked the knife from the floor.

"I was going to ask if you were planning to join a bounty-hunting team," Liam said, studying me curiously. "But I guess not since you're on parole."

"Are you a bounty hunter?" I inquired as Lyndon offered the knife to Cearra.

"Not yet," Liam replied, "but about half the guild is licensed for bounty hunting."

Half the guild? Probably the fit, dangerous looking half. I bit the inside of my cheek as Cearra positioned herself in front of the target. Considering that my extracurricular activities included regular law-breaking, membership in a guild of bounty hunters might get complicated.

"What about you, Saber?" Lyndon glanced at me as Cearra made a show of taking aim, holding the knife in a pinch grip. "What are you on parole for?"

"Murder."

Cearra's arm wobbled as she threw. The knife stuck in the upper left portion of the outer ring. She jerked toward me, staring. "Did you say *murder*?"

I *had* said "murder," and I had no idea why. I'd just said it. So much for keeping my past a secret so I'd have a chance of fitting in. Was I trying to sabotage myself? Or did part of me still want them to fear me and avoid me because that was safer?

Drew and Liam watched me cautiously, but Lyndon gave a slow nod. "You must've gone through some really tough shit."

Cearra squinted angrily at her guildmate, then blew out a loud breath. "I want another throw. She distracted me."

"Too bad," Drew shot back unsympathetically. "It's Saber's turn."

Liam grinned. "Yeah, let's see your skills, Saber!"

That was it? I'd admitted to being a murderer and they wanted to continue our game? A game which involved deadly weapons?

Lyndon nudged Drew. "Got another knife for her?"

I pulled out my switchblade. At the snap of the blade, the other four looked at it in surprise. It wasn't a throwing knife, but I'd been practicing with switchblades for years. I could throw it more accurately than a knife I'd never touched before.

Stepping in front of the target, I honed my attention on the bullseye—but it was intended for darts, not knives. If I hit it dead center, the wire that defined the sections of the board would prevent the knife from penetrating and sticking.

Choosing a spot just below the center point, I threw my knife. It thunked into the target right where I'd aimed.

"Nice!" Lyndon exclaimed.

"You beat mine," Drew observed.

"My turn now," Liam said eagerly.

"Not bad for a druid."

The last voice, unfamiliar and male, spoke near my right ear. I looked up as a man stepped close beside me. Around my age, a couple inches shy of six feet tall, and with raven hair falling into his eyes, he was one of the mythics I'd identified during my surveillance of the room as extremely fit, confident, graceful, and likely dangerous.

He ran his dark gaze over me from head to toe, then faced the dartboard. A smooth black blade appeared in his hand, and without pausing to aim, he threw it in one graceful motion. His knife flashed end over end and slammed into the board, dead center—and stuck. He'd thrown it so hard it'd cut through the section wire.

That kind of power with that level of accuracy—he was either very lucky or a true expert.

Drew sighed. "I should've just used telekinesis."

The newcomer faced me. His cool expression somehow made him more strikingly handsome. "Kai Yamada."

"Saber," I said, shaking his hand.

"Hey," Lyndon said with a mischievous grin. "Speaking of mythics on the wrong side of the law, have you ever offed anyone for the Yamadas, Kai?"

Kai's gaze slid to Lyndon. "If I told you, I'd have to kill you."

Lyndon snorted in amusement, and Drew rolled his eyes. With one more appraising glance in my direction, Kai plucked his knife from the dartboard and headed to the bar.

"He's one of our top combat mythics," Drew informed me. "He's also from a mythic mafia family."

I stiffened. "Is *everyone* here an ex-criminal?"

He and Lyndon laughed.

"No, but we're all misfits in one way or another." Lyndon clapped me on the shoulder with a large hand, his smile warm. "Welcome to the club, Saber."

5

I PROPPED MY ELBOWS on the bar top. *I'm exhausted.*

Perched on my shoulder as a ferret, Ríkr leaned against my neck. *I am remarkably fatigued as well.*

So much for showing off my "supremacy," I grumbled.

That is still an option.

I shook my head. After the knife-throwing game, Aaron had introduced me to the guild's other officers. I'd been forced to join a few hands of poker, then an old woman with a crystal ball had followed me around for a solid twenty minutes, trying to convince me to do a séance with her. Zora had rescued me with food and drinks, then several of her "teammates" had joined her and they'd reminisced loudly and with a lot of energy about their recent jobs involving more vampires than this city could possibly contain.

No sooner had I escaped that group than I'd been pulled into another one, this time by the guild's witches. Philip, a man in his fifties, had introduced another man and three women under thirty, who'd been cautiously friendly. I was surprised they hadn't been more hostile. In my experience, witches saw druids as agents of chaos and corruption instead of as magical cousins.

Stares and whispers had followed me around the pub, but they'd come from a minority of members. Most of my new guildmates had welcomed me, and more than the forced interactions, I was exhausted by uncertainty. Did they genuinely want to include me in their group? Would that change once the "murderer on parole" news spread to everyone? Would their welcome dry up if I showed my true personality? How long until they realized I wasn't "friend" material?

I'd resisted my deep-seated urge to drive people away through aggression, and I wasn't going back to faking niceties. But without those, I didn't know how to act and I was pretty sure I'd come across as awkward, stiff, and socially crippled. Which wasn't entirely wrong.

A rocks glass thumped down on the bar in front of me.

"They aren't usually this nice to newcomers."

I looked up. A woman a couple of years younger than me arched an eyebrow, then scooped ice into the glass. Her wildly wavy red hair was semi-tamed into a bun, and freckles dusted her nose and cheeks.

"When I joined a year ago," she continued in a pleasant alto voice, "almost everyone was a complete dick. Especially *that* dick."

She tilted her head, and I glanced over. The pub was half empty now, so it was easy to spot my mentor, Aaron, who was talking to the knife-throwing mafia mythic, Kai. She could've been indicating either of them, but I was betting she meant Aaron.

"Things have changed around here." She aimed a soda gun over the glass, and cola gushed over the ice. "We're a little friendlier now. Plus, everyone is really curious about you— especially after you threatened half of them with a giant-ass ice weapon."

Especially after I'd threatened them? I studied her hazel eyes, unsure how to read her expression. Had she been in the crowd I'd threatened? I couldn't remember.

She slid the cola in front of me. "I'm curious about you too."

"Just ask what you want to know," I replied flatly.

"What do you do for fun?"

What kind of question was that? I'd expected an interrogation about my criminal record. "Horseback riding, hiking, and dirt biking, I guess. I volunteer a lot, so I don't have much free time."

"Where do you volunteer?"

"An animal rescue."

"What about work?"

"I'm a vet tech and an apprentice farrier."

She gazed at me, both impressed and dumbfounded.

I frowned. "What?"

Hastily clearing her expression, she wiped the clean counter. "Nothing. I, uh, I'm just used to druids being more ..."

"More what?"

"More—*hey!*" she bellowed, pointing at something behind me. "If you throw that chair, I'll throw *you* right out the damn door!"

"Aw, Tori," a male voice whined loudly. "I wasn't actually gonna—"

"And you're cut off!" she added in a shout. "Go sober up before Tabitha puts you on ice!"

I glanced over my shoulder at a rowdy group of guys at the back. One of them was positioning a chair at a table with exaggerated, drunken precision.

"Those idiots," the bartender—Tori, I was assuming—muttered. "Sorry. What was I saying?"

"I'm not what you think druids are like."

She laughed ruefully. "I didn't mean it in a bad way. You seem really cool."

"Cool?"

"Yeah! My skills are limited to bartending, yelling at people, and—"

"—and a major-league umbrella swing," Aaron finished, stepping up beside my stool. "Your right hook is also pretty wicked."

Tori grinned at him. "Be glad I haven't used it on you."

"Just don't use it on Saber." Another guy appeared on Aaron's other side. "It's statistically impossible for one person to punch *two* druids in the face, so you'd better not try."

"Or else what?"

The new guy widened his eyes. "It'd probably break the mythic universe as we know it."

As Tori snorted, the new guy leaned around Aaron to smile at me. He was a similar height to Aaron, with bronze skin and dark, curly hair. A ridged scar cut across his left eye, which was pale white instead of warm brown like his right eye.

"I'm Ezra," he said in a quiet, smooth voice. "Nice to meet you."

"Saber," I said shortly. Kai, the ex-mafia mythic, was coming over too, and I was ready to make my escape before I had to navigate another group conversation. "I'm ..."

A slow shiver ran across my skin. I went still, stretching my senses out.

"Are we having another round of drinks?" Kai asked, joining the other two guys. "Saber, what would you like?"

I didn't answer as subtle power trickled over me. I homed in on the direction. My hand curled into a fist. Spinning on my heel, I flung my arm out in a punch at the empty space behind me.

The air shimmered and my fist smacked hard into a gloved palm.

Familiar green eyes met mine as Zak appeared from a swirl of shadows. His long leather jacket hung open, partially exposing his combat belt loaded with potions and spells. Mud splattered his clothes from the knees downward.

Shock rippled through me—then flashed into alarm.

Zak, aka the Ghost, was a wanted fugitive with a million-dollar bounty on his head, and he'd just walked into a bounty-hunting guild. His hood was up but his face was clearly visible to anyone standing nearby—which included Aaron, Kai, and Ezra, all of whom were probably bounty hunters. If anyone recognized him, he'd have twenty mythics on him in an instant.

"Holy shit!" Tori exclaimed. "Zak!"

Still holding my fist, Zak shifted his attention to the redheaded bartender. Half panicking, I looked at them too. Tori and the three guys appeared pleasantly surprised, as though an old buddy had shown up.

Glancing at me, Tori bit her lip uncertainly. "Uh, Zak ... we have a new member."

A low note of warning threaded her voice, as though she were trying to caution him about something. Did they realize he was the infamous Ghost, the most wanted mythic in Vancouver? Was she warning Zak to hide his identity from *me*?

Our evening has become more entertaining, Ríkr remarked.

Zak glanced at my fist trapped in his hand, faint amusement sparking in his eyes. "No knife? Or are you waiting for me to save your life before stabbing me again?"

"No way!" Tori gasped. "You two know each other?"

Wasn't that my line?

I wrenched my hand out of Zak's as conflicting emotions assaulted me. Who were these people to him? Why was he comfortable walking into a bounty-hunting guild? How had he known I would be here—or was it just a coincidence? Was this place a frequent hangout spot for him, his favorite pub to grab a beer after a long day doing whatever the hell he did when he ditched me without warning?

And why were these thoughts making my throat close and my eyes burn?

"Saber," Zak rumbled quietly.

He was watching me. The others were watching me too, and their eyes felt like needles piercing my skin.

I sucked in a breath, struggling to keep my face blank. "I'm leaving. Don't follow me."

Stepping around him, I swept toward the door. Footsteps thumped behind me—of course he wouldn't obey my wishes—but I didn't look back. I shoved outside and into a downpour, water sheeting from the dark sky and the streetlamps reflecting on the puddles. Cold water pattered on my head and chilled my bare shoulders. Moving as fast as possible without actually running, I careened around the corner of the building. Ríkr lost his balance on my shoulder, slid half off, then transformed into a white crow and took flight with a beat of his wings.

Heavy boots splashed in the puddle behind me. "Saber!"

Zak seized my arm and I tore it free, whirling to face him. His hood was down and rain slicked his hair to his head.

"What's wrong?" he asked.

Hurt twisted through me, but I didn't want to examine it. I didn't want to think about why him having friends at a guild had made me tear up.

"What's wrong?" I repeated incredulously. "You left in the middle of the night without telling me where you were going, and I had no way to reach you."

"I was out of cell range, and I didn't think I'd be gone this long. I planned to come right back."

"Why didn't you tell me that?"

He opened his mouth, then shut it. Flexing his jaw, he closed his eyes as though steeling himself.

"What if you didn't care?" he muttered so quietly I almost didn't catch it over the pouring rain.

"Huh?"

Eyes opening again, he grimaced. "I didn't say anything in case you didn't want me to come back."

I stared at him.

He swore under his breath. "Is that why you're so angry?"

"Isn't that enough?"

"Probably, but that doesn't seem to be the only thing."

He was right, but I wasn't dealing with the rest right now. I pivoted and sped away.

He grabbed my arm again—and an instant later, I was pressed up against the brick wall, his solid weight pinning me in place. One of his hands was behind my head, protecting it from the hard wall, and the other was gripping my waist.

"Let me go!"

"Saber," he rumbled. "What's wrong?"

I sucked in air through clenched teeth, glowering at his chin. Why couldn't I look him in the eye? "You're a fucking prick, that's what's wrong."

"Saber," he growled.

My mouth bobbed, the irrational hurt I felt rising in my throat and threatening to spill from my mouth in a tide of angry accusations. I choked them back—and a question slipped out instead.

"How do you know those people at the Crow and Hammer?"

"It's a long story, but … we've helped each other out a few times."

"So they're your friends?"

"One of them. Maybe two. Is that what's bothering you?"

I looked away. Shame spread down to my fingertips.

"Saber." His fingers pressed into my side. "Does that bother you?"

"No," I lied.

"Why does it matter whether I—"

"Because I thought you needed me!"

He'd lost everything and stopped caring about anyone except me. That's what he'd told me, and I'd felt needed. I'd felt like someone irreplaceably important to him—until the moment I'd seen his other friends and realized I'd gotten it all wrong.

Humiliation suffused me. I shoved against him, forcing him half a step back, but he rammed me into the wall, my head bouncing off his gloved hand.

And then his mouth was crushing mine.

I gasped against his lips, and his tongue pushed past my teeth. His hand fisted in my hair, pulling my head back, and he kissed me harder, consuming me like I was his last meal before his execution. His hot tongue thrust against mine, sending molten shock waves rippling out from my core. My legs trembled, my hands clutching his sleeves, my fingernails scraping the smooth leather.

He pulled back, leaving my lips cold and aching. For an eternal moment, I gaped at him, caught completely off guard. My heart thundered against my ribs, and heat burned inside me. I tried to unclamp my fingers from his sleeves, but I couldn't make them move.

"What ... was that?" I asked hoarsely.

He leaned down, bringing our mouths close. His warm breath teased my lips. "Me needing you."

A tremor ran through my limbs. I pushed on his shoulders, and he stepped back, releasing me. Sagging against the wall, I sucked in a deep breath. Rain splattered on my cheeks. My hair was drenched.

Zak turned toward the corner of the building, the guild's entrance just out of sight. "Don't you guys have anything better to do?"

At his question, a head poked around the corner—Tori's curly red hair. Aaron, Kai, and Ezra leaned out too, all four watching us with expressions varying from sheepish to annoyed as the rain swiftly drenched them.

"So," Tori drawled, "you two are a thing?"

"They're *definitely* a thing," Aaron said.

"But what kind of thing?" Ezra wondered.

Zak tipped his head back as though praying for patience, then held out his hand to me. "Let's go back inside."

"Why?" I asked irritably, in no mood to be ogled or questioned.

Bleak determination gathered in his eyes. "Because I need your help—and Ríkr's."

6

TORI SET MUGS of steaming coffee in front of me and Zak. Aaron, Kai, and Ezra had removed themselves, taking seats at the opposite end of the bar. Our corner was as private as could be expected in a small pub with twenty other people in it.

Tori propped her arms on the countertop. "How do you know Zak?"

"We … met as teens and recently got in touch again," I said. Such a nice, simple explanation for one of the worst traumas of my life. I turned to Zak, hoping Tori would take the hint. "You said you needed help."

He tapped his fingers restlessly on the bar top. "The night we got back from Hell's Gate, I left because Echo called for me."

"*Echo?*" I asked blankly.

Tori's eyes brightened with curiosity. "Was it something to do with the duel?"

Zak frowned. "What duel?"

"The dragon-chimera duel you had to referee," Tori said. "The reason you missed Ezra's birthday party."

"Oh, that." Zak lifted his mug to his mouth. "I made that up."

Tori's face darkened like a thundercloud. "Why the hell did you lie?"

"Because I was hunting a fae killer that was stealing people's hearts out of their living bodies." He sipped his coffee. "The truth might have put a damper on your party."

"Stealing hearts?" she muttered disbelievingly, then shook her head. "Whatever. Did you catch the fae?"

"It's dead."

He didn't mention my role in tracking and killing the Dullahan, and I didn't speak up.

"Is Echo a fae?" I asked, steering the conversation back to the present problem, whatever it was.

"Yes." Zak ran his finger along the rim of his mug. "His call was urgent, but he went silent before I reached him. Lallakai and I split up. I went to his territory, and she went to check with other fae in the area. I couldn't find him anywhere, and he won't answer my call."

"Didn't you say Echo has a habit of vanishing for months at a time?" Tori asked.

"Yes, but not when he wants me for something."

"I suppose—" Breaking off as a customer approached the bar, she gave us a quick farewell wave as she went to take their order.

I spun my steaming mug in a slow circle, rotating the handle clockwise. "Did Lallakai learn anything from the other fae?"

"I don't know," Zak rumbled, "because she disappeared too."

My mug stilled.

"Have you heard of the Gardall'kin fae?"

Ríkr had mentioned them once before, describing them as a "formidable medley" of warriors who'd made a place for themselves through bloodshed and brutality.

At my nod, he continued, "I've been on good terms with the Shadow Court for nine years, but I've never visited without Lallakai. I need to talk to them to find out where and when she disappeared and to see if they know anything about Echo, since their territories share a border."

"So you want me and Ríkr to go with you to ensure the Shadow Court doesn't eat you alive?"

"Yes."

Even without revealing his true identity, Ríkr could be intimidating. And with my aura sphere to boost his power, he alone could make a fae court think twice about attacking.

"I'll have to discuss it with Ríkr," I said.

Zak's gaze slid between my eyes. "Did you accept his offer to become his consort?"

"Yes."

His expression didn't change, revealing nothing. He took a long drink of coffee. "Did you drive here?"

"I took a cab." I'd abandoned my broken-down truck in a public parking lot, and by the time I went back for it, it'd been towed. Considering it was worth less than the impound fees, I was considering whether to claim it.

"I'll drive you home. Let's go."

Tightness spread through my chest at the word "home," and the feeling was as absent of logic as all my other emotional reactions tonight. Saying nothing, I followed him to the door.

I didn't know how to behave around my guildmates, and it turned out I didn't know what to do with myself around Zak either. I was a complete mess.

RAIN DRUMMED on the stable roof as I leaned on a stall door. I wasn't hiding, per se. I just didn't want to sit around in my apartment while Zak used my shower. No other reason.

At the other end of the stall, the bay mare I'd examined in the auction pens stood with her ears twitching nervously toward every sound. Dominique had purchased the mare, plus five other horses. A larger rescue had bought another ten, including the piebald gelding who'd shared a pen with the bay mare. I'd last seen the biting buckskin in a large pen packed tight with horses to be loaded on the slaughterhouse trucks.

I exhaled roughly, trying not to think about it. There was nothing else we could do, though the temptation to burn the whole auction operation to the ground was intense. Or better yet, burn down the meat factories.

A swirl of familiar magic brushed across my senses. I turned.

Ríkr's heavy cloak swished around his legs as he glided sedately down the length of the stable aisle. His white hair shone like moonlight, and his short golden antlers flashed in the harsh fluorescent bulbs overhead.

I blinked at his beautiful, otherworldly face as he stopped in front of me. Blue markings, part of his Undying magic, ran down the left side of his face like shimmering tattoos.

"Dove," he murmured in his low, even voice.

I blinked again. "Why are you in that form?"

He spread his arms, the wide sleeves of his cloak fluttering. "Does this form displease you?"

"No. And don't bother fishing for compliments," I added dryly. "Your ego doesn't need my help."

He tucked his hands into the opposite sleeves of his cloak. "You've been avoiding me. This seemed the simplest method to ensure your full attention."

Of course he'd notice I was avoiding him. "Aren't you supposed to be hiding from other fae?"

"That deception is less crucial now that you've claimed this territory. Your dominion over the energies here masks my presence, even in this form." He arched a fine eyebrow. "But let us not deviate from the topic at hand."

Leaning against the stable door, I crossed my arms. "And what topic is that?"

He gave me a pointed look.

"Zak's request," I muttered. "What do you think?"

"The Gardall'kin's territory is not one I would enter casually. They maintain an ominous reputation, and the Shadow Court comprises the most powerful and ambitious among them."

"If they turn on Zak, could you fight them?"

"Fight, yes. Defeat? Not in my current state." A faint smile brightened his pale azure eyes. "In my prime, I would have enjoyed their cowering obeisance. In this age, however, I am but a crippled old man who likes to reminisce about his glory days."

"Old man," I scoffed. His face was ageless and perfect. He didn't look any older than me.

With the clop of hooves, the bay mare stuck her head through the stall door's V-shaped opening. Her ears pricked toward Ríkr, her nostrils working as she tried to determine what sort of strange creature he might be.

"That said," he continued, "they will not needlessly offend me. I am no longer the Winter King, but I remain a Lord of Winter."

I rubbed the mare's neck. "And you're unkillable."

"An advantage to which we need not forewarn them."

Turning toward the mare, I picked a bit of straw out of her mane. "What do you think we should do? Should we help?"

"My opinion is of little consequence. What do you wish to do?"

Pursing my lips, I fiddled with the mare's mane, combing my fingers through it. Separating three locks, I started to braid them.

"Saber."

I kept braiding.

"*Saber.*"

Huffing, I abandoned the braid and turned back around.

Ríkr gave me a piercing stare. "I will not make this decision for you, dove."

"But you understand the dangers better than I do," I pointed out, hearing the note of desperation in my voice. "And you'd be taking the big risks, not me. And it's up to you whether you owe Zak a favor for helping you against Luthyr."

"Yet you must still decide," he said implacably.

My teeth pinched my lower lip. I'd been afraid he'd take this stance. I wanted him to decide for us both. I didn't want to decide. I wasn't sure I could.

Turning my back on the fae for a second time, I rested my forehead on the post between stalls.

I didn't give a shit about Lallakai, but she wasn't the one asking for help. Zak was, and over the past two weeks, he'd helped me in ways I could barely quantify. Not only had he risked his life by going against Luthyr, but he'd been beside me for every step into Hell's Gate and the painful discoveries about my parents and childhood. And he'd done all that while I was blaming him, hating him, dismissing him, and treating him like a physical and emotional punching bag.

Fuck, I was a horrible person.

On the other hand, Zak's support over the past couple of weeks didn't erase his past actions. He'd betrayed me and left me for dead. My understanding of what happened ten years ago had crucial gaps, but he hadn't once denied either of those facts. Did the boy who'd shattered me deserve my help? Doing favors for the person who'd hurt me so deeply felt like a betrayal of my fifteen-year-old self and her suffering.

My eyes slowly opened, unfocused and distant. Absently, I ran my tongue across my lips, remembering the feel of Zak's mouth—and how different it had felt from kissing him as a teenager. Then my hand moved to my pocket.

I slipped my fingers between the layers of fabric and brushed them across the rune-etched face of my river-stone pendant. I'd discovered it in my childhood home, only to lose it later. Zak had found it somehow and left it for me before vanishing for three days.

My thumb rubbed across the rune. As long as I didn't put the pendant around my neck, its magic would remain dormant. Carrying it accomplished nothing, especially since I was done hiding my druid power from the world, but I'd been putting it in my pocket every day anyway.

Pulling my hand out of my pocket, I pivoted back to face Ríkr. "I'm going to help him."

He nodded, unsurprised.

"Are you okay with that?" Uncertainty crept into my voice. "Is it what you would've decided?"

"Me?" An ancient, pitiless chill permeated his pale eyes. "I warned you before that I am not a benevolent being, dove. I would leave Lallakai to her doom, keep the Undying gift, and take her consort as mine alongside you."

My eyes widened.

"However, if you gave me permission to devour him, that would also be acceptable."

I swallowed a faint surge of nausea.

"It is your choice," he concluded, lips curving up and eyes softening, "and I will thusly dedicate myself to fulfilling your desire."

"You don't mind?"

"Not in the slightest, dove." A hint of that primeval chill lingered in his gaze. "My turn will come."

Before I could ask what he meant, blue light swirled over him. With a burst of frosty air, he transformed into a hawk. Wings beating, he soared upward and passed through the roof like it was made of smoke.

A moment later, boots thumped on the concrete floor. Zak appeared, striding toward me. He wore clean jeans and a t-shirt that clung to his muscular torso. His hair was damp and towel-mussed from a recent shower, dark locks falling across his eyes.

A faint curl of heat awoke deep in my core at the sight of him, at the memory of his devouring kiss.

I didn't know what I wanted from him. I didn't know what existed between us, this strange relationship that had formed over the past weeks. My past was chaining me to a dark emptiness where I couldn't see where to go next. How did I move forward? How did I let go?

And what should I let go of?

What I knew, without a doubt, was that I needed Zak right now. Whether that was because he was intrinsically bound to the past I had yet to face, or for some other reason, I wasn't sure, but I needed him.

And he needed me.

He stopped a long step away, his green eyes searching mine. I could see the younger version of him overlapping the adult, past and present intertwined.

I let out a soft breath. "When do we leave?"

♠ ZAK ♠
TEN YEARS AGO

THE COOL MOUNTAIN AIR *was refreshing after the gross heat of the city. I hated downtown Vancouver and the miles of concrete that made me feel like I was suffocating. I sat with my back against a tree, my eyes half closed. It was too dark to see much, and I focused on my other senses as I waited.*

Energy thrummed through the earth beneath me. The quiet power of the old forest would have felt nice if it hadn't been threaded with a clammy, rotten chill that reminded me of a corpse. The foulness was Bane's essence—his ruthless, insatiable desire for power and dominance. Some fae sensed that energy and altered their course to avoid it. Others came looking for the source.

I practiced aura reflection every waking moment, and my energy was almost undetectable. The last thing I wanted was attention from the fae drawn to Bane's evil energy.

"Plotting, young druid?"

The throaty female voice purred in my ear, and my eyes flew open.

A fae stood just behind me on my left. She was bent at the waist, her long black hair falling over one shoulder, and when I turned, our faces almost touched. I leaned back, putting a few inches between our noses.

"Lallakai," I murmured, hiding my irritation. I still hadn't figured out how she could sneak up on me like that.

Straightening, she ran her fingers through her hair. I kept my gaze on her face, not allowing her to draw it down to all her bare skin. She used her body as a weapon, and I was determined to resist it.

Her full lips curved in a teasing smile as she crouched beside me. "You have the look of a scheming mind. Perhaps I can assist."

Instead of answering, I stretched my mind toward Grenior, Keelar, Yardir, Rannor, and Dredir, checking that they were all in position.

A warm, smooth fingertip brushed down my cheek.

"So unfriendly, young druid," Lallakai complained. "You have no response for me?"

Her tone wasn't offended. We'd been playing this game once or twice a week for a few months now.

"What are you offering in exchange for an answer?" I asked her.

"Can we not partake in an amicable conversation between companions?" She looked up at me through her eyelashes. "Must everything be a bargain?"

I pushed to my feet, and she rose as well. I was two inches taller, but it didn't feel like an advantage.

"Everything will be a bargain," I told her. "Unless you're planning to become a lot more generous. Then I might consider being 'companions' with you."

With a soft laugh, she stroked my cheek, her sharp nails tickling my skin. "Naughty boy. But perhaps I'll indulge you. What gift would you ask of me?"

Wariness flickered through me. Was she actually offering me something for free? What I wanted most was to know why she was interested in me. She wanted me to believe she was considering me as a potential consort, but I didn't dare believe it. She was too insistent on hiding her presence from Bane.

"You're offering me a gift?" I clarified. "With no debt or expectation of a favor later?"

"Entirely free," she crooned. "To prove my sincerity."

Nervous tension prickled down my spine, but I decided to take the risk. "A spell."

Her eyebrows rose. "A spell?"

"Something small," I said casually. "How about concealment? You're always sneaking up on me, so you're obviously good at it."

"You think concealment is a 'small' spell?" she asked, amused.

"It'd be a good demonstration of what sort of magic I can bargain for later."

Her amusement deepened. "As you wish, young druid."

Warm, slender fingers curled around my wrist. The turning my palm to face the dark canopy of forest leaves, she pushed up my sleeve. A single druidic circle was tattooed on my inner wrist, visible even in the darkness.

She pressed her sharp nail into the center of the circle. Stinging pain sparked when she broke the skin, and as a drop of blood welled, a black rune spread through the empty circle. A thick, shivery wave of magic slid through my body, taking root.

"Touch this rune and utter my name," she purred softly, "and for the next ninety-nine beats of your heart, you will be one with the darkness. As long as no light directly touches you, you will not be seen by humans or fae."

I nodded.

She released my wrist. "I hope you appreciate my generous gift ... and will be more generous in turn."

Yeah, right. I wasn't promising her gifts, generosity, or anything else. And I wasn't thanking her. She'd said she hoped I'd be more generous, but she was really hoping I'd get stupid.

"I'll see you around," I said instead, since it was inevitable she'd seek me out again.

I walked through the trees, and her gaze followed me, a pressure between my shoulder blades, but when I looked back, she was gone. I continued forward, finding a familiar path. My steps slowed, my boots silent on the mossy ground. A light glimmered through the trees, and I picked out the silhouette of the small cabin where Bane and I lived. Adrenaline spiked through me. I stopped.

As I waited, my gaze drifted up. A dozen red-and-white talismans hung from the lower branches of a tree. They looked like tiny figurines with round heads and tassel-like skirts of loose yarn. Dozens of them swayed from the trees all around the cabin.

Minutes dragged past, then Keelar's voice whispered in my mind. Now. Go.

I sped forward as quietly as possible. I couldn't sense Bane's presence or any of his fae, and my vargs were keeping watch.

The cabin was tiny and simple. Bane had built it himself after choosing this forest as his new territory. I slipped through the wooden door. The main space was small—a crude kitchen, a table with two chairs, and storage shelves along one short wall. Stacked on the shelves were the reference texts on sorcery and alchemy I'd been studying for the past ten years. Bottles and jars, vials and pouches, wooden boxes and dried herbs—all the ingredients for my alchemy arrays were stacked with other Arcana paraphernalia.

A standing wood stove provided our only source of heat. In the corner, beside a straw mattress covered in blankets, was a small wooden chest that held my personal belongings, which amounted to basically nothing.

Light glowed beneath the door to Bane's room, but I knew he wasn't inside. My gaze flicked up, sweeping across the markings etched in the doorframe. Another red-and-white talisman was nailed to the door. They were wards against fae, not humans, but my heart still shuddered in my chest as I swung the door open. Light flooded out, and I squinted against it.

Unlike my crude mattress, Bane had built himself an actual bed and carried in a comfortable foam mattress for it. He had real pillows.

Ignoring the bed, I turned to his worktable. Books were stacked on one end, scrolls of ancient paper covered in fae writing beside them. Artifacts, vials, and small weapons were scattered across the rest of the tabletop.

Other people might've thought it was weird that Bane left important, dangerous belongings just sitting around in an unlocked room, but those people had no clue. Reaching this cabin unnoticed was impossible, and anyone dumb enough to set foot inside would never make it out again.

As for me, I could go anywhere and touch anything—if I dared. Which I didn't. His punishments for disobedience kept me up at night even years later.

I crouched and reached under the desk. Tucked in the corner was a metal case the size of four of my largest Arcana textbooks stacked together. I slid it out. A small, basic lock hung from the front, a deterrent more than actual protection. Breath hissing through my clenched teeth, I slipped delicate tools from my pocket and went to work on the lock. It popped open. I flipped the lid up, then went still, listening hard.

Grenior's quiet presence brushed against my mind, reassuring me that the pack was keeping watch.

Inside the case, narrow vials were lined up in neat rows. My fingers brushed across the tops, and I pulled one out. The label was written in Ancient Cyrillic, which I couldn't translate, but I'd memorized the name I wanted. I slid it back in and checked another.

The fourth vial I withdrew was two-thirds full of a faintly greenish liquid. This was it. I tugged the cork open and waved the fumes toward my face. A strong scent, like acidic mint with an undertone of crushed leaves, hit my nose. I tilted the bottle against my fingertip. With only a slight dampness on my skin, I touched my fingertip to the end of my tongue. The liquid had a faint, minty sweetness that was almost pleasant—until my tongue went numb.

I capped the vial, placed it back in the case, closed the lid, and clicked the lock shut.

Less than a minute later, I was striding through the dark trees, one of my alchemy texts tucked under my arm. On silent paws, my five vargs trotted out of the shadows to join me, our mission complete.

I could steal that poison. And I would. But first, I needed to come up with a substitute to replace the poison. If Bane noticed the volume had dropped, he'd know I'd stolen some. So I would mix up something faintly green, minty, and sweet that could fool him.

I was leaving nothing to chance.

My gaze dropped to my wrist, where Lallakai's new spell marked my skin.

Nothing.

8

"TELL ME ABOUT ECHO."

Zak glanced at me, then refocused on driving. The first hour of our trek north had followed the scenic Sea to Sky Highway, and I'd spent most of it gazing out the window at the choppy waters of the Howe Sound. After passing through the town of Squamish, he'd directed the truck onto a narrow highway that ran through densely wooded valleys.

We'd since left pavement behind and were rumbling along a dirt road. The gray overcast clouds hung low in the sky, spilling down toward the treetops, and eddies of fog drifted across the road like clouds fallen to earth.

"I've known Echo since I was a kid." Zak's low voice blended with the road noise. "His territory is north of Bane's old territory, so we were neighbors, in a sense."

"Friendly neighbors?" I asked dubiously.

"I wouldn't call Echo friendly. He's difficult to read, even for a fae." He drummed his fingers on the steering wheel. "I'm not sure what to make of his disappearance. He's the sort of fae no one messes with, so what happened? Even Izverg was deferential to him."

The unfamiliar name sounded extremely Slavic, like "*eez-verg*" with a rolled R. "Who?"

"Hm? Oh, Bane's fae partner, the death master." He smirked. "Izverg never revealed his real name, so Bane nicknamed him. It's Russian for 'fiend.'"

Remembering the huge jackal beast that had killed Dex, my father's fae partner, I thought "fiend" sounded like an accurate name. "Is 'death master' a title?"

"Master is the rank below Lord or Lady."

Dex had called himself a master of fire, which meant Zak and I had both ranked up from our predecessors in terms of fae partners. I glanced over my shoulder at the backseat where Ríkr was curled up in cat form, sound asleep—or so it appeared.

Zak slowed the truck as we passed through a particularly dense eddy of fog that whited out the road. "Their ranking system is pretty loose. 'Masters' are fae with particularly strong magic. Lords and Ladies are fae who've risen above other masters in power, and Kings and Queens rule courts."

"Who determines if a fae is a master?"

He shrugged. "Another fae of similar or higher rank gives them the title, as far as I know. It's the same for druid names."

"Oh, so you didn't choose 'Crystal Druid' yourself?" I asked archly.

He snorted. "No. Actually, Echo gave me that name."

"What makes a fae give you a name?"

"When you do something that impresses them, they might name you. Or if you offend them, but you won't like whatever name they give you then."

I'd better try not to offend any fae. If I was going to eventually get a druid name, I'd prefer it not be insulting. "How much farther?"

"Thirty minutes to the farm, then another five hours on horseback."

"What farm?"

He didn't immediately answer. Surprised, I watched his jaw lock up and tension line his posture.

"My old farm," he finally said. "It's the best route north to the Shadow Court, and an easy place to have Tilliag meet me."

The condition of the road deteriorated until it was little more than a dirt track. The forest had grown wilder, the towering trees blocking our view of the mountains that crowded the valley. On our right, a rocky creek raced in the opposite direction toward the Squamish River, the water frothing and white.

I peered through the windshield. "Is it just me, or does the road end?"

"It collapsed into the creek decades ago. This used to be a mining route. There's abandoned equipment scattered around the forests here."

"How do we get to your farm?"

He arched an eyebrow and spun the steering wheel. The truck swerved toward the rushing rapids of the creek.

"Zak!" I shrieked.

The wheels bounced over the rocky shore, then we plowed into the water. The current shoved at the wheels—but we kept bouncing forward, rolling over boulders hidden just beneath the rapids.

The creek was only as wide as the truck was long, and the front tires jolted up onto dry ground. I let out a breathy exhale.

Zak cast me a smug smirk. "Now you know how it feels."

"Asshole."

As an innocent party in your reckless driving competition, Rίkr growled from the backseat, *I would have appreciated some warning.*

I pried my fingers off the handle above my seat. "How'd you know you could cross there?"

"Because I created the crossing—with some fae help. You timed your question perfectly, by the way."

I scowled at him.

Fallen leaves covered the ground, disguising the narrow track that cut through the trees. The creek peeked through the foliage until the corridor through the forest curved away from the water. We drove for another few minutes, then the woods gave way to a small valley.

My heart lodged in my throat.

Once, the valley had probably been lush and beautiful. But as it was now, the word "wasteland" came to mind. The surrounding mountains were vibrantly green and bursting with life, but the valley was a uniform grayish brown dotted with the burnt skeletons of trees. It was as though a wildfire had swept through the valley, except even the worst fires didn't kill *everything.* This was something more sinister.

Tension was radiating from Zak again. He drove the truck onto the scorched, dusty earth. The creek had come back into view, winding through the center of the valley, and on its nearer side were the remains of several buildings. They, too, had been utterly destroyed.

The truck rolled to a stop beside the collapsing remains of a farmhouse. Zak cut the engine, but he didn't unbuckle his seatbelt. He just sat there, staring through the windshield at the vista of death.

"What happened?" I asked.

He started as though he'd forgotten I was there. With a click of his seatbelt, he pushed his door open. I clambered out too, my hiking boots crunching on the ashes that coated the ground. I nudged my toe through the thick layer, searching for green sprouts.

Can you feel it? Ríkr landed on my shoulder, the small claws of his jay form pricking my skin. *The land is dead. Not even the hardiest blade of grass will take root in this earth for many seasons to come.*

I closed my eyes, but all my druid senses could detect was a hollow, empty note of death. Whatever the energy here had been like before, it had been silenced.

We should not linger here. He spread his wings. *I will familiarize myself with the area. Call me when you are prepared to continue onward.*

I nodded, and he took flight, soaring north. Reaching back into the truck, I pulled two lightweight hiking backpacks off the rear seats. A larger camping pack for overnight treks sat on the floor, stuffed with supplies for a week in the bush. I hoped we wouldn't need it.

Slinging my pack onto my back, I circled the truck. Zak stood near the blackened front porch of the house, gazing up at it. I crunched across the ashes and stopped beside him, closer than I would normally have stood.

I offered his backpack. He swung it over one shoulder, then resumed staring at the wreckage. I waited.

His chest rose and fell with a deep breath. "About a year ago, I pissed off a dark-arts sorceress when I picked up a mythic teen that the sorceress had planned to make her apprentice."

I remembered what he'd said about the kidnapping charges on his MPD records—he'd been saving mythic teens from the Vancouver streets.

"The sorceress was old and powerful, with a whole network of rogue mythics to do her bidding. Making an enemy of her was stupid, but ..." His hands clenched and unclenched. "No one saved me from Bane. I couldn't let the same thing happen to that girl."

My fingers twitched toward him, but I stopped myself. What if he didn't want me to touch him?

"I sent the girl overseas and went into hiding. I thought the sorceress would forget about me. While I was gone, she found the valley, broke through its protections ... and did this."

"She did it to punish you?" I whispered.

"And to draw me out. She figured I'd come back to kill her. She was right." He gazed around at the destruction. "But it didn't change anything. It didn't bring this place back."

"Did the other kids you rescued live here too?" I asked softly.

"Yeah, they'd hang around for a few months, sometimes longer, then move on when they were ready. A few older 'rescues' managed them. I didn't do much besides bring them here."

I rubbed my temple, trying to puzzle it out. "Why do it? If you weren't taking care of them yourself, why bring them here?"

His eyes turned to mine, obscured by shadows. "Morgan was the first person I brought here. I sent all the others on their way before I went into hiding, but she didn't want to be anywhere else, so I let her stay." He pointed at the ground a few feet in front of him. "She died right there."

I looked at the spot. It was nothing more than a layer of ashes in front of the porch steps.

"I was selfish." Zak stared at the ashes. "I knew she'd be safer somewhere else, but her staying meant I could keep my horses here too."

My neck creaked unwillingly as I looked over my shoulder at the remains of another building, its shape familiar despite the damage. "The sorceress killed your horses too?"

"Burned them alive in the barn."

Horror snapped through me before a wave of grinding rage consumed it. If he hadn't already killed that sorceress, I would have started hunting her right this moment—a desire made stronger by the sight of Zak standing beside me with the look of a mortally wounded man silently bleeding to death.

I grabbed his hand and yanked him into motion. Stumbling, he extended his stride to match mine as I swept away from the burned house, heading in the direction Ríkr had flown.

"Aren't you the one who tore into me for not forgiving people for making mistakes?" I said sharply, tugging on his hand to ensure he kept moving. "That applies to you too. You need to forgive yourself."

"Aren't you the one who pointed out how some things are unforgivable?"

"You didn't burn this place down yourself. You underestimated an enemy. If it was me instead of you, wouldn't you say I should cut myself some slack?"

His mouth pressed into a thin line. "Probably, but that doesn't mean either of us can do it."

My fingers dug into his. His crushed mine. We held on to each other as we marched the length of the valley. I didn't slow as we climbed over the collapsed fence that delineated former pasture and healthy forest. I didn't slow as greenery engulfed us and the scent of green things washed away the dusty, bitter ash.

I didn't slow until we were surrounded by the vibrant pulse of life and I could no longer sense the empty death from the valley. I pulled Zak to a halt. Tugging my hand free, I turned to face him and stepped close—then I wrapped my arms around his waist, rested my cheek on his shoulder, and closed my eyes.

He stood rigidly, as though expecting a knife in his back at any moment.

"I'm comforting you, asshole," I muttered. "Should I punch you instead?"

He was silent, then with stilted motions, he settled his arms around my shoulders. He'd been a lot more confident when pinning me to a wall and kissing me. Emotional comfort was a foreign concept to both of us.

I drew in a deep breath. I exhaled, breathed in again, then began to sing.

"My young love said to me, 'My brothers won't mind, and my parents won't slight you for your lack of kind.' Then she stepped away from me and this she did say: 'It will not be long, love, till our wedding day.'"

The wrenchingly mournful tune of lost love slid softly across my lips. Zak's arms tightened around me, and he didn't breathe as I continued into the next verse about a doomed bride-to-be who would never make it to her wedding.

"Then she went her way homeward with one star awake, as the swan in the evening moves over the lake."

His hand touched the back of my head, his fingers curling into my hair. He bowed his head as he listened, his breath stirring my bangs.

"*And I smiled as she passed with her goods and her gear, and that was the last that I saw of my dear.*" I pulled myself closer to him, pressing against his chest as I began the final verse. "*I dreamt it last night that my young love came in, so softly she entered, her feet made no din; she came close beside me, and—*"

"Stop," he whispered hoarsely. "That … that's enough."

Falling silent, I turned my head, pressing my face into his neck. I could feel his pulse throbbing under his jaw, and his throat moved as he swallowed.

"I was hoping it'd be cathartic," I mumbled. "Singing works on horses."

"Saber, I'm not a horse."

"I know that. I just … I don't …" Embarrassment infused me, and I pushed away from him. "Forget it. I shouldn't have—"

He clamped his arms around me, pulling me back in so forcefully that air rushed out of my lungs. "Thank you. For trying. It helped."

I hesitated, then relaxed in his hold. "Zak … I didn't say it before, but thanks for everything last week with my parents and Ríkr and Luthyr. I couldn't have faced all that alone."

My teeth pinched my lower lip. What I should have said was, "I couldn't have faced all that *without you*."

I drew back, and this time he let me. I put two feet between us before peeking at his face. He was gazing into the trees. Lines of grief creased the corners of his mouth, his eyes dark with sorrow and regret.

Reaching out, I entwined our fingers. He glanced at our hands, then curled his fingers around mine. Considering how much we'd hurt each other, he was the last person I should be comforting and I was the last person he should be accepting comfort from. Yet here we were, just two broken people trying not to fall apart.

"Any sign of Tilliag?" I asked.

"I called for him. He'll be here soon."

I frowned. I hadn't heard him telepathically calling for the fae stallion. "Why didn't I hear anything?"

"Because you weren't listening."

"How come you can snoop in on my fae conversations so easily?" I demanded. "Is there a trick to telepathic eavesdropping?"

He tipped his head back in a husky laugh. My fingers spasmed around his, holding on tight as though his laughter might blow me off my feet.

"If you don't know how," he said with a final chuckle, "I'd rather you didn't learn."

"That's not fair. If you can do it, I should be able to as well."

"Life's not fair."

"Zak!"

He laughed again, and I couldn't do anything but stare at him as he started walking, our hands entwined as though neither of us intended to let go.

9

TILLIAG'S HOOVES THUDDED STEADILY against a thick layer of fallen leaves and brown pine needles. Astride his back, I sat behind Zak with my hands on his waist. The air had grown steadily cooler as we moved north, the sky threatening rain. I'd zipped my sweater up under my chin, and I wished I could press against Zak's body heat without getting a face-full of his slim backpack.

We'd been traveling northward for hours, and I knew we were well into the Shadow Court's territory. I could sense it in the air—the thrum of fae power. It wasn't a pleasant feeling. The Gardall'kin fae had a harsh, slippery energy that tasted of night and decay.

The woods weren't noticeably different from the landscape we'd passed through on our way here, but the shadows beneath the forest canopy were inexplicably darker. The trees were more twisted, the air thicker than it should have been. Even without my druid senses, I would've found this place eerie.

The ominous aura didn't appear to affect Grenior and Keelar. The two vargs trekked silently through the trees on our left, noses dipping toward the ground as they checked scents. They'd met us a kilometer beyond the destroyed valley that had once been Zak's home, and Tilliag had appeared a few minutes later, stomping his hooves and complaining about having to wait so long for Zak's return.

My gaze flicked to the right. Ghosting through the underbrush was a pale shape, larger than the vargs and even more graceful: Ríkr, padding through the forest in his stunning wolfhound form. His thick white fur glimmered in the overcast light, small golden antlers rising from his forehead just in front of his wolf-like ears.

He'd decided on the wolfhound for its intimidation factor, and also to reserve his humanlike form in case we needed another card to play. I hoped we wouldn't, but with not one but two tasty druids walking right into their arms, the fae of the Shadow Court might decide on an impromptu feast.

Should we expect an immediate audience? Ríkr asked, pausing between two pine trees with his ears perked forward. *Or must we demand one?*

"They already know we're here," Zak said. "Assuming it goes like normal, a few members of the court will show up to greet us."

I hope they come soon, Tilliag complained. *I have already carried you across mountains and waited while you frolicked in a human city.*

"Frolicked?" Zak muttered.

The court will greet you? Blue eyes gleamed in the gloom as Ríkr glanced our way. *Your rapport with the ruthless Gardall'kin is more intimate than I imagined.*

Zak rolled his shoulders, the muscles in his sides tensing under my hands. "Marzanna, the queen, has always favored me, and the rest of the court followed her lead. If she's changed her tune, however, this won't go well."

How did you curry favor with a Shadow Queen, I wonder? Ríkr mused.

"Queen of Death, actually," Zak corrected. "It's called the Shadow Court because the Gardall'kin all have shadow abilities of some sort, but Marzanna's most dangerous power is her death magic."

That news didn't bolster my confidence. "Is your plan to ask about Lallakai and Echo, then leave?"

"Yes. All I want is information. Marzanna might be friendly with me, but I don't want to owe her anything."

A queen's ire carries great risks, Ríkr remarked. *I will aspire to charm her of any animosity.*

"I seriously doubt that'll work," Zak replied.

Nonsense. I am very charming.

I rolled my eyes. "Unless you're going to flirt with her, Ríkr, you should focus on intimidation instead."

His annoyed chuff carried through the quiet woods. *I feel I am being doubly insulted.*

Your canine form lacks appeal, Tilliag told him. *It bears no majesty or elegance.*

Elegance of mind is required to recognize elegance of form, Ríkr replied. *You possess neither.*

"Enough." Zak pointed ahead. "They're waiting."

I leaned around him to squint through the trees. An intangible darkness blanketed the forest, and as Tilliag continued forward, it was like we were walking into an unnatural night. The gray sky faded to a midnight-blue hue, and faintly glowing, electric colors shimmered over the tree trunks. The undersides of the leaves shone silver, and the delicate fronds of ferns sparkled fluorescent pink.

We'd drifted out of human reality and into the borderlands of the fae demesne. Mist eddied among the trunks, and the buzz of fae power in the air thickened until I could taste it in the back of my throat.

The trees parted, revealing a dark glade dotted with a thousand white flowers. Hovering above them, hundreds of neon-purple fireflies fluttered in an endless dance. The remains of an ancient structure rose from the ground: smooth columns covered in moss and vines, grand archways, and carved railings. I couldn't tell what sort of building had once stood here, but what remained was alien and beautiful even as it crumbled.

Standing among the ruins, the fae of the Shadow Court observed our approach.

My hands tightened on Zak's waist. "Didn't you say *a few* fae would meet us?"

"It's usually just a few," he muttered. "Stay on your guard."

I was already guarded, tension and adrenaline winding my muscles tight. Jewel-like fae eyes tracked our every movement. The members of the court were all vaguely humanoid, but one had flesh made of twisted black vines. Another had pale skin covered in a network of bloated veins, her grayish-white hair falling in a tangle down to her bony elbows. Another had a head reminiscent of a plucked rooster with dark skin, a stained beak dominating his face.

There were a dozen in total, all monstrous, all powerful. If this went wrong, we were dead.

Tilliag halted, the fae of the court still thirty feet away. *Dismount.*

Zak swung his leg over the stallion's neck and dropped to the ground. I followed suit, my boots landing in the soft layer of flora and crushing flowers that released a sweet perfume. Back on ground level, I felt much smaller and more vulnerable.

Then Ríkr stepped up beside me and I felt even smaller. His wolfhound form was larger than a tiger, his shoulder level with my elbow.

The gazes of the Shadow Court shifted to him.

Zak took the lead, striding toward the waiting fae. I followed two steps behind, Ríkr pacing at my side. Tilliag waited where we'd dismounted, setting himself apart from us, but Grenior and Keelar had flanked Zak, their hackles raised warningly.

A hush fell as we passed beneath a stone arch and into the ruins. The shadows deepened, turning the drifting mist black. It felt like we were walking through watery ink. The Shadow Court stood in a rough half circle facing us, with a wide gap in the middle directly ahead, as though someone had yet to arrive.

Zak drew to a stop. He surveyed the line of fae, then focused on a male standing beside the empty gap. He was less monstrous than the others, with sleek ebony hair in a messy braid, two dark stripes running down his face, and black eyes. Half a dozen horns in two rows starting at his temples curved toward the back of his head.

"Lord of Shadow," Zak said quietly. "Is the queen coming?"

The horned male parted his lips, revealing a line of shark-like fangs in his mouth. "An arrogant and presumptuous question, Crystal Druid."

"Marzanna has always welcomed my visits. Has that changed?"

"Much has changed, druid. Much." His black eyes shifted to me. "You bring others. Name them."

"The other druid is unnamed," Zak said. "She is consort to the Lord of Winter beside her."

"Lord of Winter? I know of no such lord in these lands."

Omniscience is a rare talent. Ancient power thrummed through Ríkr's voice. *Unless you wish to challenge my title, Lord of Shadow, withhold your senseless protests.*

My eyes widened at his imperious order.

The Crystal Druid seeks an audience with your queen, Ríkr continued, his tone as regal as if he were still the King of Annwn. *If she will not grant it, we will waste no further time in such boorish company.*

My eyes went even wider before I controlled my expression. So much for Ríkr using his charm.

"Boorish?" the horned male replied quietly. "Should you find us so lacking in refinement, Lord of Winter, then I bid you share your judgment with our ruler."

He pivoted to face the open gap in the line of courtly fae. A moment later, a sound reached my ears—an odd rustling like something dragging across the ground. The darkness was thick and cold, obscuring my vision.

The sound grew more distinct, accompanied by the soft crunch of footfalls flattening the flowering plants that filled the glade. A silhouette, darker than the shadows, took form. It drew closer and closer, and as it stepped into the gap beside the horned male, the thick darkness parted, revealing the new arrival.

Zak's whole body went rigid. Grenior and Keelar lowered their heads, hackles raised and muzzles ridged as they snarled.

At the sight of that fae, my lungs stuttered—and when I breathed again, it was with fierce determination.

Welcome to my court, Zaharia.

The fae's voice was a hideous blend of a high-pitched whine and a deep-throated growl. Cruel amusement lined his mocking declaration as black lips pulled back from a long, narrow snout.

"Izverg," Zak rasped.

The brutish jackal let loose a high, cackling laugh.

I knew Zak had killed the Wolfsbane Druid, and I'd assumed his beastly fae partner was dead too. Clearly, I'd been wrong.

The vision I'd seen of Dex's death hadn't done justice to Izverg's ten-foot-tall frame. He towered over the other darkfae, his ribs pressed against his ragged fur coat and his shoulders bulging above long arms. Unlike in the vision, he'd accessorized with two matching gauntlets of a steel-like metal that ran up his sinewy forearms. The jointed metal covered his bony fingers, and the ends were tipped with green-streaked purple stones in the shape of talons.

One of those gauntleted fists was braced on the ground and the other was bent behind him. Still cackling, Izverg pulled something forward and tossed it carelessly onto the delicate flowers. Fireflies scattered as the unmoving heap sprawled lifelessly.

My eyes darted across long, tangled raven hair and graceful, feminine limbs. Lallakai. I couldn't tell if she was alive.

Come to collect your refuse, little druid? Izverg taunted.

Zak's hands curled into fists. "I see you're as twisted as ever."

And you smell as mouthwatering as always, Zaharia. It's been so long since I've had a taste. Looming over Lallakai's unmoving form, he ran his black tongue over his snout. *Care to bargain? Surrender to me and I'll allow the Night Eagle to live.*

"Is that why you haven't killed her yet?"

Another evil cackle.

Ríkr's shoulder brushed against my arm. *Prepare an aura sphere.*

I focused inward, gathering the ferocious inner strength I'd channeled before unleashing my screaming aura sphere in the Hell's Gate crossroad.

Izverg stretched out one long arm. He curled his jeweled talons into Lallakai's hair and pulled her head up. Her face was smudged with dirt and blood, her green eyes dull and staring.

Are you not moved to protect your lady? His jackal snout parted in a fang-laden smirk. *Heartless still, Zaharia? Bane forged you well. I remember—*

Now, Ríkr commanded.

I threw my head back and screamed. Pain ripped into my throat with the force of my cry as my rage swept out like an invisible tidal wave, washing away the slippery, rotting magic of the Shadow Court.

As my aura sphere and my voice snatched the attention of every fae, the temperature plunged below freezing. Ríkr's azure magic flashed. Sheets of ice shot upward from the ground, forming a thick wall in front of the enemy fae, blocking them from view—except Izverg.

Zak charged forward, his black sword coalescing in his hand. He leaped over Lallakai's limp form and slashed at Izverg's belly.

The jackal caught the blade, his steel gauntlet gleaming, and threw Zak backward. He landed on one shoulder and rolled. As he went down, Grenior and Keelar lunged in, teeth snapping at the jackal's legs—and I flung an ice spear at his face.

Izverg's claws snapped around the projectile in midair, and it exploded into a starburst around his hand. His arm dipped with the weight, and Grenior took advantage of his disarmed left side to tear a chunk out of his leg.

Zak grabbed Lallakai around the waist and heaved her over his shoulder. Sword in his other hand, he backed away. I called up another ice spear, aiming for Izverg's head again.

The jackal's chest swelled, then he let out an ear-splitting roar.

My aura sphere faltered and vanished as his power rippled out. The darkness deepened and the stench of rot clogged the air. The blanket of delicate white flowers melted into decaying mush, the wave of death spreading out from the jackal's feet. Ríkr's walls of white ice turned murky gray and crumbled as though they'd turned to mud.

Kill everyone but Zaharia, Izverg snarled. *Now!*

Looping circles of blue light erupted beneath his feet, then Ríkr's ice surged upward in jagged spires, engulfing the jackal.

But he'd already commanded his court.

RÍKR'S ICE WALL was still collapsing as the fae of the Shadow Court leaped over the barrier. Half of them went straight for Ríkr, but the pale-skinned female spun toward me, her hands lifting. Silvery magic glowed over her fingers—and a matching glow lit beneath my boots. I leaped backward, but the glow followed me.

Smiling malevolently, she pointed her palm at me, her magic brightening. A deathly chill rose up from my feet, numbing my limbs.

The horned Lord of Shadow appeared beside her. He shoved her, knocking her on her ass, and pointed a claw-tipped finger at me. A spear of black magic launched toward my chest. I dove to the ground and the shadow spear struck the earth behind me in an explosion of dirt.

With a loud crack, the starburst of ice encasing Izverg shattered. He appeared amidst the broken fragments, snarling furiously—and with a flash of blue light and a burst of swirling snow, Ríkr transformed from wolfhound to his humanoid form. Shards of ice whipped around him in a spiraling blizzard, tearing into the fae who got too close.

Ríkr raised his arm. The flying shards coalesced into a ribbon that twisted around him, the ice shattering and reforming so fast it was more liquid than solid. The spiraling line thickened, then thickened more until it took on the shape of a jagged ice serpent. It coiled around Ríkr, its reptilian jaw gaping hungrily.

With a bestial snarl, Izverg lunged at Ríkr. The serpent struck and ice burst everywhere, filling the glade with sparkling snow.

A dark bolt flashed past my right cheek, just missing me. I lurched around. The horned male was stalking toward me, magic swirling over his hands and up his arms. I summoned an ice spear, hurled it at him, then cast out my aura sphere again, trying to push back Izverg's foul energy.

The horned male sidestepped my spear and kept coming. He fired another black blade at me and I dove clear, rolled to my feet, and sprinted away, my gaze scouring the battlefield.

With thundering hooves, Tilliag charged past me. I raced after him.

Zak appeared in the haze of shadows, snow, and ancient ruins. Lallakai hung over his shoulder, and Grenior and Keelar darted around him, guarding his back as he rushed toward Tilliag. The stallion and I reached him together, and I helped him heave Lallakai across Tilliag's back. Zak swung up behind her, then reached down for me.

A shadow blade hit the white column beside me. Stone shrapnel sliced my skin.

Zak yanked a potion bottle from his belt and whipped it at the horned male. He cut it out of the air with another blade, and with the shattering of glass, the potion exploded into a gray cloud that reeked of iron.

I hauled myself up onto Tilliag's back, barely grabbing onto Zak's jacket as the stallion pivoted on his hind legs.

Before he could leap away, Izverg charged out of the mist, his red eyes glowing and fangs bared. Death magic clung to him in streaks of oozing, toxic black. His taloned gauntlet slashed toward Zak.

An ice spear formed in my hand and I lunged sideways, smashing it into Izverg's palm before it touched Zak. The spear burst into shards as Tilliag lunged violently forward. But I wasn't holding on. My balance was off.

The world spun as I fell, landing hard on my back.

"Saber!" Zak yelled.

"Keep going!" I gasped.

As Tilliag's thundering hooves receded, Izverg towered over me with a bestial grin. *I've traded one of Zaharia's females for another. How amusing.*

Lightning-fast, he grabbed the front of my sweater. His jeweled talons pierced the fabric, scratching my skin as he lifted me off my feet. Tongue dragging over his lips, he breathed his foul, rotten breath in my face.

Perhaps you would make a better pet than Zaharia. He has so many bad habits.

I bared my teeth. "So do I."

Grabbing his gauntlet with one hand, I rammed my switchblade into the exposed underside of his wrist up to the hilt. I got in one good twist of the blade before he hurled me to the ground. My back slammed down on the hard earth, knocking the wind out of me a second time.

The jackal's foot stomped down on my chest, squeezing the last of the air from my lungs. The leaves and flowers surrounding me browned and melted with accelerated rot. A horrific chill spread through my chest. I could *feel* death creeping through me. I could feel my cells starting to wither and die.

With a soft hiss of intense cold, frost formed over Izverg's dark fur. His eyes widened, then he stepped off me and whirled around—just as Ríkr drove an ice spear at his chest. Izverg caught it with both hands, and ice flashed over his arms.

My ex-familiar, and now fae partner, had transformed himself yet again. Ice armor glittered on his shoulders and torso, protecting his vitals. His spear was no longer a crude length of ice but a polished weapon as perfect as glass—except for the copious blood staining it.

Flee, Saber. Ríkr's telepathic voice was calm. *I will follow momentarily.*

You will not, Izverg snarled. *Shadow Court! The Winter Lord is mine. Capture the female druid. Now!*

I shoved to my feet and bolted away from the ruins—and the Shadow Court came behind me.

Four nightmarish monsters pursued me, closing fast. One had transformed into an insectile creature resembling a black, spiked praying mantis, and it sped forward on four jointed legs, drawing ahead of the others.

I ran harder, arms pumping. The trees were too far. I wouldn't make it. I glanced back—and the mantis was right behind me, its long, clawed arm reaching for my back.

The horned male dropped out of nowhere. He landed with both feet on the mantis's head, slamming it face-first into the ground. His shadow magic swirled around his arms.

I skidded to a stop and spun to face him, knowing I couldn't outrun his projectile magic. As I formed another cold ice spear, Ríkr's magical gift had never felt so insufficient. Half a dozen beasts formed a line behind the horned male, none daring to step past him after he'd crushed the mantis into the ground.

He raised his hand toward me, shadows rippling over his slender, claw-tipped fingers.

Hoofbeats exploded behind me. The sound erupted out of nowhere, almost on top of me. I jerked sideways, shocked that Tilliag had returned.

But the horse galloping toward me wasn't Tilliag.

He was lean, leggy, graceful, black as night, and with burning orange eyes. His hooves slammed down, and fire ignited beneath them. The raging flames shot forward in burning lines, blasting by on either side of me. The horned male leaped away.

I spun, half blinded by heat and smoke. The beating hooves were close. My reaching hand met silky hair.

Grabbing the stallion's mane, I swung up onto his back. He turned sharply, hooves tearing at the earth, and charged for the trees—but there was no path, just a wall of foliage. A blade of shadow magic shot past us, chilling my left ear. The impassible underbrush loomed as the stallion galloped without slowing. A strange, tingling rush of magic swept up through my body.

My vision blurred, and the trees turned to semi-transparent silhouettes.

The stallion ran full tilt into the ghostly forms like they weren't even there, leaving the Shadow Court behind.

MY LUNGS HEAVED as I caught my breath. The Dullahan's steed trotted tirelessly through the trees, following a winding game trail, and I gripped his sides with my legs, grateful that his trot was so smooth. We were alone in the dark woods, and I couldn't sense Ríkr or Zak.

Head spinning with everything that had happened, I tried to think what to do next, but until Ríkr caught up to me or I found Zak, my best option was to keep moving away from the hostile fae of the Shadow Court.

"So," I muttered, focusing on my mount instead, "I guess you went north like I suggested."

The stallion rotated an ear toward me and rambled off something in an incomprehensible language, his telepathic voice a pleasantly soft tenor.

"Or did you follow me?" I asked him with a frown. It didn't seem likely. Even a fae horse would've had trouble keeping up with a vehicle traveling highway speeds for hours, and it was even less likely that Ríkr would have missed the presence of a tagalong.

I glanced around the quiet forest. The shadows and mists of the fae demesne hid the sun. Uneasy, I stretched my senses out—and felt a familiar flicker of power. So did the stallion. He danced sideways in mid-trot, almost unseating me.

Saber.

With a flash of feathers, a white jay landed on my shoulder, and I let out an explosive breath. "Ríkr. What took so long?"

I ensured I wasn't followed. He peered at the horse I was riding. *Would this be the Dullahan's former mount?*

Resuming a smooth trot, the stallion replied in his language. Ríkr listened carefully—then replied in the same language. They went back and forth for a minute.

His name is Artear, Ríkr informed me, switching back to English. *He traveled in the direction you recommended, and while in the midst of navigating the Shadow Court's territory to more hospitable lands, he sensed your aura sphere.*

"Oh." I wanted to thank the fae for his help, but that was risky. Fae sometimes interpreted thanks as an admission of debt. "His timing was excellent."

Artear has inquired as to whether his aid was sufficient to settle the debt between you.

"Yes, of course." More than enough. He'd saved my life.

The stallion bobbed his head in a satisfied way.

He is now transporting us to the "other druid," Ríkr added.

A few minutes later, Keelar ghosted out of the shadows, her red eyes gleaming. Artear huffed restlessly, but he was willing to follow the varg. As we trekked through the forest, the sky lightened to a more natural overcast gloom and the darkness lifted.

Keelar pushed into a lope. Squinting ahead, I glimpsed Tilliag through the foliage, his neck arched and one hoof scraping impatiently at the ground. I couldn't see Zak or Lallakai.

As Artear trotted closer, Tilliag looked our way. His ears flattened. Artear pinned his ears too. His trot lost its smooth flow and turned jarring and choppy as he shifted into an aggressive gait.

I swung my leg over his back and dropped off his side, bailing before I ended up in the middle of a stallion brawl. Ríkr seemed to have the same idea, as he soared up into a tree. Leaving the horses to it, I hurried through the underbrush.

In a gap in the foliage, Zak knelt between two trees. Lallakai was stretched out on her back in front of him, and he was cupping her head as he dribbled a potion into her mouth. Her eyes were half open but glassy and unseeing. Shallow scratches marred her arms and legs, dried blood streaking her skin, but she didn't appear badly wounded.

I crouched opposite Zak. He glanced up, his face tight.

"Are you okay?" he asked brusquely, unsurprised to see me. Keelar had probably been updating him on our approach.

"Fine. And Ríkr is fine too."

Zak jerked his head in a nod and resumed trickling potion into Lallakai's mouth. "She's been poisoned, but I don't know with what. I gave her a universal antidote, and this detox potion will help her body purge the toxin."

I glanced over her pallid skin and lifeless face. "Will that be enough?"

Lines creased his jaw around his mouth. "Knowing Izverg, probably not."

A dozen feet away, one of the stallions snorted angrily. I could hear a lot of hoof stamping, but no screaming and squealing, so they must be at the intimidation phase of the challenge. I hoped that would be the extent of it.

"Did you know Izverg was alive?" I asked.

Zak set Lallakai's head gently on the ground, then sat back on his heels. For a moment, he just sat there, gazing at Lallakai, then he pressed his hand over his eyes.

"*Fuck!*" he exploded. "What the fuck is going on? How is that monster ruling a fucking court? What happened to Marzanna? Why—"

He broke off into a string of profanity, his voice growing rougher with each vehement curse. The sharp edge beneath his anger prickled along my nerves.

Exhaling violently, he squeezed his temples, his hand still hiding his eyes. "The night I killed Bane, Lallakai and I split them up. She fought Izverg while I took on Bane. I succeeded, she failed. But I escaped before Izverg returned. I never saw him again—until today."

"He didn't come after you for killing his consort?"

"Bane was just a plaything for Izverg, not that Bane ever realized it." Bitterness coated Zak's voice. "Or maybe he did and he was making the best of it. To Izverg, every living thing is a toy to slowly destroy—or quickly and violently destroy."

My fingers slipped into my pocket, but my switchblade wasn't there. I'd left it lodged in Izverg's wrist. "Now what?"

Zak slowly lowered his hand from his face. His green eyes were hollow and haunted. "We need to get the hell away from here."

My lips pressed together, but before I could decide how to reply, darkness flooded across the ground between my hiking boots. My shadow thickened and rippled upward. I recoiled, shooting to my feet—and my shadow surged up, solidifying into a solid body taller than I was.

The horned Lord of Shadows stood in front of me.

"Hold!" he cried sharply.

His demand came as Zak's shadow blade formed in his hand, my ice spear formed in mine, and Ríkr plunged out of the trees, transforming into his humanoid form in a flurry of frost. In the next instant, Grenior and Keelar were flanking Zak, snarling softly, and Tilliag and Artear had both closed in, hooves stomping.

Surrounded, the horned male stood with his hands raised and palms out in surrender, unmoving.

I leveled my ice spear at his throat, the jagged point inches from his dusky skin. "Where the hell did you come from?"

His black eyes held mine. "I hid in your shadow. No other in the court can utilize that ability. I was not followed, and neither were you."

Behind the Shadow Lord, Zak held his sword at the ready. "Why are you here, Yilliar?"

"I bid you not to depart, Crystal Druid." The fae's dark gaze flicked to Ríkr, then back to Zak. "Marzanna yet lives. I seek allies to destroy the foul beast who has overtaken my court and return Marzanna to her throne."

"Ah," Ríkr crooned. "The sweetly treacherous intrigues of court life. How I've missed those long nights of ardent scheming."

Why did he sound completely sincere?

Shaking my head, I focused on Yilliar. "All your attacks missed me, and you stomped on the other fae who were attacking me. I'm assuming that was on purpose."

"Of course." His lips curved, revealing a hint of fangs. "I do not miss."

Zak raised his sword, holding it over Yilliar's shoulder with the blade angled at his neck. "If you want to discuss the possibility of cooperating, then make us some promises."

Yilliar's dark eyes seemed to suck in the dim light. "I swear to all present here that I will inflict no intentional harm upon you nor betray you to the Lord of Death who now rules the Shadow Court."

With a grunt of acceptance, Zak lowered his arm, but he didn't dissolve the sword. I let my ice spear hang at my side, following his lead.

"How is Marzanna still alive if Izverg has her throne?" Zak asked.

"The beast poisoned her, just as he poisoned the Night Eagle. Marzanna hid herself and needs naught but a cure to regain her strength. With her, we can destroy Izverg once and for all. Do not pretend you haven't longed for his death, Crystal Druid."

Zak's face was stony. "Izverg was unstoppable ten years ago. He'll be even stronger with an entire court behind him. It's suicide."

I watched him, my lips bending in a frown.

"If personal revenge does not motivate you, what of the larger ramifications?" Yilliar's voice deepened with intensity. "Izverg already pushes the boundaries of the court's territory. His deathly poison spreads. He has held the throne for a mere fortnight, and his power will only grow. If he is not killed soon, he will become truly undefeatable."

"Izverg is your problem," Zak said flatly. "Deal with him yourself."

Yilliar bared his fangs. "When did this pathetic cowardice infect you, Crystal Druid?"

My ice spear snapped up, the point hovering at the pulse in the Shadow Lord's throat. "Impressive manners for a lord," I snarled. "Do you always insult people when you don't get your way?"

"An insult it may be, but it is accurate nonetheless."

A bone-deep chill spread through the air. "The Crystal Druid has given you his answer, Lord of Shadow," Ríkr said, his eyes bright with icy power. "Take your leave."

With a quiet snarl, Yilliar blurred into darkness and sank until his body had merged with the shadows on the forest floor.

I waited, but I couldn't sense his presence. I lowered my spear again, and then—because I still didn't know how to unmake the ice—I tossed it into a bush.

"Let's get out of here," I said. "He could pop up again any time."

Nodding, Zak dissolved his sword. I watched as he silently lifted Lallakai and carried her over to Tilliag.

I'd defended him when Yilliar had called him a coward. Zak wasn't a coward, and Yilliar deserved a spear in the throat for trying to manipulate Zak with insults. But even though I didn't want to admit it, the Shadow Lord wasn't wrong.

Because the emotion Zak was fighting, the reaction he'd tried to hide from me ... was fear.

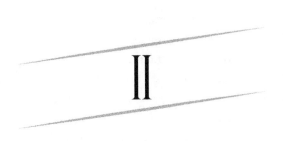

WE MADE THE FIVE-HOUR TREK back to Zak's decimated farm. In the woods a few miles north of the burned buildings was a one-room log cabin where, he'd explained, he had practiced alchemy too dangerous to perform near the teenage rescues on his farm. It had escaped the destruction that had leveled the rest of his property.

Inside the cabin was a dusty counter with cabinets beneath it, a worktable at standing height, a long wooden chest that doubled as a bench, and a freestanding wood stove. That was it.

Zak opened the chest and pulled out a tightly rolled sleeping bag. While I spread it out along the far wall, he carried Lallakai inside and laid her down on the bedding. He checked her pulse, then pulled her eyelids back to examine her pupils.

"Rapid pulse," he muttered. "Shallow breathing. Fever. Chilled extremities. Loss of consciousness." Shaking his head, he walked to the cabinets and opened them. "It could be almost anything. Her symptoms aren't specific enough to narrow down a toxin."

"Is the universal antidote helping?" I asked, moving to stand at the table. "What about a tox screen? Is that possible with alchemy?"

"To an extent." He started pulling things off the shelves. "And I'm not sure if the universal antidote is helping. Her breathing is more normal, but that's it."

As he stacked bottles, dried herbs, drafting paper, protractors, rulers, and a set of scales on the table, I glanced toward the open door. Ríkr had taken his hawk form to keep an eye out for any pursuers, and Grenior and Keelar were doing the same on foot. We were almost five hours of hard travel from the Shadow Court, but that wasn't far enough to count this location as safe—though if Yilliar was to be believed, no one aside from him had followed us.

I picked up a bundle of dried leaves, recognizing them as mountain ash. "Will Izverg hunt you down?"

"If you'd asked me yesterday, I would've said that Izverg doesn't give a shit about me." He shrugged off his long coat. "But I can't think of any reason he wouldn't kill and eat Lallakai unless he wanted her alive to lure me in."

He set his coat on the counter, his black, long-sleeved shirt stretching across his shoulders with the movement. Digging into the coat's interior, he pulled a small leather book from a hidden pocket. I watched him open the grimoire, momentarily lost in a memory of the same book in his hands ten years ago, his green eyes gliding aimlessly across its pages while I played with my red-handled switchblade.

"Lure you in ..." I repeated slowly. "Do you think Izverg might have something to do with Echo calling for you?"

Zak looked up from the grimoire, and that same sharp tightness darkened his eyes: fear. Fear at the suggestion that Izverg had lured him into a trap.

"I don't know," he growled, looking down at the grimoire again. "Like I said, Echo is powerful. Izverg used to be afraid of him."

"But Izverg is stronger now. Yilliar called him a Lord of Death. He's increased his rank since you knew him."

Zak turned pages in his grimoire, searching for something. "All the more reason to get away from him."

"What about Echo?"

"He can take care of himself."

"But he called for you."

"I'm just a druid, Saber," he snapped. "Echo can crush small towns without breaking a sweat. He doesn't need me."

I wasn't sure what surprised me more: Zak's anger or the implication about his fae ally's power.

"Zak—" I began.

"Don't fucking start." He slashed a glare across me. "I'm not a white knight. My relationship with Echo is one of convenience—for both of us. I'm not going up against the Shadow Court for a fae who only shows up to help *me* when he feels like it."

I was silent.

He slapped his open grimoire down on the table. "You know I'm not the 'loyal ally' type. I put myself first ten years ago, and I haven't changed. If you want me to be the kind of person who turns into a self-sacrificing fool the moment their friends are in trouble, too fucking bad. That's not who I am."

Bitterness suffused me at his casually cutting reference to his betrayal, but again, I said nothing. My silence only angered him more.

"For fuck's sake, Saber!" He was almost shouting. "Stop with the fucking judgmental stare. I'm a goddamn rogue. What did you expect?"

I drew in a deep breath—then I slammed both hands down on the table. "If you yell any more bullshit at me, I'll break your jaw!"

He recoiled slightly, his fury interrupted. I jumped on his hesitation.

"That's all complete garbage and you know it. Have you already forgotten how you risked your life like a self-sacrificing fool last week when we went up against Luthyr?"

Expression darkening, he opened his mouth, but I slammed my hands down again, cutting him off.

"This has nothing to do with how fucking noble you are. You aren't walking away because you're a coldhearted bastard who can't be bothered to help his allies. You're *running away from Izverg.*"

Zak's hands curled into fists.

"And," I finished, my voice softening, "that's fine. That's your choice. But quit trying to convince me it's because you're selfish when it's really because you're scared."

"I'm not—" He cut himself off, then swore under his breath.

I walked around the table. Zak watched me approach, his mouth twisted and his eyes shuttered.

I stopped in front of him. "Is Izverg more powerful than the Dullahan or Luthyr? I doubt it. But the Dullahan and Luthyr never tormented you when you were young and vulnerable. Of course Izverg scares you, Zak. How could he not?"

His jaw clenched and unclenched, a muscle ticking in his cheek. Looking away from my steady gaze, he turned to the table, unable to face me. Saying nothing, he pulled his grimoire closer. After a moment spent staring at the page, he reached for the drafting paper.

Leaning against the table beside him, just far enough away to avoid accidentally catching an elbow in the ribs, I watched as he traced out a circle and filled it with precisely measured geometric lines that connected smaller circles and other shapes. He drew in alchemic symbols with smooth proficiency, then set the charcoal pencil aside.

"The Gardall'kin fae originate from Eastern Europe," he said quietly as he pinched a leaf off an herb bundle. "From the same region as Izverg and his kin. They're all related. Competing courts or something. The Gardall'kin were driven out, so they resettled here. That's all I really know about it. I never bothered to find out more."

He crushed the leaf into tiny pieces and sprinkled it on a small oval inside the alchemy array. "When Bane moved to this country, he chose a territory close to the Gardall'kin. That wasn't a coincidence. He and Izverg were scheming from the start, and it centered around the Shadow Court." Opening a bottle, he tipped a drop of thick green syrup onto a point in the array. "That's how I met Lallakai. She's a member of the Shadow Court."

"She is?"

He nodded. "An absentee member now, but back then, she was trying to uncover Bane and Izverg's plans. She contacted me in secret and tried to manipulate me into revealing what my master was up to. I was trying to manipulate her to get whatever I could out of her. It was mostly a stalemate, but kind of fun." A faint smile touched his lips, there and gone. "She should've tried harder to get to the bottom of Bane's plans."

Pinching off several leaves from another herb, he set them on an old-fashioned scale and checked their weight. He added another leaf.

"It was all coming to a head around the time you and I met." He inhaled, then released it. "The Shadow Court then was ruled by Marzanna and Marzaniok, twin fae. King and Queen. They were more like one being in two bodies than individuals. With Bane's help, Izverg captured Marzaniok, killed him, and ate him."

I swallowed a surge of revulsion. Zak added the small pile of leaves to his array and chanted quietly in Latin. Picking up a small vial, he poured six drops in a small bowl and set it on the spell.

"Izverg …" Zak pressed his hands to the table. "A master of death like him never should've been able to kill a King of Death, but he did. Consuming Marzaniok increased his power a shocking amount. And I …"

His face went strangely blank. Concern pinched my brow, and I waited only a moment before reaching out and squeezing his arm. He jolted, his wide eyes swinging toward me—and for a second, I saw the exact same look in his eyes, the exact same fear, as I'd seen ten years ago when we'd first discussed the impossible challenge of murdering his druid master.

Then he blinked, and the teenager was gone. The adult Zak pulled away from my hand, checked the instructions in his grimoire, then reached for another ingredient.

He didn't speak again except to chant in Latin. Adding a bowl to the bottom of the array, he filled it halfway with water from his backpack, then added three drops of his blood to the circle's center point. He rumbled through another incantation, and a soft, almost imperceptible glow emanated from the array lines. The spell ingredients crumbled into ash as swirls of light spiraled into the bowl of water. The liquid turned golden-yellow, and the light faded.

"Help me feed this to Lallakai," Zak murmured as he picked up the bowl.

I followed him to the comatose Night Eagle. "What is it?"

He knelt by her head. "I can't cure her yet, but I can treat her symptoms. This will help with the fever and calm her rapid heartbeat. Then I'll start testing for toxins to narrow down the poison."

I held up her head while he fed her the golden potion a sip at a time.

"Do you want to do those tests here?" I asked as we returned to the table. "Or should we get farther away from the Shadow Court first?"

He set the empty bowl on the table, his gaze distant. He was lost in thought, his shoulders flexing every few seconds.

"If I figure out what poisoned Lallakai," he finally said, the words slow and quiet, "I could give the antidote to Yilliar."

And Yilliar could give it to Marzanna, whom Izverg had also poisoned.

"Echo might need it too." He rolled his shoulders again. "If Izverg attacked him with this poison, that would explain why he called me, and why he stopped answering. He could have fallen unconscious like Lallakai."

"So we need to figure out the poison," I concluded.

Zak's gaze slid to me. "You and Ríkr agreed to accompany me to the Shadow Court. You've done that and more already."

"Are you suggesting I go back home?" I crossed my arms. "I'm a psycho vigilante witch, remember? I live for wrecking cruel, power-hungry monsters like Izverg."

He huffed in exasperated amusement but quickly sobered. "Saber ... thanks."

I looked away, a strange tightness in my chest. "Yeah." The constrictive feeling twisted deeper. "Sure."

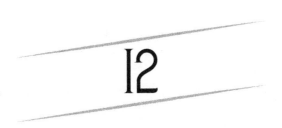

12

SINCE WE WEREN'T heading back to civilization tonight, I left Zak in the tiny cabin and rode Artear to Zak's truck, parked near the ruins of his old home. I collected our large pack of overnight supplies, slung it over my shoulders, then mounted the stallion again.

Artear swiveled his ears. His low voice chattered in my head, still unintelligible, as he crossed the burnt field and plodded into the forest. The sun had set, turning the overcast sky black. Faint light glowed around the cabin's door, guiding us back. Tilliag stood in the shelter of one wall, an almost invisible silhouette.

As I swung off Artear's back, a raindrop splatted on my nose. Another plopped on my head. I laid my hand on Artear's shoulder.

It would be safer for you to go on your way now, I told him, hoping he could sense my meaning. *You don't want to get tangled up in our mess.*

Artear turned his head, one fiery orange eye fixing on me. He rambled off something rapid.

He is already involved. Ríkr swooped out of the sky and landed on the cabin's roof, his pale form glowing in the darkness. The rain picked up, pattering steadily. *He says he will remain with us for now, and if you need a mount, he will assist you.*

Tilliag snorted loudly.

He adds, Ríkr continued in a neutral, "I'm just translating" tone, *that he is highly accomplished at protecting his rider, unlike certain others of his kind.*

Tilliag flattened his ears. *We are not mere mounts for humans, existing only to transport them.*

Artear shot back something rapid and disdainful.

Ríkr fluffed his feathers. *Bearing a rider is a demanding task for the unskilled. He understands that you may find it too challenging.*

Ears pinning, Tilliag surged out from under the cabin's eave. Artear arched his neck, ready to meet the challenge.

Rolling my eyes, I strode for the cabin before rain soaked through my sweater. I pulled the door open, light spilling out. As I closed it tight behind me, blocking out the weather, Ríkr blurred through the roof and fluttered down to land on the counter.

Zak was still at the worktable where I'd left him. The wooden top was cluttered with triple the alchemy supplies as before. He'd lit a fire in the stove, and the cabin's interior was almost stiflingly warm after the damp chill outside.

As I set the pack in the corner, he poured a drop of what looked like blood from one vial into another filled halfway with faintly blue liquid. I fished out a large water bottle from the pack, drank a third of it, and carried it over. He set the two vials on the table with a frustrated sigh and took the bottle, gulping down another third.

"Anything?" I asked.

He passed me the bottle. "Her blood is negative for everything I've tested for. I'm not surprised since Izverg wouldn't rely on a common poison, but the tests for less common toxins are more complex. I don't have ingredients for all of them, and some will take days to make."

"Will Lallakai last that long?"

"She might." Rubbing his jaw, he leaned against the counter. "She isn't getting worse. That could be because of the potions I've dosed her with, but maybe not. Marzanna is still alive after two weeks, according to Yilliar. The vast majority of poisons kill within a few hours to a few days."

I frowned. "What's the point of a poison that doesn't kill?"

Weakness, Ríkr answered. *The Lord of Death craves power, and he gains it by consuming his enemies while they still live.*

Zak nodded. "That's how Bane and Izverg took down Marzaniok ten years ago. They weakened him somehow, and ..." His eyes widened. "Wait, was it the same?"

"The same poison, you mean?" I asked, leaning forward intently.

"It's possible. Bane was working on something in the months leading up to killing Marzaniok. And he was meeting with Ruth a lot."

"Ruth sold poisons." My gaze slid to Lallakai. Was the poison in her veins one that my aunt had made? "Why would Izverg hold on to a poison for ten years, then suddenly decide to use it now?"

"Good question." Zak drummed his fingers on the worktable. "He wasn't in this area for the last nine years—I would've heard about it—which means he only recently returned. Why now?" He shook his head as though deciding it didn't matter. "As for the poison, Izverg isn't the type to carry things around with him. Was it something left in Bane's old territory that he recovered? But I took or destroyed everything useful …"

As he reached up to run his hands through his hair, the crystals hanging on cords around his neck glinted. I pursed my lips. "What about those gauntlets he was wearing? Its talons were—"

"—crystals," Zak hissed, jerking away from the counter. "Why didn't I realize it? *Those* are the poison, crystalized into a weapon. That's what Bane had Ruth make. And—" He froze. "Oh. Fuck."

"What?"

He pushed his sleeve up. Two angry red scratches ran across the back of his wrist. "He grabbed me when I was picking up Lallakai."

I seized his hand, examining the scratches. The surrounding skin was red and inflamed. "It looks like he barely broke your skin. Maybe that wasn't enough for the poison to enter your bloodstream."

His mouth thinned. He pressed down on a scratch, turning the pink skin white with pressure, then tapped his finger sharply against the scabbed line. "It's gone numb. Probably deliberate to ensure the victim forgets about the injury and doesn't start treating for a poison immediately."

I swore, anxiety building in my gut. "You're the poison expert here. If *you* lose consciousness, then what?"

That wasn't my only concern. A poison that was debilitating but non-lethal to fae might be *very* lethal for a human.

"We better not waste any time." He opened the cupboards again. "I have supplies to make another detox potion, but I gave Lallakai my universal antidote, and that one takes two weeks to mature."

I took the vials he handed me. "Do you have any other symptoms?"

"Fatigue, but I've hardly slept in days." He passed me a bundle of herbs before digging into the cabinet again. "Aside from that ... loss of appetite, I guess. How long has it been since we ate?"

"We had snacks while we were riding to the Shadow Court, but we haven't eaten a proper meal since breakfast in Squamish. So ... about twelve hours."

He rose, his mouth creasing in a frown. "Aren't you hungry?"

"No."

His frown deepened. He set a bottle of clear liquid on the counter and took the supplies he'd handed me out of my arms. "Did Izverg touch you?"

"No. Wait." My hand rose toward my chest. "He grabbed the front of my sweater."

"Strip," Zak ordered.

I didn't argue. I unzipped my sweater and slid it off. Even as I set it on the counter with his coat, I knew. I could see the small tears in my tank top that hadn't been noticeable in the thicker fabric of my sweater. I pulled the neckline down to the top of my sports bra. Three small nicks from Izverg's first two fingers and thumb marked my chest just below my collarbones, angry red against my fair skin.

"Fuck," I muttered, dread cooling my blood. "Ríkr, did Izverg scratch you?"

He landed not a single blow upon me, he replied immediately. *I am as hale as can be. Which is fortunate, as I will need to sharpen my nursemaid skills for when I am the only one left standing.*

I arched an eyebrow. "You have nursemaid skills?"

Minimally, yes. I once attended to Pwyll for a day after he was wounded in a hunt.

"And how many hundreds of years ago was that?"

He ruffled his feathers. *I may be out of practice.*

I closed my eyes, searching for logical thought. "Zak, how long until we lose consciousness?"

"I have no idea." He pulled out a new piece of drafting paper. "I can make a better guess once we start showing more symptoms. It's already been hours, but a detox potion can still slow the poison."

"But we don't have time for those complicated toxin tests."

"No."

Silence stretched through the cabin.

Zak measured a line in his new alchemy array. "I see three options. One, we go to Izverg and bargain for the antidote. He should have one, or he risks poisoning himself when he eats his victims."

I grimaced. Whatever price Izverg demanded in exchange for his antidote would be more than any of us could pay. "What are options two and three?"

"We ally with Yilliar and see if he can help us get or make an antidote, or we go back to the city and hope the Crow and Hammer's healers can save us."

"I'd rather take my chances with the Crow and Hammer."

He nodded. "Then—"

"No."

At the breathy protest, Zak and I whirled toward the cabin's far wall. Lallakai's eyes were open and turned our way. Zak abandoned his alchemy array and rushed to her.

"You're awake." He knelt at her side. "How do you feel?"

Her feverish eyes fixed on his face. "You must seek Marzanna."

"What?"

"Her twin perished because of this poison. She knows more about it than anyone alive. If she cannot reveal its secrets, no one can."

He pressed his wrist to her forehead, checking her temperature. "Are you sure?"

"Yes. Find Marzanna." With an unsteady exhale, she offered a weak smile. "Your potions are helping."

"You need hydration." He glanced at me, and I hastily passed him the water bottle. He helped Lallakai drink several mouthfuls. "Rest for now."

Ríkr flew to the worktable and perched on it, peering down at Lallakai. *What an unexpected reversal, Lady of Shadow. So recently, I was the one languishing in weakness.*

She narrowed her eyes. "Had you given me the power of The Undying immediately, I would not be in this condition."

You left without it. I am not to blame.

Scoffing, she closed her eyes. "Why not test your immortality against Izverg? His death magic will be no match for The Undying, will it?"

He clacked his beak. *I did not survive this long by gambling with my life.*

While Zak resumed working on his alchemy, I crouched beside Lallakai. "What happened after you and Zak split up?"

She didn't look enthused to be talking to me but answered anyway. "I entered the fae demesne and flew swiftly toward Marzanna's residence. Many court members were present"—bitterness roughened her normally sultry voice—"but none warned me of what waited. Izverg ambushed me. You can assume the rest."

What I could assume was that Lallakai wasn't well-loved by her court. Otherwise, someone would have tipped her off about their new leader.

"Where are we supposed to find Marzanna?" I asked.

"How would I know?"

"You told us to find her."

"Ask Yilliar." She closed her eyes, ending the discussion.

Rising to my feet, I studied Zak as he measured an angle in his array. My fingers rose to my chest, prodding the scratches Izverg had left. I couldn't feel anything, my skin numb as though the beast's claws had been coated in anesthetic.

Zak's childhood monster, and a poison my aunt might have concocted. I'd decided to come here with Zak in part to face my past, but this was more than I'd bargained for. I felt like we were spiraling back in time, falling closer and closer to that horrific night that had broken me.

A night that, I was beginning to suspect, had done just as much damage to Zak.

And neither of us was ready to go back there.

13

CROUCHED UNDER THE TABLE *in Bane's room, I lifted the poison out of the case for the second time. With my other hand, I pulled two similarly sized vials from my pocket. One was empty. The other contained a faintly greenish liquid, and I held it up next to the real poison. Their colors were almost identical.*

I pressed my thumb to the poison vial, marking the fill line at the three-quarter point, then uncorked it. The poison's minty scent seared my nose, stronger than I remembered. I poured it into my empty vial.

Keeping my thumb in place, I pulled out the cork from my substitute potion with my teeth and poured into the emptied poison vial until it was three-quarters full again. I swirled the liquid, then wafted the fumes toward my nose. It wasn't as minty as the poison. My nerves buzzed as I debated what to do. Bane had no reason to open his poison case in the next few days, and even if he did, he probably wouldn't be sniffing the vials.

No going back now.

I put Bane's poison case back where I'd found it, and with the near-empty vial of my fake substitute in one pocket and the poison in the other, I slipped out of the room. My gaze snagged on the markings etched around the doorframe. A red-and-white talisman swayed as the door clicked shut behind me.

Half a mile from the cabin, I crouched on the bank of a shallow stream. I studied the poison that the girl would use to kill her aunt, then peered at my substitute, only a few drops remaining in the bottom. Pulling the cork, I submerged the vial and used a rock to smash it into shards that disappeared in the murky water. No evidence.

Staring down at the rippling water, I tried to imagine what my life would be like without Bane. I couldn't remember anything from before him. I wouldn't even recognize a photo of my own parents. Not that I would ever see a photo. They'd lived and died half a world away from this place.

All I remembered from my life with them was my name—Zaharia—and my father's name—Andrii. That was why I'd named myself Zakariya Andrii, keeping my father's name but switching to the English version of Zaharia. I was never going back to Ukraine anyway.

So I had a name, but that was it. Maybe once Bane was dead, I could figure out who I wanted to become.

Exhaling roughly, I strode away from the stream, the poison hidden in the lining of my coat. Now I just had to prepare everything else I would need to murder the man who'd ruled my life for as long as I could remember.

FOLLOWING BEHIND BANE, *I rubbed two fingers over my inner wrist where Lallakai had embedded her spell. I couldn't test it since it was a one-time-use enchantment, and that made me nervous. I wouldn't use it tomorrow night unless I had to—but everything else was ready.*

In twenty-four hours, I would kill Bane.

Adrenaline made me jittery, and I resisted the urge to check that the poison I'd stolen four nights ago was still hidden in my coat lining.

"Zaharia," he said, his deep voice harsh and commanding.

I extended my stride until I was walking in his shadow. "Yes?"

"Govori po Russki," he barked crossly.

"Izvini," I muttered, angry at myself for slipping up. I was too distracted. "Da?"

"Tomorrow is an important night," he said in Russian.

Shocked terror rippled through me before I could stop it, and I was glad he wasn't looking my way. I cleared my expression. "It is?"

"You know I've been working on something." He glanced back at me, ambition burning in his dark, dead eyes. "Tomorrow is the night."

Was he being deliberately vague? Why say anything if he wouldn't share the details?

"All right," I said. "What do you want me to do?"

He turned so fast I couldn't react. His fist closed around the front of my coat, and he wrenched me up onto my toes, putting our faces disgustingly close. His hot breath washed over me.

"Nothing, because you are weak. Far too weak to be trusted." He opened his hand, and I dropped back onto my heels. His lips twisted in a sneering smile. "Someday soon, Zaharia, you'll learn that too."

Confusion and unease shivered through my gut, but Bane was already striding away. I hurried after him, tugging my hood up. Whatever Bane was working on didn't matter, and if he was focused on his own plans, even better. He'd be too distracted to pay attention to me.

Leaving me in front of the plain brick building, he headed inside for his next meeting with Ruth and her special poisons. I circled around to the alcove where I usually waited, and my vargs spread out to keep watch—and keep Bane's vargs away from me. Their main job was to ensure I didn't run away. They didn't care what else I did.

Leaning against the wall, I fished the small vial out of my coat's lining and examined the green liquid in the dim light of a streetlamp. If only killing Bane was as simple as slipping this into his food. He never allowed me access to his food or drink, and even if I somehow managed it, it'd take so much poison to kill him that he'd definitely notice the taste.

The girl's spell was my only chance. It had to work.

She is coming, Keelar informed me.

I slipped the vial into my pocket and rolled my shoulders to release tension. If I looked like I was losing my shit over this, she might back out of the plan.

With quiet, scuffing footsteps, she appeared in the alley, glancing around cautiously as though to make sure no one else was here. When she slipped into the alcove with me, my gaze ran down her long, thin legs. Everything about her was really thin, but I still wanted to run my hands over her smooth thighs.

Pulling my focus back up, I pushed my hood off. She smiled as she flicked her blond ponytail off her shoulder. Her shorts and tank top left a lot of her skin for me to see.

"Did you manage it?" she asked softly.

I pulled out the vial and offered it. Her teeth caught her lower lip as she held it up to the light.

She wiggled the vial, sloshing the poison. "How much will it take?"

"A few drops. It smells minty, so put it in something with strong flavor."

"Like coffee?" she suggested, arching an eyebrow.

She was so blasé about committing murder. I liked it. "Coffee is perfect."

Grinning, she pushed the vial deep into her pocket. "What will happen when she drinks it?"

"Numbness in her face, then violent trembling, then convulsions and unconsciousness, then death. It'll start in less than a minute, and she'll be dead in ten." The page from my alchemy encyclopedia flashed in my mind's eye. "I had to look it up. Never actually seen someone poisoned with it."

She tapped her pocket with the poison. "Did Bane notice anything when you stole it?"

"No." I hesitated. "Maybe."

He'd acted normally until earlier today, but he hadn't opened his poison case since I'd stolen the poison. I was positive he hadn't.

"He was watching me this afternoon," I admitted. "He might suspect I'm up to something, but he'll never guess what. He has no idea about your spell."

Her spell was what really mattered. If Bane suspected I'd stolen a poison, he'd be watching for me to poison him—which wasn't my plan. The misdirection might work in my favor.

"Did ..." Sudden unease hit me as I realized I'd handed over the poison without getting her artifact first. "Did you bring it?"

"Of course." She tapped her hand against her chest, just above her breasts. "I never take it off."

"You wear it all the time?" I asked, surprised.

"Yeah. My parents gave it to me, remember? To protect me."

Wondering what the spell looked like, I was momentarily distracted by the red straps peeking out from under her black tank top. A red bra?

I yanked my gaze back up, focusing on her face. "What happened to your parents?"

"They were helping search for a missing hiker in the mountains north of our home." *Her voice went husky, her gaze dropping.* "They knew the area really well … but they never came back. Their bodies were found a few weeks later. It looked like an animal attack, but no one was sure what kind of animal."

Assuming her parents had been witches like her, there was only one plausible explanation. "Probably a fae, then."

She nodded. "What about your parents? Bane isn't your dad, is he?"

Disgust flooded me. "We're not related." *I didn't plan to say anything else, but somehow, more words formed on my lips.* "I don't remember my parents."

Why? Why would I admit that?

Of course, she looked horrified. "Nothing?"

"Just … my father's name. That's it." *Straightening, I changed the subject.* "Will you be okay without your artifact?"

"Yeah, I'll be fine. There are no fae in the city to bother me."

"Not many."

So she lived in the city, then. I filed that away as another tidbit about her. I wanted to know more. I wanted to know her name.

She lifted her hand toward her throat. For a second, she hesitated, then she pulled a small, dark pendant from under her shirt. A smooth, brownish stone hung on a fine silver chain.

"That's it?" *I asked, watching it swing back and forth.*

It had to work. It had to.

"Yep." *She lifted the chain over her head and held it out to me.*

I cupped it in my hands, the stone warm from her body heat. I expected to feel a surge of Arcana energy but what flowed into my fingers was the unmistakable hum of fae magic. I traced a swirling rune etched in the front of the stone. Definitely fae.

"The magic in this is really powerful," I muttered, questions piling up in my head—then my senses twanged. My head snapped up, and when our eyes met, I realized that fae magic wasn't the only thing I could sense.

Spiritual energy swirled around her. It was subtle and soft, with an unexpected, jagged edge. I hadn't sensed her power until this moment, meaning the artifact had been hiding it—and hiding what she was.

"You're—" I stared at her. "Why didn't you say you were—"

Someone shouted loudly, the sound echoing down the alley. I grabbed the girl's arms, pulling her deeper into the alcove. People were stumbling around and talking drunkenly in front of the building.

After a moment, the group moved away. The girl and I listened intently, then sighed in unison. Her breasts pressed into my chest. I was holding her upper arms—holding her against me.

She looked up, and our faces were so close. The chain of her pendant was tangled around my fingers, and she slipped it free, then raised it over my head. The chain, still warm, settled against the back of my neck, and she tucked the smooth stone under my shirt.

As it slid down my chest, a strange sensation drifted through me—as though I was sinking into deep water. For an alarming second, I felt stifled, almost suffocated, then the sensation faded.

"Tomorrow night," the girl whispered, her hand resting over the pendant, "we'll meet across the street in the alley. Ruth and Bane will be dead. We'll be free."

"Free." I allowed myself to imagine what that would feel like. "What time?"

"I'm not sure. It'll depend on when Ruth has her after-dinner coffee."

I nodded. "I'll wait for you."

"I'll wait for you too. All night."

Her hand pressed into my chest, her fingernails catching on my shirt.

"And then," I murmured, my gaze falling to her mouth, "we'll leave this city together."

"Together."

As her spiritual power drifted around us, I lowered my head. Our lips met. Softly this time. Gently this time. I'd be gentle. I'd be careful. Because now that I knew she was a druid, her promise that we'd be together was no longer just an option I liked. She was like me. She could understand me. We were the same.

I needed her.

I needed everything.

Wrapping my arms around her, I kissed her more deeply. We would find a future together—as soon as we both committed murder.

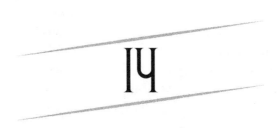

WE RODE NORTH in the dead of night.

Though the Shadow Court had every advantage in the darkness, waiting for morning wasn't an option. Zak and I had no idea how long it would take Izverg's poison to render us unconscious.

Before we left, we'd forced down some trail mix and filled our smaller backpacks with supplies. Lallakai had continued to drift in and out of awareness. It was an improvement over her previous state, and it gave me hope that the detox potions Zak had made would help us fight off the poison. But she was in no condition to travel.

Leaving Grenior and Keelar at the cabin to watch over Lallakai, Zak and I had set out alone, me astride Artear and him riding Tilliag. Flashlights would've given away our position to any searching members of the Shadow Court, so we'd split a dose of his night-vision potion. It was just enough that I could make out silhouettes and shapes. Our fae mounts moved quickly despite the darkness. Spurts of rain drummed on the hood of my jacket—a waterproof one this time.

Our plan was flimsy at best. Since we didn't know where to look for Marzanna, we were heading toward the area where Echo had called for help. According to Zak, there was a decent chance Echo knew what had befallen Marzanna. He might have been calling Zak toward her, or if we found him, he might know her location.

Instead of travelling with us, Ríkr had flown ahead in the form of an owl. He would attempt to contact Yilliar, and the Shadow Lord would hopefully reveal where Marzanna was hiding before Zak and I wasted too much time wandering around the wilderness.

Being separated from Ríkr made me nervous. Even when I'd believed he was a mostly powerless shapeshifter, his presence had been reassuring; his craftiness and confidence always gave the impression he could handle any situation. And now, knowing how powerful he was, I'd grown to rely on him even more.

I wound my hands through Artear's silky mane. Tilliag walked ahead of us on a game trail, and I watched Zak's shoulders flex and relax, only to tighten up again.

How did he feel being separated from Lallakai, Grenior, and Keelar? Did they reassure him the way Ríkr's presence reassured me? How did he feel knowing Izverg was somewhere in these dark woods? The thought unnerved *me*, and I didn't have a history with the beast.

The dense underbrush, barely visible in the darkness, thinned as we followed the trail into a shallow valley. I leaned forward, urging Artear to extend his gait, and he obliged, drawing level with Tilliag. The two stallions pinned their ears and tossed their heads, but they seemed past the bickering phase of their rivalry.

"In case we run into Izverg again," I murmured, keeping my voice quiet so it wouldn't travel, "what's the best way to fight him? Does he have any weaknesses?"

"As far as I know, he doesn't have any weaknesses." Zak gazed straight ahead. "Everything is a game to him. If he gets to hurt or kill someone, he wins. If he doesn't, oh well, there's always tomorrow."

"So we probably can't make him angry and stupid, then?"

"I've never seen him lose his head. He's a twisted sadist to his core. He only wants power so he can play games with stronger victims."

"What about physical weaknesses?"

"He's a death fae. The more you injure him, the stronger he gets."

"What?"

He glanced at me, but it was too dark to make out his expression. "You didn't know? He feeds off pain and death, including his own. What he did earlier this evening was nothing. It's when he takes a few wounds that his power really amps up."

"Shit," I muttered.

"And considering his affinity for death, I don't know what would happen if Ríkr used his Undying magic in Izverg's vicinity."

I rubbed my chest through my jacket, pressing on the numb scratches Izverg had given me. Rain pattered down, and Zak tipped his head back, letting it pepper his face. I bit my lower lip as the stallions thumped across the valley, long grass swishing around their legs.

"If I'd run into Izverg a year ago …" Zak's voice was a low, husky rumble. "I was stronger then. I had powerful fae gifts, stockpiles of spells and potions, and five vargs in my pack …"

"Stockpiles," I repeated under my breath. According to the MPD bounty page I'd looked at a few weeks ago, the majority of criminal charges against Zak were related to possessing, stealing, or trafficking illegal dark magic. He must've dedicated most of his time to his "stockpile"—until he'd lost it, along with his safe, secret farm in the mountains.

And that's when his old, undefeated nemesis had reappeared. No wonder he didn't want to go up against Izverg.

Our mounts pushed into a fast trot to cover more ground. The miles crawled past as we rode from valley to valley, heading steadily northeast toward Echo's territory. The rain stopped and the clouds broke up, giving the moon a chance to peek through the wisps.

We descended into another valley, scraggy lodgepole pines surrounding us. I stretched my legs out, then settled them against Artear's sides.

"Are we in Echo's territory yet?" I asked Zak.

"I'm pretty sure, unless we're too far north." He peered around at the trees. "I've only been to see him a few times. He usually comes to visit me instead."

"At your farm?"

"Yeah."

I fiddled with the zipper of my jacket. "I've been wondering. You mentioned you didn't have much to do with the homeless kids you brought to your farm. But why do it, then? I can't imagine rescuing animals, then ignoring them."

"That's because rescuing animals was your intent from the start. I never planned to turn my farm into a group home for teens. It just happened."

"How does something like that 'just happen'?"

Dappled moonlight drifted over him. He gazed ahead, seeming to weigh something in his mind—weighing whether he wanted to reveal more?

"It started when I was eighteen, about a year after I killed Bane." He glanced at me. "I was sixteen when we met."

My eyes widened slightly. So after I'd killed Ruth, he'd spent another year as Bane's apprentice?

"Bane's death caused unexpected issues for me," he continued. "It took me a while to get things under control. Once no one was actively trying to kill me—"

"Why—" I started to ask, but he was still speaking.

"—I tapped into Bane's old contacts in the city, and I made new contacts of my own. I asked them for any information they could find on blond, female Spiritalis mythics around seventeen living on the streets."

A strange, terrifying stillness engulfed my chest, as though all the broken shards in my lungs had frozen solid. We rode in silence for a long minute.

"A few weeks later, I got my first tip." His eyes turned to mine, silvery light dancing across his face. "But the girl wasn't you."

A tremor shook my body. Artear's ears turned backward in concern.

"It was Morgan," Zak said softly. "She looked nothing like you, and she was too old—a few years older than me—but she had the same toughness. She was scared, alone, and in a dangerous situation. She wasn't you … but I couldn't leave her there. I took her home, intending to find a safe place to send her, but she never left. That's how it all began."

My ears were ringing. His words bounced around in my skull, and it took me a moment to find my voice.

"You left *me*," I grated, my fingernails cutting into my palms. "How could you take her but leave me?"

"A lot changed in those two years. The night I left you … I regret everything about that night."

Anger ignited inside me. "You *regret* it? That's it?"

"Should I be wallowing in guilt? Is that what you want?"

My anger flared hotter. "You betrayed me and left me for dead! So *yes*, you should feel some fucking guilt."

"You have reasons to hate me, Saber. I don't deny that." His hard gaze slashed me. "But do you want to know one of the reasons I hate you?"

I faltered, then snapped, "Why?"

"Because you keep blaming me for everything, even though we were the same—both scared, abused kids trying to survive. But you made me responsible for your future." His jaw flexed. "What about me? You didn't save me either, Saber. I needed saving. You have no fucking idea how badly I needed it."

I stared at him, my chest grinding with razor shards as badly as it had ten years ago when he'd first shattered my heart. "Are you *delusional*? How can you talk like you're a victim too?" My temper ripped free from my control. "*You lied about everything and tricked me!*"

Artear tossed his head, unhappy with my sudden shout.

"You gave me a fake poison!" I yelled. "You broke the only thing I had left of my parents! You showed up just to throw it in the mud and walk away! You made me trust you and love you, then you went out of your way to crush me! How are *you* a victim here, Zak?"

Shock rippled over his face, and I realized what I'd blurted out—the confession I'd sworn to never speak aloud.

"What do you mean, a fake poison?"

My mouth hung open for a second. I snapped it shut. "You think I don't know? You gave me peppermint oil, not poison. I still can't believe I didn't guess—"

"No." He leaned sideways toward me, his eyes boring into mine with sudden intensity. "I stole the poison from Bane."

"It was fake," I repeated furiously. "Ruth knew I'd try to poison her coffee, and she knew the poison was fake. She even drank some of it to mess with me."

"Then she must have switched the poison I gave you with a fake."

"Impossible. I never once let that vial out of my sight until I poured it in her coffee maker."

"But I gave you real poison."

"Quit fucking lying—"

"*Lying?*" he yelled. "What could I possibly gain from lying at this point? Why do you villainize me like this? Fuck! This is why I can't stand you!"

"The feeling is mutual!" I shouted. "How can you pretend to—"

"Shut up, Saber! Just—*fuck!*" Snarling profanity, he threw his weight forward. "Tilliag, go!"

The stallion grunted and sped into a ground-eating gallop, his hooves pounding—and before I could tell Artear to turn back, to carry me as far away from Zak as possible, he surged after Tilliag. The wind whipped at my hair as dark trees flashed past.

Blind rage burned through me, and I let out a wordless scream. Bending over Artear's neck, I urged him faster, not caring how dangerous it was to gallop in the dark. The cold wind cut across my face, stinging the dampness on my cheeks.

Why couldn't Zak just admit he'd betrayed me? How was I supposed to accept the past and let it go when he kept changing the story? How could I have thought, even for a second, that I didn't hate everything about him?

Ahead, Zak and Tilliag were a dark shape galloping over the uneven ground. The trees had thinned, and the few that remained were even more stunted. A rotten stench hit my nose. Moonlight gleamed on water peeking through the low vegetation.

A frothing wave exploded upward, and a monster surged out of a hidden pool into Tilliag's path. The stallion swerved away from the attacking creature, his hooves splashing into water. With a harsh bellow, he went down. Zak was thrown.

Artear didn't slow. Heat radiated off him and his orange eyes glowed like embers. His hooves slammed down, and lines of fire shot forward along the ground, racing toward the creature—the mantis-like Shadow Court fae.

The mantis recoiled from the flames. Summoning an ice spear, I hurled it at the distracted creature. As the weapon left my hand, a feminine shriek of laughter erupted on my left. The pale-skinned female fae leaped out of the darkness, long talons on the ends of her fingers slashing at me.

Artear swerved away and kicked out with his back legs. The female fae evaded his hooves and cast a wave of silvery magic. It swept over us, and my limbs turned icy, as though all the blood had drained out of them.

Artear's legs buckled. He crashed down, and I tumbled off him. I landed in a puddle of reeking mud, rolled, and came up on my knees with an ice spear already forming. I flung it into the female fae's chest. She lurched backward as the ice burst into a jagged cluster.

Back on his feet, Artear slammed his hooves down and sent a cascade of fire into the fae. Silver magic engulfed her, but I didn't wait to see if she could defend against the dual attacks. I launched at Artear and hauled myself up onto his back.

With glowing magic and angry snarls, two more Shadow Court fae appeared from the darkness, closing in from behind us.

Two dozen yards away, Tilliag and Zak were up again, the druid clinging to the stallion's side with one arm over his neck while magic glowed over his other hand. He whipped his arm out, blasting the mantis fae. It ducked its insectile head, the magic rolling off its hard exoskeleton.

Artear raced toward them, and Zak swung onto Tilliag's back. With the druid barely hanging on, the stallion sprang forward. Artear galloped after Tilliag into a widening expanse of open ground scattered with stunted trees, a maze of glimmering waterways webbing across it.

But it wasn't merely a bog. Magic shivered across my skin, and between one step and the next, the world shimmered into mist.

It was a crossroads.

15

THE GROUND THUDDED weirdly under Artear's pounding hooves. The mist of the fae realm made it even more treacherous, and I clutched his mane, knowing he was one wrong step from breaking a leg—and my neck.

We'd lost our shadow fae attackers in the maze of water and mist, but we'd also lost Zak. He and Tilliag had been galloping ahead of us, a dark silhouette, when an thick cloud of fog had rolled across our path. I'd lost sight of him and he hadn't reappeared.

High-pitched laughter echoed through the pale haze. I couldn't tell which direction it was coming from.

Artear slowed to a trot, his ears swiveling nervously. Knee-high plants with narrow leaves blanketed the lumpy, moss-covered ground, and his hooves splashed in hidden pockets of water.

I scanned the mist again for movement. Zak couldn't be that far, could he? Unless he and Tilliag had veered in a different direction. The pathways through the bog were more twisted than a labyrinth, and distances in a crossroads could be deceiving.

Artear's hooves splatted into deep mud. His trot faltered—then I was flying through the air. The ground rushed to meet me, and when I hit it, my bodyweight tore right through a thick bed of moss. I plunged into icy water.

My limbs flailed, then I found the bottom—a mucky layer of decomposing mush that sucked my feet down into it. My head burst out of the water and I gasped in a breath—then gagged as a hideous stench of rot and mold clogged my airways.

Panting, I grabbed for the nearest hump of land to pull myself out of the water. It bobbed and floated away. It wasn't solid earth—it was a mass of floating vegetation. I turned, water sloshing at my chest and my lower legs sticking in the mud and silt.

A few yards behind me, Artear had sunk up to his chest. He struggled toward the solid path he'd been running on.

I wrenched my left leg free and stepped forward. When my foot touched down, it sank even deeper. The water rose to my armpits. It was way colder than it should have been, and the stink was beyond comprehension, suffocating and unbearable.

Artear got his knees up on solid ground and struggled to pull his rear legs out. I took another wading step toward him, shivering violently. He clambered out, water sloshing in his wake. I wrenched my foot free from the rotting vegetation beneath the surface.

Artear's head jerked up, ears pricked to the south. His voice rushed into my head, an urgent command I could easily guess: *hide*.

Trapped in place, all I could do was bend my knees until my chin touched the water, but I was still visible. I could hear them coming—thudding steps, a growl, a strange clicking noise that had to be the mantis fae.

Artear's orange eyes scoured across me, then he spun and trotted off into the mist. The quiet noises of the approaching fae grew louder. Shadows appeared in the mist, rushing forward. They'd spotted Artear—and they would see me too.

I sucked in the deepest breath I could and ducked beneath the surface.

Cold, slimy water engulfed my head. I held my breath as long as I could, then slowly exhaled a few bubbles at a time, fighting the screaming in my lungs. When I couldn't hold it any longer, I pushed my face back above the surface, spitting and gasping.

The mist swirled, quiet and empty. I couldn't see or sense any fae, including Artear. The shadow fae must have followed him.

With difficulty, I waded to the same spot where Artear had escaped the water and crawled onto the spongy moss. My breath heaved in and out, and I had to fight the urge to vomit. Throwing up wouldn't lessen the reek of decomposition. Black mud and hunks of rotting plants clung to my drenched clothing.

I wiped my face. The bog was silent except for the hum of insects. Flies buzzed around me, investigating the disturbed muck.

Spitting again, I trudged forward. For a few yards, the ground was solid—then my foot went through the moss layer and into a hidden pocket of water. Pain twanged through my ankle.

"Fuck," I panted, backtracking. Should I retrace my route and hope our shadow fae pursuers had continued deeper into the bog? Or should I keep moving forward and hope I made it out the other side? Which way had Artear gone?

I snapped a branch off a twisted, unhealthy pine and used it to poke at the ground. Zak had been heading north, so I'd do the same. Squinting at the sky, I started forward.

The bog stretched ahead. It was impossible to tell solid ground from unstable moss beds with deep water under them. Everything smelled so awful I could barely think. Dripping wet and squelching with each step, I made my slow way forward. Where was Artear? Was the mantis chasing him? What about Zak and Tilliag? Had Zak realized I wasn't following anymore? Would he come back for me?

A grimace twisted my mouth. Why would he?

I wiped the back of my hand across my forehead. It was easier for us to just hate each other. Our relationship had burned to a husk of bitterness and loathing ten years ago. There was no saving it. There was no forgiveness.

His voice echoed in my head. *What do you mean, a fake poison?*

It was completely idiotic of him to deny he'd given me a fake poison. The lie was so laughably obvious that it made no sense. He'd admitted to betraying me, so why deny the fake poison? It was just so stupid … but Zak wasn't stupid.

What could I possibly gain from lying at this point?

I took another cautious step. My senses stretched out, trying to detect any nearby fae, but all I could feel was the ancient power of the crossroads twining through the stagnant, rot-filled energy of the bog.

This is why I can't stand you!

Zak's voice sounded so close and so real that I looked over my shoulder. I checked the other direction. Was I hallucinating now? Was that the next symptom of Izverg's poison?

Are you completely incapable of forgiving people for making mistakes?

Stumbling forward, I shook my head. This was not a good time for me to lose my grasp on reality—but knowing that didn't make it stop.

I needed saving. You have no fucking idea how badly I needed it.

"How was I supposed to save you?" I growled. I'd been trapped in my own nightmare. There was no way I could've fixed his.

A monster like you has no right to be within a thousand feet of any child.

I jerked to a halt. That wasn't Zak's voice—that was my father's. I dug the heel of my hand into my ear. Why did it sound so real? What was wrong with me?

Be careful with your temper, Saber, he said sternly. *There are some words you can never take back.*

"Dad," I whispered, squeezing my eyes shut. I could see his face, his grave disapproval, but I couldn't remember what mean, childish thing I'd shouted at him in a fit of anger.

You smell as mouthwatering as always.

I jolted at Izverg's hideous voice. Eyes flying open, I turned in a sharp circle, scanning the bog. Patches of water rippled softly, ethereal mist drifting through the vegetation. It was so quiet.

Your ability to reason your way through a problem is utterly crippled.

Ruth's cold voice cut through me like a knife, more real than any memory of her I possessed. I went rigid, my breath hissing through my clenched teeth. Why was I hearing these voices? What was happening to me?

When someone deceives you, you're hopelessly dense.

"Stop," I growled.

Ungrateful bitch.

"*Stop!*" This time I shouted it. Jaw clenching, I hurled my energy outward in an aura sphere. The mist swirled and danced, then thinned.

The moonlight cast silver beams on a hump of soggy moss a few yards away. The hill swelled, growing larger—and larger—and larger. Taller than me, it quivered, moss and muck clinging to what looked like a boneless mound of slimy, quivering black flesh.

It twitched and pulsed. A dark line creased its fleshy front, then split open into a mouth, lined with curved fangs pointing inward, big enough to engulf my head.

Do you even grasp how pathetically dense you are, Rose?

The horrendous mouth moved in time to the words as Ruth's voice filled my head. I pressed my hands to my ears to block out the sound. Another crease in the slimy mass peeled apart.

Worthless, the first mouth sneered.

The second mouth curved into words. *This is why I can't stand you!*

Zak's voice hit me like a blow to the gut, but the first mouth was still moving.

Ungrateful bitch.

I needed saving.

You're hopelessly dense.

As the voices battered me, a third mouth popped open, flashing more curved teeth.

Perhaps you would make a better pet than Zaharia.

Stupid, traitorous whore.

Sometimes I really fucking hate you.

"No!" I screamed. "Stop it!"

The bog monster loomed over me, the mouths opening wider, the slimy throats inside them pulsing. I stumbled backward. Another pair of lips peeled apart, the fourth mouth gaping.

My foot landed on moss that dipped warningly, then tore. My leg sank into cold water, and when I staggered for balance, my other foot went through too. I plunged into the swampy water up to my shoulders.

The mouths were all moving, all speaking. Ruth's voice, Zak's voice, Izverg's voice, my father's voice. They pummeled me, hitting every wound, every scar. And as they attacked, the bog monster arched over me, ready to plunge down and engulf me.

Roaring at the top of my lungs, I ripped my arm out of the water. Cold rushed over my hand, and I smashed an ice spear into the monster's closest mouth. As it exploded into a starburst, I summoned another one. Screaming to drown out the voices, I smashed spear after spear into the creature until all I could see were jagged stalagmites of ice.

My scream faded, and in its place, silence.

I sloshed backward, my legs sticking in the mud at the bottom. The bog monster, half of it engulfed in ice, didn't move, its mouths frozen. I struggled away, reaching for something solid.

I hauled myself onto a flimsy moss bed. Covered in reeking muck all over again, I crawled away from the water until the ground stopped bobbing. I thumped it with my fist. Solid. My legs quivered with post-adrenaline weakness as I climbed onto dry land and sat heavily.

I should keep moving. My screaming and aura sphere might have attracted attention. I should keep moving—but I couldn't make myself stand.

My limbs shook, and it wasn't merely from fright and exertion. The words, the voices, they still echoed in my head. Weaker now, memories instead of magic-spawned recreations, but they still hurt. They hurt so much, and my breathing hitched with a weak sob.

"G-get up," I told myself, my voice almost as raspy as Zak's. "Saber!"

My head jerked up again, neck twinging as I twisted. A shadow in the mist. Thudding hooves. The haze swirled, and Zak appeared, astride Tilliag, riding toward me.

"Zak?" I whispered.

"Saber!" he called, urging Tilliag into a faster trot.

He'd come back for me.

Even after what I'd said, the way I'd treated him, he'd come back.

I pushed up onto unsteady legs as Zak swung off Tilliag in mid-trot. He strode to me, covered in almost as much stinking muck as I was, mud splattered over one cheek, his brows furrowed over green eyes.

"Saber, are you okay?" he asked, reaching for my shoulder.

My entire body quivered. "You came back for me."

His hand paused. "I asked you to come here. How could I leave—"

I threw myself at him.

He grunted as I collided with his chest. Stumbling, he landed on his ass. I went down with him, clutching his arms, my forehead pressed to his shoulder.

"I'm sorry," I gasped. "I'm sorry I called you a liar. I'm sorry I'm so mean to you."

He didn't react, his limbs rigid.

"We were just kids." A sob shook me. "That night, you were so cruel. You hurt me so badly. But saving me wasn't your burden. I can't blame you for that. You were just a kid too."

His breath rushed out, and he wrapped his arms around me, squeezing so hard I couldn't breathe. Clinging to him just as tightly, I felt like I was fifteen again. Fifteen and holding him the way I'd wanted to that night, after Ruth had beaten me, after I'd walked across the city, after I'd waited hours in the rain for him to come.

If only that night had been different. If only …

"I tried to find you, Saber."

I shuddered at his raspy whisper. Tears welled in my eyes.

"I couldn't fix what I did. I helped all those other kids because I couldn't help you. I—" His voice hitched, broke. "I don't hate you, Saber. I just—I just hate everything."

The tears spilled down my cheeks. "It's all so fucked up."

"Beyond fucked up." He pushed me back enough for his eyes, dark with pain, to meet mine. "Saber, I swear I stole the poison for you."

I touched the corner of his mouth, trying to smooth away the creases in his jaw. "All this time, I thought you'd tricked me from the start and none of it … nothing that happened between us was real."

"No," he whispered. "I meant it, Saber. I tried to kill Bane that night, just like we'd planned. But he knew."

"He knew as well?" I swallowed the sick feeling in my throat. "How? How did they find out what we were planning?"

"I don't know."

I leaned into his enclosing arms, trying to steady my breathing. There was more I needed to know, so much more, but I was too exhausted. And far too fragile. I needed to recover my equilibrium.

He held me for a minute longer, then loosened his arms. Together, we climbed to our feet. Zak glanced at the half-frozen bog monster but said nothing. He boosted me onto Tilliag's back and swung up behind me.

For the first time in a very long time, I could no longer feel those grinding, broken blades in my chest.

16

I KNEW WE'D REACHED the edge of the seemingly endless bog when I heard the sound of burbling water. Tilliag's ears pricked forward, and he broke into an eager trot. I didn't blame him for hurrying. All three of us stank so badly I could barely breathe through it.

A narrow, quick-flowing river snaked along the edge of the valley, its energetic ripples gleaming in the faint light growing on the eastern horizon. Tilliag didn't slow when he reached the pebbly riverbank. He plunged right in.

I slid off his side, landing with a splash, and moved far enough that I wouldn't get stepped on, then went down onto my knees. Water pushed against me, trying to carry me away, but it was only a few feet deep. Holding my breath, I dunked my head into the cold flow and vigorously scrubbed my hair.

When I pulled my head out, I spotted Zak a few yards away in a deeper section of the river. He'd pulled off his backpack and shirt and was sinking the latter into the water. We washed, scrubbed, stripped, and scrubbed some more. In my bra and underwear and nothing else, I helped Zak wipe down Tilliag so he didn't have to stink either. I wondered where Artear had ended up. I hoped he was okay. Would he be able to find us again?

I sat on a smooth boulder at the water's edge, holding an armful of wet clothes and my drenched backpack, most of its contents ruined. "I never want to see another bog again."

"I never want to *smell* another bog," Zak grumbled. Standing in ankle-deep water, he wrung out his jeans, the thick muscles in his upper arms bunching. His boxers were plastered to his skin, and the rest of his tight, muscular body was on full display.

My gaze traveled down, then made its way slowly back up. When I got to his face, I found him watching me, his gaze dark and heated. We stared at each other for several heartbeats before simultaneously looking away.

I combed my fingers through my hair, then started braiding it. "Where are we?"

"No idea. I didn't know this crossroads existed." Glancing at the pre-dawn horizon, he splashed to the shore. "We're either in Echo's territory, or we missed it and we're on the northeastern edge of the Shadow Court's land."

"What do we do now?"

He tossed his wet pants over a rock and stepped closer to me. As I looked up, he pressed his wrist against my cheek. Pushing my bangs aside, he checked my forehead, then his.

"We're both running fevers, so for now, we should find shelter, dry our clothes, eat something, and dose up on potions."

We'd scrubbed our clothes, but it'd been a wasted effort. The only way to rid them of the bog stink was to burn them. Using Zak's least contaminated shirt, we slung it over Tilliag's back like a saddle blanket and mounted him in our underwear. I sat in front and Zak tucked up behind me, the rest of our soggy garments stuffed in our dripping backpacks.

His warm hand rested on my waist, skin on skin. His legs bumped mine. His breath was hot on the back of my neck.

Tilliag plodded downstream, following the river. The sky gradually lightened, the shadows receding, and a faint pink stain appeared above the mountains in the east. The river flowed into a narrow ravine, and steep, rocky walls closed in on either side of us.

Ears swiveling, Tilliag came to a halt. *Shall I turn back?*

Zak swore under his breath. "Yeah, I guess we—"

Breaking off, he sat up straight as though listening.

"What's wrong?" I asked.

"I heard …" He exhaled. "I thought I heard something. Or maybe I sensed it. It was faint, but … Tilliag, keep going."

Tilliag splashed into deeper water. It rose up to his belly, the current pushing against him. If Zak and I had tried to wade across, we'd have been swept away. The shadows deepened as the ravine narrowed. The sides were too precipitous to climb. If we were attacked, we could only go forward or backward.

I tightened my grip on Tilliag's mane. "Is this a good idea?"

"Probably not," Zak muttered.

Tilliag waded farther downstream. The current roughened as the ravine curved in a tight bend. His hoof slipped on the rocks beneath the surface, and he stumbled, almost dislodging me and Zak.

"We should—"

"No," Zak interrupted. "I can sense something."

Tilliag tossed his head. *As can I.*

I exhaled, unable to sense anything unusual. As the ravine bent to the north, a dark spot in the rocky wall came into view. It almost looked like a shadow, but it was too dark.

"Is that a cave?"

Zak leaned into my back, my pack squishing wetly. "The presence is coming from there."

What presence?

Tilliag halted in the shallows near the dark crevice in the ravine wall. It was twice the stallion's width but our heads would barely clear the top while mounted. The three of us peered into the darkness inside the gap.

"What sort of presence?" I asked doubtfully. Just because he sensed a fae didn't mean we wanted to get friendly with it.

He swung off Tilliag's back, dropping into the knee-deep water, then climbed onto the rocky lip at the cave's edge and stepped into the darkness. Swearing quietly, I jumped down and hurried after him. Everything about this felt stupid—not only invading some fae's hidden lair but doing it soaking wet in our underwear.

Inside, the cave was just large enough for Tilliag to follow us into the dim shelter, his hooves clacking loudly on the rock floor. As my eyes adjusted to the darkness, I picked out the damp, mossy walls. The cave was about twelve feet across with no fae in sight. Relieved, I glanced around for the least uncomfortable spot to sit. A feverish ache throbbed in my muscles, and I felt hot and cold at the same time. The poison was definitely setting in now.

At the back of the cave, Zak was examining the rocks. As I opened my mouth to ask what he was doing, he stepped into the wall—no, *through* it. A dark crag split the stone, almost invisible and just wide enough for Zak to squeeze through. Whatever was on the other side was too dark to make out.

With another curse, I shuffled into the gap after him.

Light bloomed. Zak's silhouette appeared ahead of me. He stood at the edge of an open space three times the size of the cave entrance. Water dripped somewhere, and the air smelled faintly of mold. I stopped beside Zak, squinting in the light emanating from one of the crystals hanging around his neck.

The cavern wasn't empty.

Tucked against a rough wall, a bed of embroidered blankets had been arranged with great care. Several woven baskets, stuffed with supplies, were stacked nearby, and an ornate lantern emitted a glow so faint we hadn't seen it from the antechamber. Someone lay across the bed, their slim frame buried beneath blankets, leaving only a mess of raven hair visible.

"Marzanna," Zak muttered.

He strode toward the slumbering figure, and after a shocked moment, I hastened to follow. He crouched and swept tangled hair away from the fae's face, revealing the delicate features of a young woman, her eyes closed and skin as white as snow.

"This is the Queen of Death?" I stared down at the fae. "You sensed she was here?"

Zak pressed his wrist to her forehead. "That, or she's semi-conscious and purposefully got my attention."

"What's she doing here, of all places?"

"It's a good hiding spot." He moved his fingers to the pulse in her thin neck. "The crossroads' magic makes it harder to detect her power."

I lifted the lid off a basket. Inside was an assortment of colorful but unrecognizable fruit. "She didn't bring all this with her. Someone brought her supplies. How much do you want to bet it was Yil—"

The shadow behind Marzanna, cast by the faint lantern light, swelled upward. It rippled into a humanlike shape, and with a burst of cool wind, it solidified into a fae. The horned Shadow Lord's black eyes narrowed suspiciously as he crouched over Marzanna.

"Yilliar," Zak greeted calmly. "Good timing."

"How did you find this spot?"

"I sensed Marzanna's presence. Why did you suddenly show up?"

"I heard from the others that you'd been sighted at the crossroads." He rose to his full height, his crown of horns catching the faint light. "Have you reconsidered your decision?"

Zak stood, facing him. "I'm not risking my neck to kill Izverg for you and Marzanna."

"Yilliar, have you seen Ríkr?" I cut in. "He was trying to find you."

"I have not." The Shadow Lord stepped over Marzanna's unmoving form, forcing me and Zak to back up. "Why have your ally seek me out if you refuse to aid us?"

"I'm not getting involved in a battle for the throne," Zak rumbled, "but I need an antidote to Izverg's poison. If I'm making one, I'll prepare some for Marzanna too—for a price."

Hope brightened the fae's dark eyes. "Name it."

"We'll barter once we know that I can make one." Pulling two potion vials off his belt, Zak held them out to Yilliar.

"Lallakai said Marzanna has knowledge of Izverg's poison. Give these to her, and we'll see if she wakes."

The Shadow Lord accepted the vials. He studied them in the faint lantern light, then turned a slow smile on Zak that revealed his sharp teeth. "I'm pleased to have your assistance, Crystal Druid."

"Don't be too pleased, Yilliar. My help doesn't come cheap."

Yilliar's smile widened, and as he turned to Marzanna with the potion vials, I wondered if we should have taken our chances trying to get back to the Crow and Hammer.

WRAPPED IN A BLANKET from the stash of supplies Yilliar had stockpiled for Marzanna, I sat at the back of the outer cave, watching the small river sparkle in the morning sun. Tilliag had wandered off to explore the area in case we needed to make a fast escape, but I suspected he just didn't like standing in a cave.

Leaning against the cave wall, I suppressed a yawn. I'd volunteered to take first watch, but staying awake was more difficult than I'd expected. My fever was worsening despite the potion Zak had given me half an hour ago, and a dull ache had set into my muscles. The only thing making my life slightly less miserable was the bowl beside me. The bluish liquid filling it had come from a vial in Zak's backpack, and once exposed to air, it'd begun emitting steady, pleasant heat. No wood, fire, or smoke needed. As much as I hated alchemy, it was undeniably useful.

After promising to find Ríkr and return as swiftly as possible, Yilliar had melted into the shadows. I didn't trust the fae, but since I had no way of contacting Ríkr, Yilliar was my best bet. I hoped the Shadow Lord found him soon. I didn't like being separated when everything was so uncertain.

With a soft scuff, Zak appeared from the crevice that led deeper into the cave. A purple blanket, embroidered with black vines, was draped over his shoulders. Otherwise, he wore only his boxers. We'd laid all our clothes out in the cave to dry, and we had nothing else to wear.

Zak sat beside me and wrapped the blanket around himself. "I can't sleep, so you can go lie down if you want."

I made a quiet, noncommittal noise. I was tired, but I doubted I could sleep either. "Any sign of Marzanna waking up?"

"Not yet."

"What if she doesn't know anything useful about the poison?"

"Then we head for the Crow and Hammer as fast as possible."

We'd never make it. We'd have to cross the bog crossroads or detour around it, and with the Shadow Court hunting us, that'd be impossible. Plus, if we left, we'd be condemning Marzanna to death and giving Izverg the chance to devour her, which would increase his power further.

Little sunlight reached the back of the cavern, and Zak's face was deep in shadow. When I'd first met him—again—a few weeks ago, he'd seemed like a person who never backed down from a threat, yet he had no plans to confront Izverg. What was it about the jackal beast that had Zak in a defensive retreat?

"If you could go back in time," I murmured, studying him, "would you run away with me that night?"

"If everything else still happened the same way?" He gazed toward the river. "If we had run, Bane would have hunted us down in no time. He'd have fed you to Izverg and punished me for trying to escape."

My fingernails found a loose thread of embroidery on my blanket. I tugged on it. "What if we'd killed Bane and Ruth first?"

"Then yeah, I'd have gone with you." He tipped his head back, resting it against the wall. "I wanted to go east. There are big, old forests in northern Ontario with lots of fae. We could've set up a territory there. It would've been a good source of alchemy supplies, too. I know my way around black markets, and I would have sold poisons or artifacts for money."

I bit my lower lip.

"Venturing into new territories as a druid is always dangerous. I would've taken it slow … finding somewhere to stay at the edge of the city first, then exploring the wilds a bit at a time. Smallfae are easy to befriend and they can provide a lot of information about the more powerful fae nearby."

"Did you have all that planned ten years ago?" I asked haltingly.

"I wouldn't call it a plan. They were just vague ideas."

"I see," I mumbled.

"What's wrong?"

A soft, bitter laugh escaped me. "Your 'vague ideas' were ten times more detailed than anything I'd thought of. I'm realizing really fucking late how completely unprepared I was. You had all sorts of survival skills, and I knew shit. I had nothing to contribute."

"It doesn't matter, because that's not what happened. You have lots of skills now." He glanced at me. "We should work on your druid skill set, though. You need a tattoo for that rune from Ríkr, and your aura reflection is awful."

"And yours is perfect, is it?"

"Yes. It's a necessary survival skill."

"Hmph." I relaxed against the cold stone wall and rested my head on his shoulder. "Fine, you can teach me."

His arm twitched slightly, as though he was surprised I'd agreed. Maybe he'd expected me to say he was the last person on earth I'd let teach me anything. Maybe he was waiting for me to lash out again, tell him I hated him, and try to stab him.

A couple of weeks ago, I might've said that. Maybe even a couple of days ago. But everything was changing—*I* was changing.

"Zak ..." I stared down at my hands, gripping the blanket. A faint, painful grind scraped across my ribs. "After this is over ... you should come back to the rescue with me. Stay at my place for a few days."

"A few days?" he repeated softly.

"Yeah." I concentrated on breathing. "You can show me druid things. And ... we can talk about everything. Really talk about it."

A long pause. "All right."

My gaze lifted to his, and fear climbed through me, closing my throat. "Will I hate you when you tell me everything?"

"Maybe." Pain and regret darkened his eyes. "Probably."

The pounding of my heart filled my ears. "I don't want to hate you."

"What's done is done. We can't change it now."

The tight fear in my chest intensified. I remembered that moment outside the Crow and Hammer when I'd told Zak that I'd thought he needed me, and how upset I'd been that it'd appeared he didn't.

And I remembered the way he'd kissed me.

Whatever this strange, traumatic, painful relationship between us was, whether it was healthy or destructive or something else entirely, we needed it. It didn't make any sense, but right now, we needed each other.

My hand floated toward him, moving as though I had no control over it. His bare skin looked pale in the darkness, heavy shadows sculpting the muscles banding his arm. My fingers curled around his forearm. The jagged shards in my chest quivered, but I ignored the warning.

I pushed onto my knees. The blanket slid down my back, cool air washing over my bare skin. Holding his arm with one hand, I gripped his jaw with the other. His eyes widened as I pulled his face up. I stared into those familiar green eyes, every molecule in my body vibrating.

This wasn't smart. It wasn't safe. It wasn't good for me. But I couldn't stop myself.

I leaned down.

I kissed him.

His mouth was slack with shock, but I didn't care. My heart was skipping wildly. My gut twisted, fear and need competing. I pulled away. Our eyes locked. No longer surprised, his gaze burned. But he didn't move, waiting to see what I would do next.

Grabbing his face with both hands, I crushed our mouths together.

His hands closed around my waist, hot against my skin. Lips parting, mouths open, tongues sliding together. I pressed into him, arching over him. My knees straddled his legs, my thighs against his torso. Skin on skin. His blanket wasn't between us. I didn't know where it had gone.

His fingers slid down to my ass, then he pulled my hips down into his. I gasped against his mouth. Scorching desire spread through my body. I needed him. I'd needed him since the night we'd held knives to each other's throats in a dangerous, darkly flirtatious game. Since we'd made out against the stable wall. Since he'd taunted me in the hotel bathroom. Since he'd kissed me—devoured me—outside the Crow and Hammer.

And now I was kissing him, and it wasn't enough. My hands were clutching his shoulders, fingernails digging in, and it wasn't enough. I ground against him, my hips rocking—and it still wasn't enough. My hand dragged down his chest, his abs. Found the waistline of his shorts. Slid under them—

He grabbed my wrist, stopping me. "Saber."

I froze, my mouth hovering an inch above his.

"I—" He let out a rough breath. "I don't think we should do this."

Rejection slammed through me. Baring my teeth, I shoved off him—and he grabbed my arms. We tipped, rolled, then I was on my back on our discarded blankets and he was pinning me down.

"Don't lose your shit, Saber," he rasped. "I'm stopping because I don't want to hurt you, not because I don't want you."

"I like it rough, you idiot," I snapped.

"I don't mean *that*," he snarled, then his mouth collided with mine, teeth and tongue and fire. He pulled back, leaving me panting. "I don't want you to regret doing this now ... before we've talked about everything."

The burning emptiness in my core didn't care about any of that, but his words made the broken shards of my heart quake.

"That's why it has to be now." I curled my hands over the back of his neck and tried to pull his mouth down. "It has to be now, because after we talk ... the truth ..."

His expression was losing heat. Something else gathered in his eyes, softening the lust from his features. His fingertips brushed across my cheek.

The fear I'd buried in heated desire flushed through me like icy water, and I realized tears had welled in my eyes. My limbs were shivering, but not from cold. I inhaled unsteadily.

He lowered himself onto the blanket beside me and pulled me into his arms. I buried my face in his chest, fighting the tears.

Zak might not have betrayed me in the way I'd thought, but he'd still hurt me. I'd been permanently damaged by the pain he'd caused me, and once I had the whole story, once I knew why he'd shattered my heart, I wouldn't be able to pretend anymore that I could possibly forgive him.

I wouldn't be able to pretend anymore that a future existed where we could be anything but pain for each other. That future had died ten years ago. All I could do was delay the inevitable moment I faced our past and all its anguish.

And I couldn't delay it much longer.

17

AT THE MOUTH of the cave, I crouched on the riverbank and splashed cold water over my hot face. Though it was only midafternoon, the sun had dipped out of sight behind the towering trees and steep sides of the ravine. We'd wasted half a day, and with each passing hour, Zak and I got sicker.

I braced my hands on my thighs as I rose. My muscles felt tired, as though I'd run a marathon instead of slept, and my chest ached, though that feeling might've been the result of emotional turmoil more than my fever.

I adjusted the blanket on my shoulders. My clothes were mostly dry, but a faint, moldy odor permeated the fabric. I wasn't looking forward to putting them back on. As I turned toward the cave, a cool prickle of familiar power ran across my skin.

I went still with surprise, then spun to face upstream.

In the center of the river, his long white cloak billowing around him, Ríkr strode toward me. Instead of wading through the rushing water, he walked on top of it, the liquid freezing beneath his feet with each graceful step. The large pack of supplies we'd left at Zak's cabin hung casually from his shoulder, adding a strikingly human element to his fae garments, snow-white hair, and golden antlers.

The only thing that could have improved my mood more was if Artear had been at Ríkr's side. Instead, it was Yilliar hastening along the narrow bridge of ice Ríkr was creating. The Shadow Lord carried Lallakai in his arms, and Grenior and Keelar followed on his heels.

"Ríkr," I exclaimed softly, relief leaving me lightheaded.

"My lovely dove." As he stepped from his ice bridge onto the rocky shore, he scanned my mostly nude body. "I would say I am pleased to see you well, but that assessment seems inaccurate."

"Pretty inaccurate, yeah." I reached eagerly for the heavy pack he carried, more than ready to put on clean clothes. As he passed it to me, I tilted my head toward Yilliar. "So who found who?"

"Let us call it a mutual discovery," Ríkr replied with a faint smirk.

Yilliar shouldered Ríkr out of his way, then tipped his arms forward. He all but dumped Lallakai on her feet before striding into the cave with his mouth twisted in disgust. The two vargs trotted after him, eager to be reunited with their druid.

Lallakai swayed, and Ríkr extended a hand to her. She grabbed his wrist, breathing heavily.

I swung the pack onto my shoulders. "I see you and Yilliar are on good terms."

She cast me a weak glare with dull green eyes. "Yilliar's ego is unbearably inflated from years spent in Marzanna's favor. Under better circumstances, I could crush him."

Even if she hadn't looked minutes from death, I wouldn't have believed her.

"Did Yilliar bring you up to speed?" I asked Ríkr, moving to Lallakai's other side and offering my arm as well. She reluctantly took it, using Ríkr and me as crutches as she hobbled into the cave.

"I believe so," Ríkr replied. "How fares the Queen of Death?"

"She's improved somewhat. Zak thinks she might wake up soon."

"Excellent news."

The three of us squeezed through the crevice into the larger cavern. My gaze swept across the dimly lit space, seeking Zak. He was crouched beside Marzanna's nest of blankets, and Yilliar knelt a few feet away, his arms gently encircling a slim figure. Marzanna was sitting up—barely—and at the sound of our footsteps, she raised her head.

Limp raven hair hung around her narrow shoulders like curtains, its length spilling across the blankets. Her face was deathly pale and surprisingly young. She looked no more than sixteen, though that meant nothing when it came to fae.

"My Queen," Yilliar crooned, "I rejoice that you have awakened."

"Have her drink," Zak said, shoving a bottle of water into the fae's hand. "She's dehydrated."

Rising, Zak hastened toward us, his brows pinched with concern. He took Lallakai's arm and pulled it over his shoulders, murmuring questions about her symptoms. I watched silently as he led her to the blankets where he'd been sitting earlier and helped her down, then pressed his wrist to her forehead to check her temperature.

Heaving a bitter sigh, I set the pack on the ground and leaned against Ríkr's arm.

"Dove?"

"I'm exhausted," I whispered.

"You are ill." Worry glinted in his inhuman, crystalline eyes. "You are weakening."

I nodded since there was no point in denying it.

His mouth thinned unhappily. Taking my wrist, he strode toward the Shadow Court's Queen.

"Let us proceed immediately to the most pressing matter," he announced. "Marzanna, what do you know of the poison that afflicts you?"

Her huge eyes, black as bottomless pits, rose to his. "I do not know you."

"My identity is of little importance when you linger on the cusp of death. Answer me."

Yilliar curled his arm around her thin shoulders, keeping her upright. "These two arrived with the Crystal Druid. They are our allies against the beast."

She blinked slowly, and as her eyes opened again, Zak stepped past me and crouched in front of her. "You know what this poison is, don't you?"

"She knows." Lallakai's sharp voice echoed through the cave. Leaning against the wall ten feet away, she sneered at Marzanna. "She obsessed for years over how Bane and Izverg killed Marzaniok."

"You dare speak of his death in front of your queen?" Yilliar snarled. "Your incompetence is the reason—"

Marzanna fluttered her hand, and Yilliar fell instantly silent.

"I was obsessed," she whispered. "I scarcely ate or slept in the long months following his gruesome demise, craving answers more than rest or sustenance. I uncovered all I could of the Wolfbane Druid's schemes and the beast's weapons. His unsightly gauntlets bear poisonous claws—a poison brewed to reduce his enemies to a weakened state whereupon he may devour them at his leisure, as he did to my beloved brother. With much effort, I divined the nature of the vile toxin and its counter."

Zak leaned forward. "What is it? What's the counter?"

"A flower," she sighed. "A flower that only grows in the care of dragons."

"You mean Dragon's Breath? It has magical properties, but I didn't know it could be used as an antidote. How is it made?"

"I know not." She closed her eyes in another slow blink. "I had an ally knowledgeable in poisons create the antidote for me."

I leaned forward intently. "You already have the antidote? Where is it?"

"I suspected, even then, that the beast would use the same cowardly strategy he had used upon my brother to bring me down." She leaned into Yilliar's supporting arm. "I hid the antidote in the bone eater's lair, where neither the beast nor his minions could reach it. It is ironic, is it not ... that I could not reach it in time either."

Her eyelids drooped, and she sagged against Yilliar's side. He gently laid her down, his face tight. "Her breathing is weaker. Druid, you must strengthen her."

"I'm out of potions. I need to make more." Zak sat back on his heels. "But what she really needs is the antidote."

"Then we should go get it," I said. "Where is the bone eater's lair?"

Yilliar brushed Marzanna's hair off her pale forehead, his touch gentle and anxious, then rose to his feet. "I know its location, as do all members of the Shadow Court."

I frowned. "How is that a good hiding spot, then?"

A chuff of breathless laughter came from Lallakai's corner. She rested her head against the rock wall, feverish eyes rolling our way. "It is most safe. The bone eater preys on any and all fae unwise enough to wander within its reach. Not even the lords and ladies of the court would test their strength against it."

"She is correct." Yilliar didn't sound happy to be agreeing with Lallakai. "The bone eater is unassailable and utterly deadly. I would surely die if I tried to enter its lair. Only Marzanna can retrieve the antidote."

Ríkr tucked his hands in his cloak sleeves. "I am not familiar with this creature. Why Marzanna alone?"

"The bone eater is blind, but its senses are acutely attuned to the presence of our kind. Marzanna, however, is the Queen of Death. She can assume the form of death and pass the bone eater undetected."

Assume the form of death? Did he mean she could become a zombie at will?

"So any fae who is not dead or faking death can't get past the bone eater?" Zak asked. "Ríkr, what if you and Yilliar attacked it together?"

"Impossible," Yilliar declared. "Attacking it with enough force to kill it would undoubtedly destroy the antidote as well."

Silence fell over the cave.

"What about making a new batch of antidote?" Yilliar asked Zak. "You know the crucial ingredient and where it grows."

Surprise flickered through me. "You know where it grows?"

Zak nodded. "It isn't that far from here. I could be there and back in four or five hours depending on how far east we are right now. But the potions I've used it in weren't for consumption. I have no idea how to prepare it as an antidote. I either need more information about Marzanna's antidote or I need to examine it myself."

"Then we're back to the bone eater," I muttered.

"We might need both." He pushed to his feet. "Marzanna had the antidote made for herself. I doubt there's enough for all four of us, and Echo might need it too."

"Then what do we do?"

"We divide and conquer." Ríkr's eyes gleamed eerily in the dim light. "You and Zak will procure the antidote's crucial ingredient so he can prepare more, while Yilliar and I challenge the bone eater for the existing antidote."

Unease rippled through me. Yilliar had already explained why fighting the bone eater wasn't an option, and Marzanna wouldn't recover enough to get it herself. We needed another option for sneaking past the bone eater—and I had the perfect solution. Or I would've, if I'd brought my river-stone pendant with me.

I'd carried it around for three days straight, but when it'd come time to pack for our excursion to the Shadow Court, I'd decided to leave it at home so I wouldn't lose it again.

"The bone eater senses the presence of fae," I said, "but what about a druid?"

"All fae notice druids," Ríkr replied. "I doubt this creature is an exception."

Yilliar ran a fingertip back and forth over his jaw. "It is possible, if the druid kept their energy exceptionally well hidden and a fae with a strong presence were nearby as a distraction."

Zak crossed his arms. "My aura reflection is as close to perfect as it gets. I could—"

"You need to get the Dragon's Breath," I interrupted.

His eyes narrowed.

"Divide and conquer, like Ríkr said," I continued. "We don't have time to all go get the Dragon's Breath, then sneak into the bone eater's lair. The longer this drags out, the weaker we'll get. What if we take too long and you lose consciousness before you can make more of the antidote?"

Zak's jaw flexed. "So you're volunteering to sneak into the bone eater's lair? You don't even know how to do aura reflection."

"I can instruct her," Ríkr offered. "And though Yilliar and I cannot safely attack the bone eater, we can provide a spectacular distraction."

"Not too spectacular," Yilliar countered. "We must not draw the attention of the court."

"I don't like this," Zak growled.

"Neither do I, but I like dying even less."

Crossing the cave to our large pack, I knelt and unzipped it. Not having expected to ruin two outfits at once, I only had one more change of clothes—a tank top and the jeans I'd worn to the Crow and Hammer the night before we'd left.

Zak crouched beside me, holding the pack open while I fished around for socks. "Saber ..." A brief pause, then he let out a harsh breath. "I hope you can learn aura reflection as fast as you learned aura spheres."

I hoped so too. "Where's the soap?"

He dug into the bottom of the bag. His searching hand hesitated, then he pulled out his alchemy kit. I raised my eyebrows as he unrolled the heavy leather satchel, pretty certain he didn't keep soap in there.

He took stock of his supplies. "Unless the antidote is extremely simple to make, I might not have all the tools I'll need. We'll have to go back to my farm."

Could we afford to add half a day of hard travel onto the time it would take to collect the Dragon's Breath, examine the existing antidote, and concoct more? Zak and I were already feverish and weak. Would we last that long?

I bit my inner cheek, using the sting to counter the hopeless dread weighing down my limbs.

"What ..." Lallakai coughed weakly. "What about Bane's former abode?"

Zak twisted toward her, frowning. "What about it?"

"You left alchemy supplies behind, did you not? It's significantly closer than your farm."

"I ..." He trailed off, his gaze going distant. "I only took his artifacts and valuables, so the rest might still be there."

I shifted uncomfortably. "Do you mean ...?"

He nodded, his face pale and his eyes haunted. "My old home ... where I lived with Bane."

18

"MY DEAREST DOVE," Ríkr drawled, his soft tone almost disguising the scrape of frustration, "I am beginning to wonder if you are trying."

I gritted my teeth. An exceptionally patient hunter Ríkr might be, but he wasn't a patient teacher. At least not today, when so much relied on me learning one basic druidic skill.

"Shall I repeat my instructions," he continued, "or are you simply ignoring them?"

On second thought, maybe he *wasn't* hiding his frustration.

"I'm trying, okay?" I snapped. "Aura spheres were easy because I'd done them before, even if I hadn't realized it, but I've never had to hide my energy. You were draining it all, remember?"

Behind us, Lallakai chuffed with derision. I glanced back. Tilliag plodded along the narrow game trail behind me and Ríkr, the ancient forest blocking most of the evening sunlight.

Lallakai sat astride the stallion, her long hair flowing across our large pack, which was slung over his hindquarters.

Zak had prepared another batch of potions for us, and the recent dose had given Lallakai enough strength to sit upright, but she was in no condition to walk. We'd agreed she should ride Tilliag, but no one—especially Tilliag—was all that happy about it.

Trailing a dozen steps behind Tilliag was Yilliar, his dark form almost lost in the shadows. He'd insisted Lallakai accompany us to Bane's former territory instead of waiting in the hidden cavern. I wasn't sure if it was genuine paranoia or his intense dislike of the Night Eagle, but he'd refused to leave her alone with Marzanna.

Since we needed Yilliar to help us find and sneak past the bone eater, we'd had no choice but to bring Lallakai along. Having her as an audience for my aura reflection lesson wasn't helping me focus.

"Sense the energy around you," Ríkr murmured, softening his voice as he paced beside me through the old forest. "Immerse yourself in it and feel nothing else."

I half closed my eyes, trying to sink into the quiet thrum of ancient life all around me. My foot caught on something and I stumbled.

"Your impatience and frustration radiate outward." Ríkr's long, heavy white cloak fluttered as he stepped gracefully over the fallen sapling that had tripped me. "It is a clear beacon to fae."

"I know," I growled. "It's hard not to feel anything, you know."

"You may still feel, dove. You must do it *within* the energy around you. It is the difference between wading gently through a still pond and charging into the water."

Squinching my eyes mostly shut, I held back a complaint about his lack of concrete instructions. Again, I tried to calm my emotions and immerse myself in the surrounding energy. It had a distinct feel, almost like a harmony of musical notes.

"Better," he said softly. "But I still sense a discordant air of apprehension. Do not fear the bone eater, dove. Master this and you will be safe."

I bit my lower lip. It wasn't the prospect of the bone eater that caused anxiety to buzz across every nerve in my body. It was Zak's absence.

When we'd left the cavern, Yilliar, Lallakai, Tilliag, Ríkr, and I had headed west, cutting across the northern edge of the bog. Zak had gone east. He wasn't strictly alone—his two vargs had gone with him—but how much protection could they offer? Zak didn't even have Tilliag for a fast escape. If the Shadow Court caught his trail and followed him, he'd be a sitting duck.

The others seemed to think he'd be fine since he was heading away from Shadow Court land, but even if he didn't run into Izverg's minions, the wild mountains contained plenty of dangerous fae—and Zak wasn't at his best. If he felt anything like me, he'd be feverish, fatigued, and a bit shaky. His potions were only slowing the effects of the poison, not stopping it.

Sending him off alone wasn't ideal by any stretch of the imagination, but I needed Yilliar to lead me to the bone eater's lair and Ríkr to teach me aura reflection. Tilliag was transporting Lallakai, who couldn't walk, and later, he would carry me away from the bone eater in case it chased us. Leaving Marzanna alone had also been a last resort, but at least she was well hidden.

"Your feelings of dread are *increasing*, dove."

I exhaled roughly. "I'm trying. Controlling my emotions isn't my strong suit." Evening out my breathing, I flexed my spine to release tension. "What if I can't do it? What then?"

"I'll attempt to freeze this bone-devouring creature into a solid block of ice." He arched an eyebrow. "I have no intention of allowing you near its lair with anything less than a perfectly undetectable aura."

"That's not going to happen. No way I can master it that fast."

"Of course not, if you waste precious time complaining instead of practicing."

Narrowing my eyes angrily, I bit back a retort. Again, I focused on the forest's energy. Worrying about Zak wouldn't change anything. I had to get this right or it'd be a repeat of our fight with Luthyr, where everyone had depended on me and I'd blown it. Out of habit, I slid my hand into my pocket, searching for the comfort of my switchblade handle.

My fingers met a leather tie. Brow furrowing, I tugged it out of my pocket. The tie came free, a grape-sized brown stone swinging from it.

I stopped in the middle of the trail, staring at my river-stone pendant. But ... I'd left it at home, hadn't I? My mind rushed back over our hasty packing spree the night before we'd left. I'd intended to put the river stone somewhere safe, but in the midst of planning and packing, I'd spontaneously added these pants without checking their pockets first. I'd brought the pendant without realizing it.

"What is that?" Yilliar asked.

I looked up, finding three pairs of curious fae eyes watching me. Instead of answering, I dropped the cord over my neck and tucked the stone down the front of my shirt so it rested over my heart.

Ríkr's eyes lost focus. "Ah. Impressive."

"I sense but the faintest flicker of your energy," Yilliar said with muted disbelief. "What is that item?"

"An artifact my mother's fae partner made to hide me from fae as a child," I said. "Is it working?"

Yilliar dipped his chin. "Most definitely. It is a more complete concealment even than aura reflection. You will be able to walk past the bone eater unmolested, I am certain."

"It is remarkably effective," Ríkr murmured. "Why did you not reveal it sooner?"

"I didn't realize I had it." A grin spread over my face. "This is perfect. No aura reflection needed."

Yilliar made a shooing motion. "Then let us continue with haste to the bone eater."

I started down the trail again, Ríkr pacing beside me. One problem solved, but now I had nothing to distract me from my concern for Zak. I peeked at Ríkr out of the corner of my eye.

"Ríkr," I murmured. "Can I ask a favor?"

"Anything, dove."

I steeled myself. "Since I don't need you to teach me aura reflection anymore, will you go find Zak?"

He gazed at me blankly. "Leave you? Dove, you may have an excellent concealment spell, but that does not guarantee your safety."

"My safety is more guaranteed than Zak's," I insisted. "He's out there alone. His vargs aren't enough to protect him, and if anything happens to him, I die too, remember?"

If tragedy befalls Zak and he cannot concoct more of the antidote, I will kill Yilliar and Lallakai so you may consume the antidote unchallenged.

Ríkr's telepathic voice slid quietly into my mind, and I shivered at his ruthless, matter-of-fact calmness.

The bone eater won't be a problem now, I replied, switching to telepathic communication as well. *So you can—*

You are my priority, dove, he interrupted implacably.

But ... I bit my lip, getting my thoughts in order. *This isn't just about me. If we don't save Marzanna, Izverg will rule the Shadow Court unchecked. He'll keep expanding his territory and spreading his death magic until it reaches our home. You can't fight the whole court alone. If we don't stop him, it'll be like Rhiannon and the Summer Court all over again. Do you want to run from another court, Ríkr?*

He considered my words in silence. The crown-like black headpiece that covered his forehead shone faintly in the dim light, the markings of The Undying running down the side of his face.

I am weary of retreat, he finally replied. *I will go to Zak, as you wish.*

My tension melted away. *Thank you, Ríkr.*

But understand, dove. The bone eater is not our only foe. Yilliar will protect you until you retrieve the antidote, but his priority is Marzanna. At worst, he will kill you before rushing the cure to his ailing queen. Without me to block him, you must ensure he does not betray you.

I clenched my right hand, a rush of cold flowing from the rune on my inner wrist. If I asked him how the hell I was supposed to fight off a Shadow Lord by myself, Ríkr would insist on staying with me. I'd have to figure it out on my own.

"I'll handle him," I murmured.

Azure eyes moved across my face, seeing right through my bluff, then the former Winter King smiled faintly. "Be safe, dove."

"You too."

My heart squeezed uncomfortably as blue light shimmered across him. He melted into the form of a white hawk, and his wings thundered in the air as he soared upward, vanishing into the forest canopy.

BANE'S FORMER BASE looked no different from the surrounding forest. The only sign a human had ever set foot among the trees was a small log cabin with an overgrown garden behind it. The structure had weathered ten years of complete neglect fairly well, but it wasn't much more than four walls and a roof. Its single window had wooden shutters, one broken, and no glass. A rusted metal chimney stuck out from the slanted roof.

The rough-hewn door was closed, and I stood in front of it, feeling vaguely nauseous. This was where Zak had grown up. This was where Bane had trained him ... and abused him.

It was so small and crude. I doubted it had electricity. No way it had a bathroom. There was probably an outhouse nearby. Ancient forest surrounded the structure, and unlike Zak's destroyed farm, no hidden roads led here. It was pure wilderness, untouched by humans except for this lone cabin and its former druid inhabitants.

My life with Ruth had been miserable, but I'd never lacked a dry, warm bed, access to clean running water, or the ability to shower whenever I wanted. I'd gone to school. I'd had a closet full of expensive clothes. In the light of Ruth's constant emotional and physical abuse, I'd never appreciated those luxuries—but looking at this plain wooden structure, I appreciated them now.

"Glamorous, isn't it?"

I turned. Lallakai was sitting against the trunk of a tree, gazing at the cabin. Hanging from the branches above her were odd talismans made from faded red and white twine. With round tops and tassel-like bodies, they resembled the little tissue-paper ghosts children made as Halloween decorations. They dotted the lower boughs of trees all around the cabin.

"I am unpleasantly familiar with this place," she said, her voice lacking its usual sultry purr. Her cheeks were sunken, her skin pale. "For six months, I spied on the Wolfsbane here, attempting to uncover how he and his beast were plotting against the Shadow Court."

I stepped away from the cabin door, unwilling to open it and see more of Zak's childhood neglect. There was no point in going inside. Yilliar, Tilliag, and I would leave for the bone eater's lair as soon as Yilliar finished checking that this spot was safe. Lallakai would wait here for the rest of us to complete our respective missions and return. Then Zak would use the cabin's alchemy supplies to create more of the antidote.

I crossed the carpet of pine needles and stopped a few feet away from Lallakai. "You tried to get information out of Zak. That's how you two met, isn't it?"

"Indeed. He was stubbornly reticent despite my efforts." She pursed her lips. "He remains aggravatingly stubborn even now. A habit of his I could not break."

I didn't like the way she said "break."

"Had I understood then that he would never cross Izverg," she added in a murmur, "I would have altered my strategy."

"Never cross Izverg?" I repeated. "What do you mean?"

"Have you not noticed?"

"Noticed what?"

"How Izverg terrifies him."

I'd recognized that Zak was plagued by a lingering fear of Izverg from his childhood, but I wouldn't describe his reaction as terror. "I don't think—"

"There is no more apt description," she interrupted. "He's spent years building his power so as to never yield to the likes of Bane and Izverg again, yet fear of them still paralyzes him."

I crouched beside her. "And you're disappointed in him because of that?"

Surprise flickered over her wan features, as though she hadn't realized that was how she felt.

"When you're a kid, your abusers seem invincible. That isn't a feeling you just forget, and part of Zak probably still sees Izverg the same way even now." My hands curled into fists. "Which is all the more reason why you should be grateful to him, not disappointed. He might still be afraid, but he attacked Izverg head on to get you away from him."

Her brow furrowed, and she mulled over my words for a surprisingly long moment. "Izverg is not an easy opponent," she conceded. "I battled him twice before, and on both occasions, I escaped with my life but not victory."

"Is it because you lost that Marzaniok died? And that's why Yilliar hates you?"

"Yilliar hated me long before Marzaniok's demise. I was the king and queen's most trusted subordinate, and he jealously yearned for my status." Her mouth twisted. "We all, Marzanna included, underestimated the beast and his druid, but she blamed me entirely for her brother's death. She cast me from her side to become the lowest peon of the court, sneered upon by all."

Bitterness rolled off her in waves. "For a long year, I sought to regain a shadow of my former status, but I was ruthlessly scorned. Nothing short of vengeance for Marzaniok would save my position in the court, so I set out to find the beast and his druid."

"To find them?" I waved at the cabin. "They weren't here?"

"Bane distanced himself to avoid the Shadow Court's bloodthirsty retribution. However, it did not take me long to track them down." Her emerald eyes regained a spark of intensity. "As before, Zak remained Bane's obedient apprentice. Yet he was different."

"Different how?"

"He was more calculating, more ruthless, and"—her lips curved up—"far more intriguing. This time, when I appeared before him, he did not play games. He offered himself to me in exchange for my help killing Bane and Izverg."

How desperate had Zak been to escape that he'd sold himself to Lallakai? "So the two of you killed Bane but not Izverg?"

"Killing Izverg was my task, and I failed." She fluttered her hand as though the details of how she'd lost to Izverg didn't matter. "I occupied Izverg long enough for Zak to kill his master, and I hoped that would be sufficient. Alongside my new consort, I returned to the Shadow Court with the news of Bane's death, but Marzanna's resentment was unrelenting. She offered Zak more courtesy than she did me."

My brain stuck on the words "my new consort."

"Scorned again, I forsook the court and turned my attention to Zak, encouraging him to build his power however he saw fit." She ran her tongue across her upper lip. "With my help, he rose to heights that rivaled his former master, becoming the dominant druid for hundreds of miles and the most notorious rogue in Vancouver."

While Zak had been conquering the city's rogue underground and building his druid powers, I'd been patching together the best life I could while on parole. Once again, I was struck by the stark differences between us.

"So you gave up on the Shadow Court?" I asked. "You don't care anymore about regaining your position?"

She settled back against the tree. "Marzanna's hatred for me is as everlasting as her grief for Marzaniok. As long as she is queen, I will never be more than a pawn beneath her foot. I've maintained my connection to the court only to benefit Zak."

Thoughts churning, I rose to my full height. "How do you really feel about Zak?"

A soft, breathy laugh vibrated her throat. "Jealous, little druid?"

My lips pressed together.

"You have no understanding of our bond. I am more than a companion, confidant, guardian, or lover." She smiled when I gritted my teeth. "I am so much more. I took an immature boy and shaped him into one of the most powerful druids of this age. I *created* the Crystal Druid. He belongs to me, and he will for the rest of his life."

My jaw clenched harder. Turning on my heel, I strode away from her. Not long ago, Lallakai had promised to change how she viewed and treated Zak, and for most of that time, she'd been unconscious from poison. I couldn't expect a long-lived fae to evolve her attitude overnight. Fae weren't like humans.

Their minds worked differently and they saw the world in ways we couldn't imagine.

Ríkr's voice whispered in my memory, calmly promising to kill Yilliar and Lallakai to save me. He and Lallakai were both loyal to their druids. They would both protect their druids however they saw fit—whether their druids agreed with their methods or not. Lallakai was too controlling and invasive, but Ríkr's habits of manipulation and deception hadn't left me unscathed either.

My hand closed around the front of my shirt, squeezing the river-stone pendant. I wished I could ask my parents for advice. I wished I could speak with them one more time now that I knew what I was—and what they'd been.

A final conversation was impossible, but at least I had the pendant they'd left me. I wasn't facing this next challenge alone. Wearing it now felt like their hands reaching through time to protect me.

And I was about to stake my life on the strength of that protection.

19

EXHALING SLOWLY, *I lowered the chain over my neck. The cold stone slid down my chest under the neckline of my shirt, and as it settled over my heart, that faint sensation, like I was sinking into cold water, engulfed me again.*

Well? I asked Keelar, my heart drumming against my ribs.

The dark, wolfish fae stood close to my left leg, and her red eyes studied me for a few seconds that felt like an eternity. I cannot sense your druid power, only a faint hint of spiritual energy, like that of a weak witch.

Relief and something like terror swept through me. It was working. It was actually working, just as the girl had promised—and that meant I was going ahead with my plan. I was killing Bane. Tonight.

I turned, staring through the trees, but I was too far into the wilderness to see anything. A few miles south of here was Bane's second lair, where he did business with humans instead of fae. It was on the northern edge of North Vancouver, a thirty-minute drive from the Downtown Eastside where I would meet the girl.

My hands trembled and I clenched them into fists. Was I really doing this? Was I killing Bane tonight?

Zak, Keelar murmured. I sense the Night Eagle.

Lallakai was here? But we were three hundred kilometers from Bane's primary territory, and I'd never seen Lallakai anywhere else. The only reason she might be here was because she'd followed us.

I tapped the pendant under my shirt. Which way?

Keelar ghosted through the trees on silent paws, and I followed her, almost as quiet. The late afternoon shadows were deep and the overcast had dulled the sunlight to a cool, unpleasant gray. I stretched my senses out, but Lallakai was good at sneaking around undetected. She'd snuck up on me so many times.

Maybe with the pendant, I could sneak up on her for once.

Keelar and I crept through the trees, moving toward Bane's house. I didn't want to get too close. If any of his vargs spotted me, they might realize my presence was completely hidden. That was why I'd gone so far out into the forest to test the enchantment.

Just when I was about to turn back, I felt a shiver of cool, dark power. I crouched behind a thicket and peered ahead, Keelar beside me. It took a moment for my eyes to pick out Lallakai's shape among the shadows.

As soon as I spotted her, it was like a veil was lifted and I could see clearly. She was standing in the shelter of a towering spruce, her arms crossed. In front of her was a floating smear of darkness that might've been a fae or some sort of magic.

Slowing my breathing, I focused on the faint sense of her presence and "listened" with my mind instead of my ears. After a moment, I caught a soft, feminine voice.

—searched high and low for that foul, dog-headed beast. *Lallakai directed her words at the dark shape in front of her.* It is probably chewing carrion bones in a cave.

I couldn't hear what the dark shape said in reply.

Lallakai tossed her head, her long hair shimmering. What more do they expect of me? I cannot be in two places at once. Either I observe the druid or I track the beast, though both tasks are beneath me.

The dark shape rippled in agitation.

Utter foolishness, *she complained.* I have been watching them for two seasons. They accomplish nothing of interest, let alone concoct sinister plots. I tire of the queen's endless paranoia.

She listened, then huffed in exasperation. If she is so concerned about her brother's whereabouts, I will return to help her search for him.

With a final ripple, the shade faded away. Lallakai glanced toward Bane's house, then swept her arms outward. Shadows swirled over her body, and she transformed into a black eagle. I ducked behind the thicket as she flew off through the trees, heading north.

When the sound of her wingbeats had faded, I stood up. So she was a spy for the Shadow Court. I wasn't surprised. I'd known all along she wanted something from me. If she'd only been interested in making me her consort, she would've done it by now.

It was too bad, though. She seemed powerful, and she was way more pleasant than Izverg. I could do a lot worse.

I pressed my hand to the pendant, then tugged it out from under my shirt and slid it into my pocket. The artifact worked. I had no more preparations to make. If I was killing Bane, it had to be tonight—because, like Lallakai had said, Izverg wasn't here. For whatever reason, he'd stayed behind when we'd left for this trip to the city.

This was my best chance, and I wouldn't waste it.

I WAS READY.

The muggy heat clung to my bare arms. I'd stripped down to a t-shirt and jeans, eliminating any clothing that could snag on anything. A ten-inch knife was strapped to my thigh, three potions were attached to my belt, and three crystals hung on leather ties around my neck.

Breathing at a slow, deliberate pace, I pulled the girl's stone pendant from my pocket. It was too dark in the trees to see the etching on the front. Gripping the chain, I looked down. Keelar once again stood beside me, her scarlet eyes gleaming.

The others are distracting Bane's pack, she told me.

And no sign of Lallakai? I asked. It'd been hours since she'd flown off, but I didn't want her suddenly returning and screwing everything up.

No, Keelar confirmed. We are ready.

Bane's house was a hundred yards away through the trees. The toxic energy of the city was stronger here, and combined with my aura reflection, my presence was almost undetectable. When it disappeared entirely, it'd take Bane's varg pack a few minutes to notice—but I'd still have to move fast, before the pack realized I'd "vanished" and started searching.

I grabbed a potion from my belt, tore out the cork, and downed it. Enhanced strength.

The second potion flowed across my tongue like oil. Enhanced speed.

Tipping back the third potion, I poured the fizzy liquid down my throat. Scent masking.

I dropped the vial and seized a crystal hanging around my neck. Latin rushed over my lips, and a tingle of Arcana magic answered. Sound suppression.

Gripping the second crystal, I uttered another incantation. Cloaking spell.

Lastly, I dropped the chain over my neck and pushed the pendant down my shirt to rest against my heart. Aura concealment.

Keelar's intent stare swept over me before she rushed away, paws thudding softly. She and the others would distract Bane's pack, and the rest was up to me. Only I was hidden from fae senses, physical and otherwise. Only I could do this.

I sped through the trees. The combination of increased strength and speed could be disorienting, but I'd practiced. I moved smoothly. The scent-masking potion meant none of the vargs would catch wind of me, and the sound-suppression spell would prevent them from hearing me. The cloaking spell wasn't as good—it made me look blurry and shadowy—but that's why my vargs were running interference.

We'd been pestering Bane's familiars like this for months. It wouldn't seem out of the ordinary. Nothing to raise their suspicions too soon.

The house came into view. Small, but way nicer than the cabin where we normally lived. The windows glowed warmly, but Bane wasn't in there. I swerved toward the detached double garage, approaching it from the back.

I blinked rapidly, focusing my eyes on the fae demesne. Mist washed over the landscape, and the garage lost its solidity, becoming a shadowy shape.

Reaching the building, I slunk along the wall. Around the corner, light shone from an open overhead door. Bane was inside, working on whatever big thing he'd had planned for this night. Lallakai should've paid more attention to what Bane was up to. I didn't know his plans either, but she was underestimating him big time.

Three vargs lounged on the grass near the driveway. They hadn't noticed me, but I had no way of getting past them.

Grenior and Yardir appeared on the opposite side of the garage. I didn't try to eavesdrop on what they said to the other vargs, not wanting them to notice me, but whatever taunts my vargs made, it had the others on their feet and snarling in an instant.

Two of Bane's vargs rushed off after Grenior and Yardir, who retreated into the trees. But one stayed behind, too lazy for dominance games.

I silently swore. I couldn't sneak past him. Only one option.

I crept to the edge of the building. The varg had lain back down in the shadows. No direct light. I touched two fingers to the dark rune on my inner wrist and whispered Lallakai's name as softly as I could.

Cool magic swept up my arm, and the shadows all around me deepened. I was submerged in darkness, and no one would be able to see me—or so Lallakai had promised.

I slipped away from the cover of the garage. Silent, scentless, unseen. My knife slid from its sheath, and I pounced. One hand pinned the varg's head to the ground and the other drove my knife into the base of his skull, severing the spinal cord. Instant death. No chance for the varg to sound an alarm before he died.

Pulling the knife free, I darted toward the open garage door. Bloody knife in one hand, I crouched at the threshold and gripped my last crystal spell. One hit with this spell would stun Bane for five seconds. And in those five seconds, I would slit his throat.

I peeked inside. Light from the interior touched my face, and Lallakai's spell disappeared.

Bane stood at a table in the center of the garage, his back to me. For a single shocked heartbeat, all I could do was stare.

The woven red-and-white talismans that decorated the trees around our cabin lined the edges of the table. And lying across it was a slim fae wearing dark clothing. One graceful arm, lean but masculine, hung off the edge. His fingers were missing, blood dripping from the stumps. Black hair was matted around his head, roughly hacked off a few inches from his scalp. His face was tilted toward me—young, androgynous, with dull, dark eyes gazing at nothing.

Lallakai had definitely underestimated Bane.

I whispered an incantation. A faint violet glow lit up my final spell, and a sphere of arcane energy formed in my hand. I took aim at the spot between Bane's broad shoulders. I drew my arm back to throw it.

A chill like the breath of death itself washed over me.

I looked up.

Izverg's blood-red eyes leered down at me. He was right behind me, leaning over me. For a disbelieving, terrifying moment, I couldn't move.

Found you, *he gloated.*

TILLIAG TOSSED HIS HEAD. *The scent of death is everywhere.*

I didn't need him to tell me. Even I could smell the distinct odor of decomposing flesh permeating the forest. It hung in the night air, tainting every breath I took. Flies buzzed in repulsive numbers, the hum of their wings louder than the rustle of leaves in the faint breeze.

Yilliar walked ahead of us, his steps slow. He'd moved quickly for the past hour, using his shadow magic to leap between patches of darkness while Tilliag alternated between trotting and cantering to keep pace, but now he crept forward cautiously, his painstaking progress illuminated by moonlight.

Gripping Tilliag's mane, I squinted at the fae lord's back. Ríkr's warning repeated in my head. Would the Shadow Lord turn on me as soon as I had the antidote?

I pinched the oval river stone through the front of my shirt, the pendant hidden under my clothes. *Tilliag, my spell is still working, right?*

I sense but the faintest energy.

Reassured, I tried to relax, but it wasn't easy. The danger of our mission aside, using the river-stone pendant again was strangely unsettling. Ten years had passed since I'd worn one.

Yilliar raised his hand, and Tilliag halted with an unhappy snort.

The bone eater's lair is just ahead, the Shadow Lord revealed, speaking in our minds. *The druid and I will continue on.*

I swung off Tilliag's back. An achy twinge ran through my muscles as I landed. The latest round of Zak's potions was wearing off. In another hour, I'd be weak and lightheaded with fever.

Through the trees, I could just make out a rocky bluff where a portion of the mountainside had been sheered away eons ago. A rough semicircle cut into the rocky barrier, forming a sort of open grotto, and at the back, a stream of water plunged into a tiny basin. A mess of fallen trees and leafy shrubs covered the ground around the waterfall and the trickling stream flowing away from it.

The bone eater is an ambush hunter, Yilliar told me as I joined him at the edge of the trees. *Do you see the large cluster of fallen logs? The creature waits in a pit beneath it.*

Uncomfortably reminded of a trapdoor spider, I studied the grotto. Near the basin, collapsed trees with wilting leaves formed a sort of shallow pyramid that hid whatever was beneath it. The debris had been dragged there, which meant the bone eater was at least as strong as a draft horse.

I exhaled slowly. *Start your distraction.*

Shadowy magic rolled off him like heatwaves, and he stepped out of the tree cover, moving cautiously toward the stream. I followed a moment later, angling toward the stack of full-size trees the bone eater had torn from the ground to form its hideaway.

The stench of decomposition grew stronger, and I swatted at the flies buzzing around my head. Water splashed as Yilliar treaded into the stream. His attention was fixed on the logs, his limbs tense and ready. He was primed to leap away at the first sign of movement.

I pulled the neckline of my shirt over my nose, breathing through the fabric as I crept toward the fallen trees. The gap beneath them was too dark to make out anything. I crept closer and closer, placing each foot with care. The moonlight barely lit the ground, and every step risked a noise that would give away my presence. The bone eater might be blind, but no one had said anything about it being deaf.

A dozen yards away, Yilliar paced at the stream's edge, magic rippling off him. The bone eater should be focused on him, but if it wasn't, I was probably in its striking range now.

My heart drummed against my ribs as I inched alongside a log, climbing over branches. The darkness beneath the debris pile was ominously still. I was almost close enough. A few more feet and I'd be able to crawl through a ground-level gap into the creature's lair.

I glanced at Yilliar, and he let off a flare of shadowy power that buzzed across my skin. Exhaling, I sank onto my hands and knees and fumbled at my hip. A flashlight from our supplies was clipped to my belt loop, and I flicked it on, shining the beam into the darkness beneath the tangled logs.

The beam flashed across a bare patch of dirt. There was no pit and no monstrous fae. This wasn't the bone eater's lair.

Shoving backward, I launched to my feet and spun. Yilliar tensed, surprised confusion widening his eyes.

Horror slammed through me. "*Behind you!*"

My scream was drowned out by a sudden racket of snapping branches as the innocuous cluster of shrubs behind Yilliar exploded upward. Long, bone-white arms shot out of the flying debris, huge hands grabbing at the Shadow Lord. The rest of the bone eater followed: a huge, thin body with a mass of sharp, bony protrusions sticking from its humped back; powerful hind legs; and a bony tail that whipped behind it.

It smashed down onto Yilliar, cutting off his hoarse shout.

I summoned an ice spear and threw it with all my strength. It flew across the distance and struck the bone eater's side in a burst of icy shards. The creature jerked its head up.

Its face resembled a human skull with a grotesquely elongated forehead ridged with bony spines. Jaw hanging open and its fangs stained red with blood, it turned its empty eye sockets in my direction.

Blades of black power slashed upward, catching the bone eater under the chin. As it reared back, a wraithlike creature appeared—as dark as obsidian, shadows dripping off him like black ink spilling down his skin, and a crown of horns upon his dark head.

Yilliar's true form.

The Shadow Lord flung a hand up and a bolt of power smashed into the bone eater's face. But the monstrous creature was four times Yilliar's mass, and with a silently gaping jaw, it seized the shadow fae, claws tearing. Shadows whirled over

Yilliar. A piercing black spear tore into the bone eater's shoulder.

I sprinted toward the two fae. Swerving past the bone eater, I ducked under its writhing tail and dove into the pit it had appeared from.

The stench of rot hit me so hard that my diaphragm seized, my body trying to eject the toxic air. I slid into the dark, reeking hole. The flashlight bounced wildly from my hip, its bright beam flickering across a bed of yellowed bone splinters—the scant leftovers of fae skeletons.

Gagging on the stench, I spun the light across the graveyard of shattered bones. The beam hit something dark and glossy. At the back of the pit, tucked neatly into a little crevice between tree roots, was a small black case.

I crunched across the bones, not worrying about making noise as magic pulsed and flashed behind me. I fell on the loose mat of splinters, shoved up, and lunged for the box. Grabbing it, I wrenched the lid off. Inside, a black stone vial with a silver cap was nestled in a bed of embroidered fabric.

I stuffed the vial deep in my pocket, then whirled and threw myself at the nearest edge of the pit. I scrambled up it and tumbled into a shrub. Tearing free, I sprinted away.

"Yilliar!" I screamed over my shoulder. "I have it!"

Behind me, the wraithlike form of the Shadow Lord unleashed a whirlwind of black blades. As the bone eater recoiled, Yilliar's rippling form plunged into the ground—and the shadow beneath my feet bulged upward. Yilliar, still in his wraithlike form, surged out of my shadow, and we spun around to face our enemy.

The bone eater crouched in front of its reeking pit, its long back legs folded like a frog's, ready to launch at its prey. The damage Yilliar had inflicted was already healing. Its hideous, eyeless face was turned toward us, and its tail lashed slowly back and forth. Its teeth, stained with Yilliar's blood, flashed hungrily as it opened its mouth wide, beckoning us closer, but it didn't move away from its lair.

You have the antidote? Yilliar asked.

I tore my gaze away from the bone eater and looked at the Shadow Lord. His horns were the most solid thing about him. The rest of him was draped in rippling shadows. Even his face was more shadow than flesh, his eyes the faintest gleam.

"Yes," I said hoarsely. "Let's get back to Zak."

Yilliar's ethereal head dipped in a nod. I curled my hand, ready to summon an ice spear—but the Shadow Lord turned wearily toward the trees where Tilliag waited. Either he was too injured to fight me, or he'd never intended to break his word. Sighing in relief, I took a step forward.

A deathly chill washed over me.

What have we here?

The scraping voice pushed into my head, and I whirled around, Yilliar copying me.

A shadow moved in the darkness beneath the tree, and with a soft rustle, a beastly form stepped into the moonlight. Izverg's eyes glinted like spots of luminescent blood in the night, and his silver gauntlets clinked as he rested his fists on the ground.

On either side of him, dark silhouettes shifted closer—more shadow fae.

It's a sneaky little druid, Izverg observed, his lips peeling back in a vicious canine grin. *And a filthy traitor begging for punishment.*

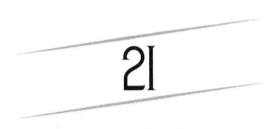

21

PANIC BURST THROUGH ME, emptying my head of everything but fear. For a second, I couldn't move—then I shoved the feeling away and focused on the heat of adrenaline in my veins.

Beside me, shadows writhed over Yilliar. *Get the antidote to Marzanna,* he whispered. *No matter what, druid.*

He thrust both hands out. A twisting spiral of black magic blasted toward Izverg. It struck the jackal beast in the chest, and he staggered backward, blood spraying.

Izverg cackled madly as blood drenched his short, ragged fur. A stale, icy breeze whipped out from him, and in its wake, the foliage melted into dark, soggy goo. The trees blackened, rotting before my eyes. The wave of death expanded, sucking the life out of everything in its path.

Yilliar's draping shadows deepened, and in a silent rush, he leaped into the cloud of death around Izverg.

As he charged, two fae darted out of the dying woods—the pale, veiny-skinned female and a creature the size of a tiger that ran on its hind legs, its charcoal gray fur striped with jagged red lines.

I reeled backward, flinging an ice spear, but they both dodged it. I couldn't win this fight. They were too fast, their magic too strong, and I only had one attack.

My heart clogged my throat as I whirled toward the grotto. The bone eater had retreated halfway into its pit, its skull-like face turned toward us and its back legs coiled, ready to leap at the first victim to step within its reach.

I ran straight at it.

The two shadow fae streaked after me, but my focus was on the bone eater—on those coiled hind legs. Its clawed toes dug into the earth. Behind me, the pale female cast a wave of silver magic at my back—and the bone eater launched forward.

I dove for the ground.

The bone eater shot over my head, and the female screamed. I landed on my front and slid into the pit of bone shards. Rolling onto my hands and knees, I peered out.

Crouched on its weirdly elongated limbs, the bone eater had the female crushed under one huge hand and the tiger-like beast pinned under the other. Both fae struggled violently. Two dozen yards beyond them, the forest was disintegrating into rotting mush as Izverg and Yilliar battled.

The bone eater retreated, dragging its victims into its lair. I stumbled away, turning to the rear of the pit. Grabbing handfuls of tree roots, I scrambled up the dirt wall—but the back was much steeper than the front. The roots tore and I slid down and landed on the bed of bones with a crunch.

I froze in place as the bone eater folded itself into the pit with me, dragging its two victims with it as they writhed in vain. The pale female cast a wave of silver magic over the bone eater, but her enchantment had no effect. With a revolting *pop*, it unhinged its jaw and crammed the tiger beast into its gaping maw. Fangs crunched through bone, and blood drenched the ground.

I cringed back, trying to quiet my breathing. My fingers clenched around the river-stone pendant through my shirt.

It didn't feel right.

As the bone eater swallowed noisily, I tugged the pendant out of my shirt. The glow from my flashlight gleamed across its face, illuminating the deep, ugly crack that had split the rune in half.

Numb disbelief blanked my brain. It was broken. The rune had cracked. When? How?

"No!" the female fae screamed. "Don't—please—don't—"

Her cries cut off with a wet crunch, and my brain snapped back to the terrifying reality of where I was—feet away from the bone eater without a spell to hide my presence. The only reason it hadn't noticed me yet was because it had tastier prey in its mouth.

I snapped a glance at the steep wall of the pit, then pressed my back against it and switched off my flashlight. As darkness plunged over the pit, I focused on the energy radiating from the earth. The bone eater's long presence here had tainted the land. The pure power of the stream and rocky earth was veined with violence and rot, and my skin crawled as I sank all my senses into that feeling.

The wet, sloppy chewing of the bone eater went quiet. Skeletal splinters creaked and snapped under its weight as it twisted in the cramped pit. In the faint moonlight, a blank skull face with a gaping mouth loomed in front of me.

Panic spiked in my chest and I squeezed my eyes shut, feeling the energy of the earth. Immersing in it. Drowning in it. I wouldn't even breathe. Foul, bloody breath washed over me. I squeezed my eyes tighter, concentrating with everything I had.

Come out, come out, pretty little druid.

Izverg's taunting call raked across my mind, breaking my focus. My eyes flew open. I stared into the eyeless countenance of the bone eater—then it spun around, coiling its body for another pounce. It faced the opening of the pit, waiting with the end of its tail twitching feet away from me.

Little lady druid, Izverg called. *Where are you?*

Gasping silently, I pushed up on trembling legs, just enough to peek between the jagged spines that covered the bone eater's back. A dozen paces away, just outside the monster's striking range, Izverg stood. Moonlight shone on the blood matting his fur, but he showed no signs of pain or weakness.

With one gauntleted hand, he held Yilliar by the throat. The Shadow Lord wasn't moving.

Druid, druid. Izverg's blood-red eyes scanned the grotto. *Where did you run, sneaky druid?*

My gut wrenched, and I sank lower, concentrating on the energy of the grotto. Aura reflection could hide me from Izverg as well as the bone eater—if I could stay focused.

Izverg waited a minute more, then lifted Yilliar up to his eye level. *Such a shame, Shadow Lord. I thought she might bargain for your life, but you're as worthless to her as you are to Marzanna.*

No, I thought silently, desperately.

The jackal's lips peeled back from his fangs, an insatiable hunger burning in his canine face. *Don't despair. Your power will live on in me, and I will use it to slay Marzanna—ah.* A sharp laugh. *That is no comfort to you, is it?*

If Yilliar responded, I couldn't hear it—but I heard it when Izverg slammed the Shadow Lord into the ground and tore into him with his fangs. I heard every tearing bite, every wet swallow. Yilliar died as I cowered in the bone eater's shadow, frantically strengthening my aura reflection as horror and guilt broke through my concentration again and again.

The sounds of ravenous eating finally fell silent, and when the bone eater relaxed its terse, tightly coiled pose, I knew Izverg had left.

The bone eater stretched out its long arms and pulled uprooted bushes toward the pit. While it fumblingly reburied itself to prepare for its next ambush, I crept slowly to the opposite side of the pit, timing my steps with its movements. As it arranged a particularly large shrub on its back, I climbed out of the pit and scooted silently to the stream. The gargling water hid the sounds of my footsteps as I paced slowly and deliberately away.

When I reached the spot where Yilliar's blood drenched the ground and stained the stream's pebbly bank, I stopped. For a long minute, I stared down at his remains, my chest grinding so painfully I couldn't breathe.

Then I launched myself into an urgent, near-hysterical sprint. My boots splashed in the pools of decomposing mush that had been healthy trees less than an hour before. I ran through Izverg's circle of death and into the forest, following the stream until it met a large creek.

I threw myself into the water. Cool liquid plunged over me, engulfing my head. I burst upward again, hands rubbing my face. I splashed water over myself, then grabbed handfuls of sand from the creek's bottom and scrubbed my skin.

I could still smell it. The stench of decomposition from the bone eater's lair. The wet reek of Izverg's death magic. The coppery tang of Yilliar's blood.

With frantic motions, I scrubbed until my skin burned, then sat weakly on the creek's bottom, the water breaking over my chest. My fingers pressed against the obsidian vial of antidote tucked safely in my pocket.

Breathing hard, I lifted my river-stone pendant out of my shirt and tilted it toward the moonlight. The crack through the rune had appeared at some point after I'd arrived at the bone eater's lair. But nothing had struck me in the chest. Nothing had touched the pendant.

The crack was in the same spot as the one on the pendant Zak had returned to me ten years ago.

Confusion joined the maelstrom of remorse and exhaustion spinning through my skull. My limbs ached in the cold water, and I pushed unsteadily to my feet. My fever was back. I could feel it.

It took several seconds too long for the rhythmic splash of footfalls in the water to register in my brain.

I whirled toward the sound—and my knees gave out. As I sat heavily in the water, Tilliag trotted swiftly upstream toward me, his ears pricked forward. And behind him, Artear's burning orange eyes glowed in the darkness, his black coat shimmering.

"Tilliag," I said weakly. "Artear. You're both okay."

Tilliag grunted as he stopped beside me. *I sensed the presence of this one*—he flicked an ear toward Artear—*and deviated from my spot to investigate. Had I not …* He blew out a noisy breath. *Had I not been distracted, I could have warned you of Izverg's approach.*

"Or Izverg would've killed you." I levered myself to my feet with effort and grabbed Tilliag's mane for balance. "I'm glad you aren't hurt. You too, Artear."

The black stallion rambled something unintelligible in my head, but it carried a note of relief, as though he too were happy I'd survived.

I tightened my grip on Tilliag's mane, trying to convince my trembling legs that I had the strength to leap onto the stallion's high back. Before I could try, Artear shouldered past Tilliag's hindquarters. He bent his knees, sinking into an equine bow that lowered his back to my level.

Releasing Tilliag, I slung a leg over Artear and wrapped my arms around his neck. He lunged to his feet. Lying across his back, I didn't immediately right myself.

I could have done that too, Tilliag grumbled.

"Just get us to the cabin," I whispered.

Artear turned carefully and started forward, his steps smooth so I wouldn't slip off him. My wet skin was so cold but my torso felt so hot. My limbs were numb. I didn't know if I had the strength to hold on to Artear.

But I had to. The antidote was in my pocket, and all I needed to do was get it to the cabin where Zak would be waiting with the Dragon's Breath. This nightmare was almost over.

Or so I hoped.

22

SITTING ON A WOODEN BENCH with my back propped against the wall, I studied the interior of the cabin where Zak had lived with Bane. A wooden counter ran along one wall and a roughly constructed table had been shoved up against a bookshelf scattered with old texts. One door hung open, revealing the dark woods outside, and another door was closed. Spread across the table was a mess of Arcana paraphernalia, illuminated by a battery-powered lantern from our supplies.

Standing at the table, Zak worked with single-minded focus. I didn't understand what he was doing, but I assumed it would result in more antidote. The obsidian potion vial had held only a few tablespoons of syrupy gold liquid, and he'd used half of it in whatever alchemic processes he'd needed to figure out the antidote's composition.

Near his elbow was a bundle of freshly picked plants. Its flowers resembled candle flames with pale yellow throats and ruffled, bright orange petals. Dragon's Breath, the rare ingredient that would save us from Izverg's poison—if Zak could prepare the antidote. I had no idea what degree of skill it took to deconstruct a potion and recreate it, all without instructions, a recipe, or any knowledge of how it had been made in the first place.

A swirl of hissing steam rose from his alchemic circle. He lifted a white bowl from its center and studied it intently. He swirled its contents, then brought it to his mouth and took a large swallow.

I straightened on the bench, watching anxiously. He took another swallow.

"Well," he said after a minute. "I don't feel worse. No idea if it's working or not."

I pushed off the bench, and he passed me the bowl. Golden liquid the consistency of maple syrup filled it halfway.

"Two mouthfuls will be enough," he told me.

I tipped the liquid past my lips. It was strangely slimy on my tongue, with a taste reminiscent of turmeric. My throat burned faintly after I'd swallowed. I took another generous gulp, then handed the bowl back. He carried it to the open door. I followed him as far as the threshold, stopping to lean wearily against the jamb.

Night lay heavy over the woods, silvery moonlight dappling the forest floor. Sitting under a tree decorated with weathered red-and-white talismans, Lallakai lifted her head at Zak's appearance. He crossed to her, crouched, and offered the bowl. She drank her two mouthfuls without hesitation.

My gaze roved slowly over them as they spoke, their words too quiet for me to hear. I pressed my hand to my chest, where the river-stone pendant was hidden under my shirt.

I retreated inside and sat on a sleeping bag left on the floor. My body ached and throbbed.

With a quiet rustle, Zak sank down beside me. "If we don't feel noticeably better by sunrise, then it didn't work."

"What will we do then?"

He leaned his head back against the wall. "We'll be too weak to travel by that point, but Ríkr could get you to the Crow and Hammer."

Even if he did, I'd likely be too far gone for their healers to save me. If the antidote didn't work, it was over. We were dead. Izverg won. What would Ríkr do then? Would he move on or seek revenge?

The sound of the jackal's teeth tearing into Yilliar's flesh shuddered through me. I was pretty sure Ríkr was more powerful than Yilliar had been, but was he powerful enough to defeat Izverg and his entire court? Not even close, especially now that Izverg was that much stronger from having consumed the Shadow Lord.

"Marzanna needs the antidote too," I mumbled. "I promised Yilliar I would get it to her."

"She's a fae queen. She can hang on a bit longer."

I didn't argue. Neither of us was in any shape to trek back to the hidden cavern. The only one who could go was Ríkr, and he wouldn't leave me. He was outside, circling the cabin in hawk form and watching for any sign of danger.

Zak closed his eyes, exhaustion aging his face. His cheeks were hollow, and stubble darkened his jaw. His chest rose and fell, his breathing labored. If the antidote failed, we would soon slip into fevered unconsciousness.

A slow breath slid from my lungs, and I tugged the leather cord of my river-stone pendant out from under my shirt. The rune had split cleanly in half, and I stared at it with a mixture of bewilderment and grief. I'd finally reclaimed a keepsake of my childhood, only to ruin it a week later. But how? It just didn't make sense.

My gaze flicked to Zak, his eyes still closed. My old pendant and this one had cracked in exactly the same way. That couldn't be a coincidence. Whatever had broken this stone must have broken that one too, which meant Zak hadn't done it—at least, not intentionally.

If he hadn't ratted me out to Ruth, and he hadn't given me a fake poison, and he hadn't deliberately broken my precious pendant, then the only crime left on the mental list I'd held against him all this time was the way he'd cruelly abandoned me.

I closed my eyes, squeezing them tight. I'd blamed him for everything, including his failure to take on the burden of my future. But that had been my burden to carry, not his. As a teen, I'd seen his strength, not his vulnerability. I'd known he was being abused too, that he was scared too, that he was desperately trying to survive just like me, but I'd still pinned all my hopes on him.

It hadn't been smart or fair, and I could see that now.

But the one thing I couldn't explain, couldn't ignore, was the "why." Why had he rejected me in the cruelest way possible and gone back to Bane?

That was the mystery I needed to solve. That was the answer I had to have. Not to cement my grudge or validate my hatred, but to *understand*.

"I never should have involved you in this."

I started at Zak's quiet rasp. His eyes were open, and he was gazing blankly at the closed door across from us.

"It was a suicide mission from the start," he continued bleakly. "If I'd suspected Izverg was involved, I never would have …"

That dark flicker in his eyes. I'd seen it before.

"Zak …" Panic shivered through me, then faded away. "What really happened that night ten years ago?"

"You want to talk about that *now*?"

"We might not get another chance."

"Not exactly a pleasant note to end on, Saber."

"Doesn't seem like it'll be pleasant either way." I let out a long breath. "Before, I couldn't stand the thought of reliving it all. But now, I can't stand not knowing. I need the truth."

His teeth pinched his lower lip in an uncharacteristic expression of uncertainty. I was ready, but maybe he wasn't.

The cracked river stone was hidden in my left hand, but I stretched my right hand toward him. My fingers closed around his. "You said you wanted the truth."

"There is no truth. I wanted to know how Bane learned what I was planning to do. I thought you had something to do with him finding out, but it's obvious now you didn't."

"If we compare what happened to us that night, maybe we can figure it out." I squeezed his hand. "You were going to sneak up on Bane using my pendant, right? What happened?"

"I …" A tremor ran through his limbs. "Bane was in the garage. He and Izverg had captured Marzaniok, but I didn't know that."

He went silent, staring straight ahead with hollow eyes. I squeezed his hand again. I'd thought, when we finally discussed this, he'd be forcing his explanation on me while I fought tooth and nail not to hear it. I'd never expected I'd have to pry the words out of him.

"I'd prepared with spells and potions to ensure I wouldn't be detected." His throat flexed as he swallowed. "Bane had his back to me. I had a spell to incapacitate him so I could slit his throat. I was about to throw it at him when …"

His breathing rate increased. All color left his face.

"Zak," I whispered.

"He wasn't supposed to be there."

"Who?"

"He hadn't come with us." His pupils dilated with adrenaline. "He wasn't supposed to be there."

"Who was there?"

He dragged his blank stare to mine, and for a terrible second, hatred twisted his features. Utter, untempered loathing and disgust.

All directed at me.

Then his face went cold and empty, and when he answered me, his voice was just as lifeless.

"Izverg."

23

THE BRIEF MOMENT *when I stared up at Izverg, looming over me with that gloating canine grin, stretched into an eternity of terror—then I threw myself away from him.*

His jaws crunched down on my right shoulder. Fangs pierced my skin. My collarbone snapped. He grabbed my forearms, claws tearing, and both the spell and my knife dropped from my spasming hands. I should've been faster than him. I'd used potions to enhance my speed and strength—but it hadn't been enough. It was never enough against Izverg.

He lifted me off the ground, his fangs grinding into my shoulder. Agony tore through me, and I couldn't stop the rough scream that erupted from my throat.

Grenior! Keelar!

They didn't answer me, and that's when I heard it—the distant sounds of canine yelping. Bane's pack had outmaneuvered them. Just as I'd been outmaneuvered. Bane hadn't turned around when I'd screamed. He knew what was happening. He'd been waiting for me—and so had Izverg.

But how?

How how how—

Izverg threw me to the ground, knocking the wind out of me. His claws raked my back, tearing through my shirt. His huge hand shoved me into the hard driveway, forcing the air from my lungs and sending agony shooting through my broken collarbone.

Naughty druid, *he cackled.* You've been very bad, haven't you?

He flipped me over and pinned me again. I panted, lightheaded with pain, unable to fight his impossible strength and size. He crouched over me, a huge black monster filling my vision.

Drool dripping from his black lips, he put a claw on my chest and slid it down, opening a new wound that had me screaming again. His dark tongue licked hungrily at his muzzle as he opened another wound. Then a third. As hot, wet trails ran across my torso, he lowered his head and dragged his tongue through my blood.

I scrunched my eyes shut, jaw clenched, rapid breaths hissing through my teeth.

Block it out. I had to block it out. Don't think. Don't feel. Shut down. Ignore his claws slicing me again, the pain, the blood, his hungry stare and rough tongue and high-pitched laugh. Block it out.

But I couldn't, not completely, because one word kept repeating over and over, screaming through my head like a siren. HOW?

"That's enough."

Bane's voice seemed to come from a great distance. Izverg cackled shrilly as he grabbed my ankle and dragged me into the open garage. The concrete scraped my bare back, but I hardly felt it through the burn of my other wounds. Light fell across my face, half blinding me, then a shadow blocked it.

Leaning over me, Bane curled his lips in a sneer. He knelt, pinched my jaw open, and poured a potion into my mouth. The sour taste of a blood-replenishing elixir flooded my tongue, and I wanted to spit it in his face.

I swallowed the potion. Bane released me, then reached for my throat. Sharp pain stung my neck, followed by a snapping sound.

He held something above me. The girl's stone pendant, its chain broken.

"I can see it in your face." His voice was low and scathing. "You're wondering why you failed. I'll tell you: because you are weak."

The pendant swung back and forth.

"You're weak because you relied on others." He didn't sound angry. He sounded disgusted by my deficiencies. "You're only as strong as the weakest fool you put your trust in. I warned you yesterday."

He'd known even then? But … how?

"Others are weak. They're selfish, gullible, impulsive, dull-witted, and they always have their own agenda. If you want to be strong, Zaharia, rely on your own strength. Trust no one. Rely on no one." He dropped the pendant. It bounced off my bloody shoulder and clattered on the floor. "You shouldn't have tried to kill me until you were ready to do it alone. Putting your faith in someone else … you have much to learn."

He rose to his full height. My breath rushed in and out, speeding toward hyperventilation. This wasn't over. My punishment was just beginning—and Izverg knew it too. His lips peeled back in a grin, and he stretched an eager hand toward me.

Bane shoved Izverg's arm away. "Not yet. Give the potion time to work or he'll die from blood loss."

Izverg growled.

"You have a better meal waiting." Smirking, Bane turned away. "I'm done with the King of Death. He's yours now."

Izverg turned toward the dark-haired fae lying across the table. Sprawled on the cold ground, all I could do was watch as Izverg engulfed the fae's delicate head in his huge hand and inhaled greedily. From between Izverg's fingers, the king's dark eyes met mine, dull but conscious.

And he was still conscious when Izverg began to eat him.

THE KING *of the Shadow Court was dead.*

It'd taken him a long time to die, but even though Izverg had dragged it out on purpose, the king hadn't made a sound. He'd kept his pride until his last breath.

Lying on the concrete where I'd been for the last hour, I wished I could be that strong, but no matter how many times I'd promised myself I wouldn't scream for Izverg, I always ended up screaming anyway.

You're weak.

Bane's scathing voice repeated in my memory.

You're weak.

You relied on others.

The words merged with the throbbing agony in my body until they echoed with each pulse of pain. I was weak. I'd relied on someone else. I'd trusted the girl.

The girl ... but how could she be responsible for this? It didn't make sense. Something had gone wrong, but it couldn't be her fault ... could it? Bane wanted me to blame her. He was trying to manipulate me, but I knew better. I'd failed because I'd fucked it up, and I couldn't blame anyone else.

Izverg tossed his head back as he swallowed a final mouthful and licked his chops. Blood dripped off the table. Bane stood at the counter at the back of the garage, admiring his new collection: vials of blood, braided locks of black hair, dismembered fingers, and samples of flesh and organs in jars of preserving potion.

Body parts of a fae king. He'd sell them on the black market for millions.

Bane glanced at Izverg. "How was it?"

Izverg grinned. I can already feel his magic infusing me. He was as powerful as his reputation suggested.

"Good." Bane snapped the case of body parts closed. "Bring the boy."

Izverg's clawed feet scraped the concrete as he stalked toward me. His muzzle was wet with the king's blood, and when he peeled his lips back, red stained his fangs. He reached for my throat.

Darkness plunged over the garage.

An earsplitting screech rang out. The darkness swirled—and two black blades slashed across Izverg, tearing through his ragged fur coat. He lurched backward.

His attacker appeared in a swirl of darkness, an ebony blade in each hand and semi-transparent eagle wings arching off her back. Lallakai. Her face was twisted with rage and her chest heaved violently.

"You killed him." She hissed the words, then screamed them. "You killed him!"

And she hurled herself at Izverg.

I rolled out of the way as shadow magic exploded off her like bands of black electricity. Izverg roared with laughter and unleashed a wave of his strength-draining, life-sucking power.

Panting, I shoved onto my hands and knees. The girl's stone pendant glinted on the ground. I grabbed it and crawled away from the battling fae. Bane was shouting something, Izverg was laughing, and Lallakai was screaming. No one was looking at me.

I pushed onto my feet. My knees tried to buckle, and I staggered—then I was running toward Bane's truck.

Grenior! *I threw his name toward the trees, hoping he was close enough to hear me.* Take the others and run away! I'll find you later!

I pulled the truck's spare key from my pocket. I'd planned to use the truck to get away once I'd killed Bane so I wouldn't have to deal with his varg pack—but I hadn't killed him. And now I was running away.

But what else could I do?

I slid into the driver's seat and jammed the key into the ignition. The engine turned over, and I floored the gas. Tires spinning, the vehicle shot forward. I glanced in the rearview mirror. Izverg and Bane were both attacking Lallakai. She would lose. Probably die. I didn't care.

All I cared about was getting the girl and running. Running as far as I could, as fast as I could. Running forever.

How had it gone so wrong? How had Bane figured out my plan?

The city lights flashed past as I sped down the highway. Everything hurt. Wounds throbbing. Bruises throbbing. Head throbbing. My vision blurred in and out, and I let off the gas as I blinked, trying to focus.

You're weak. You relied on others.

The girl had known I would try to kill Bane tonight and that I would use the pendant she'd lent me. But she couldn't have told Bane. That didn't make sense. Had she been playing me from the start? I couldn't believe that. I wouldn't have fallen for an act.

I turned the truck off the highway. I was driving through downtown Vancouver. It was late and the roads were empty. Rain spattered the windshield, a few drops at first, then falling harder. I switched on the wipers. My vision kept blurring.

How had Bane figured it out? How!

You're weak. You relied on others.

I smashed the heel of my hand into my forehead to silence Bane's voice. The girl's pendant bounced off my chin, the chain tangled around my fingers. I'd been holding it this whole time. As I lowered my hand, light caught on the stone's face.

A thick, ugly crack had split the rune in half.

My eyes widened in disbelief. It was broken? But how? When? Bane had pulled it off me, but he hadn't done anything to it, had he? Or had Izverg—

My gaze jumped from the pendant to the road—and I slammed the brakes. The tires locked up, and the truck skidded into the back of a parked car. The airbag exploded in my face. The truck jolted to a rocking stop, and I sagged in my seat, breathing hard.

The windshield was a spiderweb of cracks, but the engine was still running. The car I'd hit was in way worse shape, its flimsy hatchback obliterated by the steel deer guard on the front of the truck. Fumbling for the keys, I cut the engine, then pushed the door open and dropped out of the truck. My knees buckled and I clung to the door to keep upright. Rain drummed on my head.

My blood-splattered face stared at me, reflected in the driver's window. My shirt was in shreds, punctures and scratches all over my chest, blood everywhere. I could still feel Izverg's rough, hot tongue.

I leaned over and vomited onto the asphalt. Once my stomach had calmed, I climbed onto the back tire. There was a duffle bag of supplies in the box, and I dragged out my leather coat and put it on.

Zipping it under my chin, I pulled the hood over my head. My gloves were in the pockets, and I put those on too.

Gripping the stone pendant in my fist, I walked away from the truck, my boots splashing in puddles. My head was spinning, and walking in a straight line was hard, but the alley wasn't far, and she would be there. Then maybe I'd understand how I'd failed.

I squeezed her pendant. Would she blame me for breaking it? How would she react when she found out I hadn't managed to kill Bane?

You're weak. You relied on others.

The words pulsed with my throbbing wounds.

The alley was just ahead, and I could see her sitting on the ground, curled in a ball, face hidden, blond hair soaked. My steps slowed. Ten paces away from her, I stopped. Something inside me turned brittle at the sight of her.

She raised her head. Bruises. Swelling. Blood smeared by the rain. Tears on her cheeks. Pain and desperation all over her face. And … relief. Relief that I was here.

Weak.

But I wasn't the weak one.

She was.

I could see the weakness all over her. She'd been beaten—by her aunt, an alchemist. A human. Not a ten-foot-tall beast with claws and fangs and impossible strength and speed I couldn't even fight with potions.

She was weak, and because I'd relied on her, I'd become weak too. If not for her, this wouldn't have happened. I wouldn't have tried to kill Bane before I was ready. I wouldn't have counted on her artifact—a spell that had broken.

She was weak.

And as she looked at me with desperate, tearful relief, hatred welled up in my chest like acid. I hated her relief. I hated her unspoken expectation that I, the strong one, would protect her. I hated her bruises and the way she was all curled up like a helpless child. I hated her weakness.

I stepped forward. She watched me walk closer, her hopeful expression faltering. I could see it so clearly now: she was dead weight. I'd never survive with her hanging on to me.

Stopping in front of her, I pulled her pendant from my pocket and tossed it onto the ground. It was weak, just like her. It'd failed, just like she had.

She stared at her beloved artifact, then lifted her gaze to me. The look in her eyes was like a knife through my chest, but I was already in so much pain. I didn't need her piling it on. I didn't need her at all.

I turned and walked away.

I didn't look back.

Dawn was just beginning to turn the sky yellow when I parked the truck in the driveway. As I climbed out, Bane stepped out of the garage. He waited as I walked toward him. Two steps away, I stopped and stared into the face of the man who'd raised me, trained me, and tortured me. I hated him. I fantasized about killing him. I wanted him dead.

But I wasn't strong enough yet, and if I ran, I never would be. So I would stay. I was his apprentice, and he would make me stronger. Because that was the deal. He would make me as strong as him, and then I would kill him.

His eyes bored into mine.

"I understand now." My voice was a rasp. "I learned the lesson."

"Good." He reached out. His heavy hand settled on my shoulder—and squeezed my broken collarbone, his fingers digging in. "There are no allies, Zaharia. Only tools."

My last sight of the girl's face, of her eyes, burned through me, carried on a wave of pain from my shoulder. I was glad I'd never learned her name.

"Yes," I told my master. "I understand."

There were no allies. No rescuers, no heroes, no friends, no family. There was only me and my strength.

And I would hone that strength until the day I killed Bane.

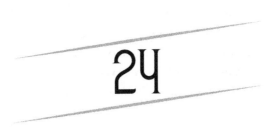

24

ZAK FELL SILENT, and I didn't prompt him to continue. What more was there for him to reveal? I finally had his side of the story, and the broken shards in my chest were tearing into my lungs like never before.

"So that's it," he said after a long minute, sounding steadier than he had while describing his state of mind as he'd walked away from me that night. "I don't know how Bane figured out what I was planning, or how you ended up with a fake poison, or how the pendant broke. I don't have any answers."

Closing my eyes, I concentrated on breathing, hoping that might relieve the grinding agony in my chest. When I opened my eyes, I found him watching me with exhausted resignation, waiting for my hatred to crash down on him.

I uncurled my fingers, revealing the cracked river stone I'd been clutching. He frowned at it, then his face lost what little color it had regained.

"Is that ... you kept it all this time?"

"No," I murmured. "I left it on the street where you threw it, walked back to my aunt's house, and stabbed her in the throat."

His eyes widened.

"I should've run for it after that, but I just sat beside her body until the police came. I wasn't all there at the time." I rubbed my thumb across the cracked stone. "This is the pendant I found when we went to my childhood home."

"I don't remember it being cracked."

"It wasn't. I used it to sneak into the bone eater's lair, and it cracked then. I have no idea why it broke, but this crack looks exactly the same as the one from ten years ago, doesn't it?"

He nodded slowly and held out his hand. I passed him the stone, and he examined it carefully.

"The enchantment is gone," he murmured. "The spell failing probably cracked the rune."

"I wore the pendant for years without problems. Why would it suddenly fail?"

He handed the pendant back to me. "Did you come into contact with any fae magic while at the bone eater's lair? Different magics don't always play nice with each other."

"Not that I noticed. What about you?"

"I don't think Izverg used any magic on me. He didn't need it, and—" His eyes went out of focus. "He didn't use magic on me, but I ... Saber, did you make any ice spears while you were wearing the pendant?"

My fingers curled around the river stone, a sick feeling clogging my throat as I realized the direction of his thoughts. "Yeah."

"I used a concealment spell Lallakai gave me," he said quietly. "I broke the pendant with her magic. And you broke this one with Rίkr's magic."

The enchantment's sole purpose had been to hide my telltale druid energy. Concealing fae magic must have been beyond its capabilities. I pressed my thumb into the rune. I'd broken it purely by accident, and so had Zak. As useful as it had been for hiding a druid child, it wasn't an effective tool for a practicing druid.

"Lallakai's spell …"

Zak's whisper pulled me from my thoughts. He was staring at the closed door across from us, a deep crease in his forehead.

"Lallakai's magic …"

I frowned at him. "Zak?"

He pushed to his feet. Moving slowly, as though in a trance, he walked to the door and stopped inches away, staring at the wood. Alarmed by his strange behavior, I hastened to his side as he brushed his fingertips over the doorframe. Markings had been scratched in it, lines and runes that circled the top half of the threshold, and a dusty red-and-white talisman hung from a nail in the door.

"These are wards against fae magic." His voice was a quiet, terse rasp. "I knew that. *I knew that.*"

"Zak?"

His hand shook and he curled his fingers, pressing his fist into the frame. "*Fuck!*"

I gripped his arm. "Zak, what's wrong?"

He bowed his head, a bitter laugh shaking his shoulders. "It was my fault. It was my fault all along."

"What are you talking about?"

"The wards." He pulled his fist back—then slammed it into the doorframe, shaking the wood. "These fucking wards. Bane warded this room against fae. But I asked Lallakai for a spell. I let her put fae magic into my body, and then I snuck through this door to get a look at the poison I was going to steal for you."

My gaze skittered across the etched spell markings.

"As soon as I crossed his wards, that bastard knew someone had trespassed. He must have swapped his entire poison stash out for fakes to prevent me from stealing anything dangerous. And I didn't fucking notice. I was too worried about my substitute being convincing."

He was quiet for a second, then he laughed again—a horrible, grating laugh. "I tripped the wards again when I went in the second time to steal the poison. He'd have been watching my every move after that. How much do you want to bet one of his familiars was spying on us when we exchanged the poison and your pendant?"

Nausea bubbled in my gut. "He tipped off Ruth."

"Then they both waited for us to make our moves, knowing exactly what we were planning." His head was still bent, his face turned away. "If I hadn't gotten greedy and asked Lallakai for a spell, I wouldn't have tripped the wards. Or if I'd been smarter, I would've realized I couldn't carry fae magic through his wards."

I stood silently beside him, absorbing everything. So that was it. We'd failed because Zak had overlooked a small detail. It hadn't been a malicious betrayal, just a mistake. And we'd both gone through hell because of it. I couldn't dump all the blame on him; I'd been equally responsible for our plans. Or I should have been. I'd let him shoulder all the preparation and risks alone, assuming we had everything under control without ever understanding what he was up against.

I touched his arm. He flinched as though he'd expected me to hit him.

"Now we know," I said softly. "We were desperate kids, and we both made mistakes. What you went through that night, and afterward … I can't imagine. But like you said, what's done is done. We can't change it now."

He lifted his head, his pain-shadowed eyes meeting mine. "You should be angrier."

How could I be angry after hearing what he'd suffered that night? He'd done everything he could to succeed. Yes, he'd turned against me by the time he'd met me in the alley. And yes, it hurt to hear that he'd seen me as a liability. But I couldn't blame teenaged Zak for failing to withstand Bane and Izverg's combined physical and mental assault.

I'd blamed him enough already.

"We have the answers we needed," I murmured. "Now we can leave it all behind. It's been ten years. It's time to move on."

"Move on," he repeated quietly, turning his back on the door. The pain faded from his eyes, but something dark lingered in his gaze. "Yeah, you should."

My eyes narrowed. "What about you?"

With a rough exhale, he leaned against the wall. "Izverg has me in his sights again. He loves the slow hunt. Even if I escape this time, he'll keep hunting me. Whether it's tomorrow or a decade from now, he'll devour me. The more paranoid I am in the meantime, the more fun it is for him."

Loathing for the beast burned in me.

Zak closed his eyes. "Seeing him is … it's like I'm sixteen again."

I stepped in front of him. "If Izverg is going to keep hunting you, then you know what we have to do."

He opened his eyes again. "It's impossible."

"You said the same thing about killing Bane."

"Bane was mortal. Izverg is—"

"Everything we've ever done has been impossible, yet here we are." I tapped the center of his chest. "We killed the Dullahan. We killed Luthyr. And we'll kill Izverg."

"You don't have to do anything. Izverg isn't your problem."

"He became my problem when he poisoned me." I hesitated, then threw out the next words. "And I won't sit back and let you do this alone. We'll handle it together."

He stared at me for a long moment, as though unsure he'd heard me right—then he pulled me close and lowered his head. Our lips met. It was a soft kiss, layered with hurt and uncertainty and regret, but there was something else in it— something that made the grind in my chest go still and warmth light my insides.

Drawing back, he rubbed his thumb across my cheek. "Let's wait to see if we survive this poison. Then we can worry about Izverg."

I pursed my lips. "We could start planning, at least."

"Planning how?"

My gaze slid to the open door and the dark forest beyond. "Like asking Lallakai how to free the Shadow Court from Izverg's control."

LALLAKAI SWEPT her dark hair off her shoulders. "Free the court? Why bother?"

"Because killing Izverg will be much easier if he doesn't have a small fae army backing him up," I replied impatiently.

"Oh?" Ríkr murmured. "We're killing him now?"

"Maybe," Zak grumbled. "Saber is getting ahead of herself."

The four of us had gathered in the cabin's musty interior. A small fire in the freestanding stove warded off the night chill. Dawn was a couple of hours away, but we didn't need to wait any longer to know if the antidote had worked. The ache in my limbs had faded and Zak's complexion appeared healthy for the first time since he'd been poisoned.

Lallakai's recovery was the most significant. Since drinking the antidote, the color and vibrancy had returned to her face. She was no longer weak and unsteady, and aside from the hollowness of her cheeks and the scabbed scratches on her creamy skin, she seemed back to her usual self.

"Izverg is a dangerous enemy to leave unchecked," Ríkr said from the wooden bench, his feet crossed at the ankles. "I'm inclined to ensure he perishes swiftly and thoroughly before returning home."

I nodded. "I don't want him coming after any of us. Or getting any stronger." I glanced between Ríkr and Lallakai. "Back to separating Izverg and the court. What about Marzanna? Yilliar planned to return her to the throne. That suggests some courtiers are still loyal to her."

Picking up a hairbrush she'd taken from our supplies, Lallakai collected a handful of long locks and brushed at the ends. "Marzanna has been in a state of near death for a fortnight. Even with the antidote, she will be useless for some time. How long do you plan to linger here, waiting on her recovery?"

"She need not be at full strength," Ríkr mused. "She could occupy the court's attention while we strike at Izverg."

"How do you propose to kill him, hmm?" Lallakai worked the brush through a knot in her hair. "Your cold and ice won't shield you from Izverg's death magic the way it protected you from Luthyr's summer magic. Were your power of the same caliber as when you reigned as the Winter King, you could overwhelm him with brute force, but"—she quirked an eyebrow mockingly—"Ríkr is but a pale imitation of Arawn."

"How fortunate, then, that among our company is a Lady of Shadow with experience in combat against him and who can spearhead an attack."

Lallakai scoffed. "Do you think me a fool? Why risk almost certain defeat and death for a queen who despises me?"

"Perhaps she will despise you less," Ríkr suggested, "if you defeat her nemesis and save her court."

"What about Zak?" I asked her frostily. "Izverg will keep hunting him."

Her emerald eyes flicked to her consort, a faint crease between her brows. "Izverg will be too busy playing king to bother us further. That aside, you have never sought to take revenge on the beast."

Leaning against the worktable, Zak turned the obsidian vial, refilled with antidote, around and around in his hands. "It wasn't that I didn't want to, but it was easy to make excuses. I don't have any excuses left. Leaving him alive is more dangerous than challenging him."

He looked up, his gaze moving from Lallakai to me. "I want to kill him. I want his shadow out of my life forever."

I smiled faintly.

"I see." Lallakai set the hairbrush on the counter and arched her eyebrows at Ríkr. "This is what you desire as well?"

Frowning, I wondered why she was asking him.

"It is my preference," Ríkr confirmed.

"Then if I am to risk life and limb against Izverg, I will wait no longer for my promised reward." She lifted her chin imperiously. "Lord of Winter, I demand you fulfill our bargain without further delay and give me the Undying gift."

I bit back a curse.

"With the power of The Undying, I can confidently challenge Izverg. It is rightfully mine, and I will accept no more excuses."

Ríkr pushed off the bench. Rising to his full height, he faced Lallakai with his eyes glittering like chips of ice. "Our bargain specified no timeline, Night Eagle, nor do you have any means by which to force me to comply."

I almost relaxed, relieved that Ríkr wouldn't be sharing his dangerous power.

"However," he continued, "a promise made must be a promise kept. I will gift you the Undying magic now on the condition that, regardless of who strikes the killing blow to Izverg, *I* will be the one to consume his power."

"You cannot add conditions to a bargain after it's been struck," she snapped.

Ríkr's lips curved in a smooth smile. "It is in poor taste, I agree."

She hissed furiously. "Fine."

Cold dread sank through my middle, but there was nothing I could do. Ríkr had already promised to share his power, and if he hadn't, we all would've died in Hell's Gate. I just hoped Ríkr knew what he was doing.

25

"THAT'S EVERYTHING," I said, stuffing the rolled sleeping bag into our large pack.

Standing at the table and studying his open grimoire, Zak nodded absently. I glanced around the cabin. The signs of his recent alchemy work had been cleared away, and the antidote was stored safely on his belt of potions. Our supplies were packed, and all that was left was to leave.

But Zak was still studying his grimoire with a deep frown.

I stepped up beside him, glancing at a page written in an alphabet I'd never seen before. "What's the matter?"

"Huh? Oh, just ..." He flipped a few pages half-heartedly. "Searching for something that could give us an advantage over Izverg."

Our first order of business was getting Marzanna the antidote so she could regain her strength. After that, we'd come up with a concrete plan on how to bring down Izverg.

"Marzanna might have some ideas," I suggested. "They have similar powers, don't they?"

"Similar, yeah, but Izverg isn't on the same level as Marzanna. Although he may have added a new trick or two in the years since he consumed Marzaniok." His frown returned, but this time he was staring at the door to Bane's room. "Hm."

"What?"

Striding to the door, he plucked the red-and-white talisman off it. "I wonder ..."

"Wonder what?"

He studied the red and white threads a moment longer, then stuffed the talisman in his pocket. "Can you check if Lallakai and Ríkr are done?"

Rolling my eyes at his lack of explanation, I headed out into the cool pre-dawn air. Ríkr and Lallakai had retreated to a quiet spot where he could share his Undying gift with her, and though part of me was curious about how that all worked, I wasn't enthusiastic enough to go watch. Zak had no problem with his fae partner becoming more powerful, but I didn't like it.

Leaves and pine needles crunched under my hiking boots as I walked into the trees, following a faint glow. As I drew closer, I made out their silhouettes facing each other with their left hands clasped together. A soft azure glow swirled over Ríkr, and a similar radiance shimmered over Lallakai in shades of deep emerald.

I slowed my steps, worried about interrupting them, but the glow was fading. Biting my lower lip, I continued forward. The last of the soft radiance vanished, and Ríkr released Lallakai's hand. As I stepped into the small gap in the foliage where they stood, she stretched out her left arm. A band of markings, identical to Ríkr's, ran from her left hand up her arm, over her shoulder and neck, and up the left side of her face. Instead of bright blue, the pattern shimmered greenish black. Lallakai was now undying.

Grimly unhappy, I turned to Ríkr—and gasped. Icy disbelief plunged through me as I gaped at his face. At his unmarked skin. The blue pattern that had run down the left side of his face and neck was gone.

A few feet away, Lallakai smiled smugly as she admired her newly adorned arm.

Panic boiled in my gut and I grabbed Ríkr's wrist, my fingers digging in. "Ríkr—where—your markings—I thought you were *sharing* your Undying power, not giving it away!"

His eyebrows rose at my obvious desperation. "I can neither duplicate nor divide Hafgan's gift. I can only pass it to another."

"But—but you—" I spluttered incoherently. It'd been bad enough when I'd thought he was making Lallakai as invincible as he was. But now she was invincible and he was unprotected? "I can't believe you agreed to this! You're—"

"—alive," he cut in. "Which I wouldn't be had Lallakai not assisted in killing Luthyr. You, too, would be dead."

"But—"

"It feels glorious," Lallakai purred, stroking her slender fingers down her arm. "I will recover instantly from any injury?"

"Near instantly, and nearly any injury."

I wanted to smack the indulgent smile off his face. Why was he so calm? He'd just given away his greatest power, the gift that had kept him alive against all odds for centuries! He wasn't the all-powerful Winter King anymore. He was vulnerable to attacks from other fae.

Lallakai paused, dragging her attention off the new markings. "What will I not recover from?"

"Ah." That edge of glittering ice was back in Ríkr's eyes. "That is the question, isn't it?"

She lowered her arms. "This power is not infallible. There are ways to kill The Undying, as Pwyll killed Hafgan and as Luthyr almost killed you."

"Indeed."

Her eyes narrowed to slits. "How did Pwyll defeat the Undying magic?"

Ríkr smiled—and said nothing.

"Tell me!" she snarled, stepping toward him. "This is my power now, and I must know."

"I have fulfilled my promise. You now bear the gift of The Undying—both its extraordinary benefits and its detriments. Do enjoy, Lady of Shadow."

Baring her teeth, she surged toward him. Wintry cold swirled out from Ríkr, covering everything around him in a layer of frost, including me.

"Careful, Night Eagle," he murmured.

Halting her rush, she curled her fingers threateningly.

"Attack me," he crooned, his eyes glinting with ancient cunning, "and we will swiftly learn which is more powerful: your new ability or my knowledge of it."

Lallakai's jaw clenched, her beauty lost in the furious twist of her features.

He tucked his hands in his cloak's sleeves. "I bestowed you the Undying power in trust, Lady of Shadow. The moment you turn on me, I will take back what is mine."

They stared each other down, two powerful fae unwilling to yield. But Ríkr was the former King of Annwn, ruler of the Winter Court, and Lallakai was no match for him. With a furious snarl, she swept away, stalking through the trees toward the cabin.

I let out an explosive breath, then spun on Ríkr. "You just gave her every reason she could possibly need to kill you. As soon as Izverg is dead, she'll go for you next."

"Then it is well and good that, upon Izverg's death, I will gain a great deal of deadly power well suited to battling a Lady of Shadow, isn't it?"

My eyes widened. He'd *planned* this when he'd demanded she let him consume Izverg's power? "You're ..."

"Impressively strategic?"

"Insane."

"Ah."

I lowered my voice. "You shouldn't have told her you'll take the power back."

"She would have soon realized as much herself." He tilted his head back, gazing at the dark sky. "Her ambitions are shortsighted. Were she more cunning, she would have foreseen the danger in taking the Undying power without killing its previous bearer."

I wrapped my arms around myself. The shift of the Undying magic from Ríkr to Lallakai had pitted them against each other, with Zak and me caught in the middle of a conflict that would end up with one of our fae partners dead.

"What a mess," I muttered.

Ríkr canted an azure eye toward me. "Fret not, dove. One doesn't live as long as I have without a measure of deviousness."

Somehow, I wasn't reassured.

LALLAKAI WAS the only member of our group in a good mood. She kept holding her arm out as she walked, turning it from side to side to watch the Undying pattern shimmer, as though it were a new piece of jewelry instead of Ríkr's most powerful magic.

He walked a few steps behind her, and I couldn't get a read on him. He seemed quietly amused, but I wasn't sure I trusted that. There was no way he didn't feel exposed. He'd shed the impenetrable armor that had protected him for centuries, and I felt like I'd lost my armor too. Ríkr's indestructibility had been a comfort. I'd thought I could never lose him—but now I might.

Astride Artear, I glanced at Zak riding beside me, our heavy pack slung across Tilliag's hindquarters. Judging by his tension and the distracted distance in his eyes, he was too busy worrying about how to kill Izverg to give the transfer of Ríkr's Undying power any real thought.

Dawn had stained the horizon pink and purple, but deep shadows stretched across the shallow valley as we approached the bog and its hidden crossroads. As much as I'd have loved to never set foot in the bog again, we had to cross the upper edge of it to reach Marzanna's cave.

"Once we've dosed Marzanna with the antidote," I said quietly, "what's the plan?"

Zak flexed his shoulders, his hands resting on Tilliag's mane. The two stallions were walking side by side. Their competitive feud had fizzled out—or maybe they were too tired for posturing. Grenior and Keelar brought up the rear, their dark fur blending with the shadows.

"We need to move Marzanna farther from the Shadow Court while she recovers," Zak replied. "We'll head east into Echo's territory. I still need to find him."

His hand moved to his hip, where the obsidian vial of antidote was stored. It contained two doses plus a little extra, enough to save Marzanna and Echo—assuming the latter was poisoned as well. I hoped he was strong enough to cling to life until we found him.

The familiar but unwelcome stench of rotting vegetation clogged my nose as the scattered trees grew stunted and standing water glinted in the growing light of sunrise. Lallakai led the way into the bog, familiar with the route. The ground thudded under the horses' hooves.

My nerves prickled, memories of the bog monster fresh in my mind. Ethereal mist rose from the mossy ground as the fae demesne blended with the mortal realm, and power hummed along my nerves. I had no real idea how long it'd take us to reach the other side. My first trek across the bog hadn't been linear.

"Saber." Zak's voice was quiet, almost too soft to hear over the stallion's thudding hooves. "You said before … that after all this was over, I should come back to the animal rescue with you."

Tightness spread through my chest, making the grinding edges behind my ribs vibrate. He was silent, maybe waiting for me to respond, maybe unsure what to say next.

"Do you still want me to?"

My breath hitched. I'd suggested he come home with me so we could talk about what had happened between us ten years ago. But we'd had that discussion and gotten our answers. I'd dwelled enough on that soul-shattering night, and I didn't want to think about it anymore. I wanted to move on.

But did I want to move on *with him*? Was that possible? Could I let go of the hurt I'd suffered with a reminder of it all right in front of me? Or did I need to cast him out of my life in order to live?

Zak was waiting for my reply, and I didn't know what to say. I needed time to think, to process. But if I said the wrong thing—and "I don't know" might be exactly the wrong thing—he would make the choice for me.

I opened my mouth, closed it, then tried again. "I—"

Lallakai threw her arms up.

A band of black magic swept out from her in a curving wall—and flashes of red magic exploded against it, feet from her face. She reeled back a step, hands pressing against the dark barrier. The crossroads' humming magic rippled and shivered, and the sour taste of death rolled across my tongue.

Silhouettes appeared in the eddying mist. They drifted closer, faint splashes betraying silent footfalls when they met water. Directly ahead, a dozen feet in front of Lallakai, the largest shape loomed, its bulky shoulders and long arms supporting a bestial head with blood-red eyes.

Izverg bared his fangs in a malevolent grin. *We meet again, Night Eagle.*

Adrenaline buzzed through my limbs as I scanned left and right, picking out the silhouettes of a dozen fae on both sides. Izverg had brought the Shadow Court with him.

And we were surrounded.

26

LALLAKAI'S BARRIER fizzled out, and she slid backward a step, putting herself closer to Ríkr. He shifted so they stood side by side, facing Izverg. A Lady of Shadow and a Lord of Winter against the King of Death—and his entire court.

You seem much rejuvenated, Izverg observed with a hissing laugh. *I will enjoy your struggles as I devour you.*

"*That* is your most intimidating threat?" She flipped her long hair over her shoulder. "A classless beast, as always, Izverg. The lords and ladies of the court must find your utter lack of sophistication refreshing."

"I was about to remark on his lack of intellect and poise," Ríkr murmured.

"His flaws are near limitless."

Izverg let out a screeching laugh, unfazed by their insults. And for good reason. Insulting him was about all we could do.

Artear's neck arched, his ears swiveling. Beside us, Tilliag stamped a hoof, his nostrils flared. His attention fixed on Izverg, Zak slipped a vial off his belt, popped the cork, and downed it in a gulp. He pulled a second vial, swallowed its contents, then touched one of the crystals hanging around his neck and murmured an incantation. A flicker of light ran across him as the spell activated.

I didn't have any spells and potions. All I had was an endless supply of easily breakable ice spears.

This is too easy. Izverg ambled forward using his long front arms, his deadly gauntlets clinking. His hungry gaze raked across his two fae opponents, then lifted to me and Zak. *One of you may continue on untouched. I will allow you to decide which.*

I tightened my grip on Artear's mane. Zak had been right. Everything was a game to Izverg.

Something bumped my side. Zak's hand. Without looking away from our enemies, I reached down and closed my fingers around his. He held a small, hard object. I slid it from his grasp and he stretched his arm out in front of him. A black rune flared across the back of his hand, the magic bleeding up his arm. His shadowy sword took form, his fingers curling around the hilt.

I squeezed the object he'd handed me: the obsidian vial of antidote.

We didn't stand a chance against the entire court. Lallakai had the Undying gift, but Ríkr, Zak, and I would never survive the combined assault of this many fae. Marzanna might be able to stop the court from attacking, but she was still in the cavern and barely clinging to life. Even if I gave her the antidote, she wouldn't recover in time.

It was impossible. It was—

Zak's green eyes met mine, fierce and commanding. He wasn't prepared for this. None of us were. But ready or not, it was time to fight—time to risk everything on the slimmest chance of survival.

We'd survived the impossible before.

Artear! I clutched his mane and threw my weight forward. *Break through their line!*

A mortal horse would have balked. Even Tilliag might have hesitated. But Artear had been the Dullahan's mount for who knew how long, carrying the lethal fae through centuries of bloodshed and death. From charging into a swarm of armed humans at the horse auction to luring shadow fae away from me, he'd never given in to fear.

And he didn't start now.

With a bellowing scream, he launched away from Zak and Tilliag, veering toward the shadow fae lurking in the mist. Flames burst over his hooves, but they didn't streak outward in burning lines like before. Instead, the fire raced up his legs. With a burst of scorching heat, his mane ignited into rippling orange and red, and behind me, his tail whooshed into streaming flame.

I almost let go of him, but though the heat was painfully uncomfortable, it didn't burn me. Fire streaked behind him as he galloped straight at a cluster of three fae, and I felt like I was in the center of an inferno, seconds from being consumed.

With the huge, fiery black stallion bearing down on them at full tilt, the three fae scattered.

We flashed past them. I twisted to look over my shoulder as Izverg's hideous cackle rang out—then ice exploded upward, engulfing the three fae Artear had charged past before they could attack us from behind.

As though Ríkr's ice had been a signal, magic exploded from all sides, and the crossroad's energy seethed at the violent unleashing.

"Don't slow down!" I cried. "Get to Marzanna!"

Artear stretched out, fire surging over his hooves. The ground shuddered, dangerously unstable. Galloping through the bog was madness, but if we slowed, we'd never make it back in time to help.

Magic shivered across Artear and through my body. The mist thickened, the mossy ground losing its greenish hue. It grew semi-transparent, and shining water was suddenly visible, glowing against the dark ground. Twisting pathways spread out before us, weaving through the maze of water and fog.

Artear had shifted us farther into the fae demesne, and with our path revealed, he blazed ahead at top speed. The boom of magic behind us faded, and ahead, the bog ended at the frothing water of the river.

The world solidified again, and the fire died from Artear's hooves and mane. Slowing to a fast trot, he plunged into the river and sloshed downstream toward the ravine and Marzanna's hidden cavern. The rocky walls were just ahead. We were almost there.

A foreign presence crackled through the river's surging energy.

In a flash of darkness, a three-foot-long smear of black energy smashed into the side of Artear's neck. Hot blood sprayed across me as the stallion bellowed. He reared up, front legs kicking as the streak of darkness shot above us, floated for a moment, then rocketed toward his face.

An ice spear flashed into my hand and I swung it above Artear's head. I expected the spear to pass through the shadowy streak, but it connected with something solid and burst. Jagged shards engulfed the dark shape and it tumbled out of the air to land in the water with a splash.

Artear spun around, water breaking across his chest.

Three more dark shapes hovered twenty feet in the air. I could just make out bodies within the encasing shadows—something like a cross between an oversized dragonfly and a fish, with hooked claws instead of fins. They floated in place, their insectile wings beating so rapidly they blurred, then they dove.

Whatever the hell they were, they were *fast*.

I summoned another ice spear, jabbed at the oncoming creature, and missed. Claws slashed across my arm, and Artear jerked as a second one sliced his shoulder. I whipped the spear around, but it was like trying to hit a zigzagging baseball that was actively avoiding the bat.

In desperation, I threw the spear and missed again. Claws raked across my thigh as another creature shot past me. Artear surged back and forth, half rearing, but he couldn't fight them off—and because he was belly deep in water, he couldn't drive them away with flames either.

Cold flared across my hand, but another spear wouldn't help. I needed different magic, a weapon other than a spear—

Ríkr's voice popped into my head, telling me about his magical gift—that with practice, I could control the shape of the ice.

I swung my arm out, and as ice flowed off my palm, I concentrated on the shape I wanted. The weapon took the form of a stocky club. I whipped it in an arc. The blunt end smashed into a shadow creature, and it plunged into the river, frozen inside a crystalline starburst. The remaining two creatures zoomed upward, out of reach.

"Keep going," I panted. "I'll fend them off."

Artear pivoted to face downstream. I twisted, keeping the two creatures in sight. They followed, cautious now, and I curled my fingers, waiting. Artear splashed into the narrow ravine.

The creatures dive-bombed us.

I flung my hand out. A barrage of shards flew in a wild arc, catching another creature. It fell, and the last one retreated into the sky, shadows fluttering around it.

Artear pushed forward, and the dark opening of the cave came into view. He climbed onto the rocks, hooves clattering, and I ducked as he rushed into the cave.

I swung off him. "Wait here."

He faced the cave opening, his orange eyes glowing with power. I raced to the crevice at the back of the cave and squeezed through. Yilliar's small, magic-fueled lantern glowed softly, illuminating the petite figure sitting on a mound of embroidered blankets.

Marzanna's dark eyes fixed on me.

"You're awake," I said breathlessly, jogging to her. I sank into a crouch and fumbled for the vial. "Drink two mouthfuls of this."

She took the vial, untwisted the cap, and without the slightest hesitation, drank two generous mouthfuls. Passing it back to me, she let out a slow breath. Her cheeks were hollow, her black hair stringy, and beneath her silk garments, she was all bones. The poison had taken a terrible toll on her, but the detox and vitality potions Zak had given her before we'd left had helped. She was more alert than when we'd left her.

"Druid," she whispered. "Tell me. Has Yilliar perished?"

My throat tightened. "Izverg ambushed us at the bone eater's lair. He killed Yilliar."

She gazed unblinkingly ahead, her eyes glassy. To my shock, tears spilled down her face, running over her sunken cheeks. "I knew when he did not answer my call. He has always answered."

"I'm sorry."

"First my brother, now my dearest companion."

"Marzanna." I gripped her thin shoulder. "Izverg and the entire court have Zak, Lallakai, and Ríkr surrounded. You need to call off your courtiers. They'll listen to you."

Grief and despair clung to her. "They will not obey a weak queen while a powerful king commands them."

"Izverg isn't powerful. He's just evil. Is there any way to boost your strength, even temporarily? They're all going to die, and no one will be left to help you regain your throne."

She blinked slowly, and I almost screamed with impatient urgency.

"You are a druid." Her stare fixed on me. "Your energy is powerful. Give it to me."

"What?"

"Give me your energy. It may be enough."

I didn't have time to waste questioning her. "Tell me how."

"Do you know … an aura sphere, as the Crystal Druid calls it?"

"Yes."

"Create one." She pressed a hand to her chest. "Here."

Make an aura sphere inside her? I had no idea how to do that, but again, we had no time for questions or explanations. I swung around in front of her and pushed my palm against her chest. Fierce desperation burned through me, and I filled myself with it.

"*Above, the thunder crashes,*" I sang, letting the rhythm of the battle hymn fill me. "*Around, the lightning flashes. Our heads are heaped with ashes. Victory art nigh!*"

My energy flooded the cavern, and Marzanna's eyes widened.

"*For lo the foe defaces with fire our holy places, he hews our homes in pieces, our maids more than die.*"

Her thin fingers closed around my wrist, holding my hand against her chest. My power swirled into her. Concentration tightened her face—and ravenous euphoria lit her dark eyes.

"*But we, with storm and thunder, pursue him with his plunder, and smite his ships in sunder. Victory, hear our cry!*"

My voice trailed off, and I pulled on my hand. For a long second, she didn't release me—then her grip loosened and I yanked my arm back, breathing hard. Dizziness rolled over me, and I braced my hand on the rock wall. I felt weakened but also strangely electric, as though my song had intensified the energy I had left.

"Impressive, nameless one." Marzanna raised her hands, palms tilted upward. "Your energy is potent. I owe you a debt."

I pushed to my feet. "Pay me back by saving Ríkr and Zak."

She flowed to her feet and plucked a folded garment from a supply basket. Shaking it out to reveal a silky cloak, she swung it over her shoulders, then swept toward the crevice. I was right on her heels, squeezing through after her. She glided past Artear toward the bright opening of the cave.

A black streak shot into the cave entrance, flashing straight for Marzanna.

I lunged past her, ice coalescing in my hand. Instead of a rough spear or a bulky club, a crystalline sword took shape, its razor edge gleaming. I slashed it through the air. It hit the shadow creature dead center. A starburst exploded over it and instantly shattered—shattering the creature with it.

Sparkling crystals danced in the air. Marzanna half turned, her delicate eyebrows arched. "I see my guardian is capable. Let us continue to the foul usurper."

Her gaze flicked to the drifting bits of ice, then returned to me. A faint smile graced her lips.

"Lead the way, Bladesong Druid."

27

SPIRES OF ICE jutted out of the bog like twenty-foot-tall stalagmites.

Artear flew across the wet, mossy ground in a full gallop, his hooves pounding. Marzanna rode in front of me, petite and frail from illness. Despite her poor condition, her attention fixed on the flashes of magic ahead.

How long had I been gone? Fifteen minutes? More than that? Long enough for Izverg and the Shadow Court to have killed Zak and Ríkr.

But it wasn't over yet. Who was still fighting?

Another cluster of crystalline spikes erupted in a burst of snowflakes. Ríkr. I couldn't see him, but his magic was unmistakable. Fifty feet away from his ice, a spiral of black shadow whooshed into the sky, and I glimpsed a pair of dark eagle wings. Lallakai was alive—of course, because she was Undying. The Shadow Court had divided into two groups to attack Ríkr and Lallakai, splitting the pair up so they couldn't work together.

Halfway between the two battles, something moved. A hulking shape with long arms. Izverg. He swung a gauntleted fist, and a smaller shape darted out of the way.

Zak was fighting Izverg—alone.

"Marzanna, get your court under control," I barked. "Artear, protect Marzanna!"

Before either fae could argue with me, I shoved backward off Artear. I hit the ground and fell into a roll across the spongy moss. The stallion kept going, swerving toward Ríkr's ice spires. Shooting to my feet, I sprinted toward Izverg and Zak. I couldn't see Grenior, Keelar, or—

No, I could. Two dark lumps among the moss, two dozen feet from Zak. The vargs weren't moving. No sign of Tilliag. He had no combat-worthy magic that I'd seen, so he'd probably fled.

Zak and Izverg circled each other, shadows dancing over Zak's black sword. Izverg was grinning. He was playing. That's why Zak was still alive. It was all a game, and Izverg didn't want it to end too quickly.

Zak's movements were stiff. He'd shed his jacket, and scratches scored his chest. He was hurt, bleeding, and slower than normal. But he didn't falter as he faced his childhood monster.

My foot plunged through the moss into a pool of water. I crashed onto my knees, shoved up, and kept running.

Zaharia, Zaharia, Izverg mocked. *Something about this seems almost familiar, don't you think?*

The sword in Zak's hand flicked side to side as he debated his next move—then he lunged in. His blade snapped out, swift and deadly, but Izverg twisted, impossibly agile for his size. The sword grazed his leg as he thrust his claws at Zak.

Zak flung his left arm up. A rune on his inner wrist flashed and Izverg's hand collided with a transparent shield that rippled under the impact before breaking into silver sparkles. Zak swept his sword out again, and a wave of darkness crashed into Izverg's lower abdomen, blood splattering.

The beast didn't flinch. His clawed hands plunged through the shimmers of the shield spell, and he grabbed Zak's shoulders, lifting him off the ground.

Ah, Izverg cackled. *Now this is familiar.*

My breath seared my lungs, my legs burning. I was almost close enough. Almost—

Izverg's jaws opened and his head snapped down. His huge mouth engulfed Zak's right shoulder, his fangs sinking deep. For a second that lasted forever, he savored the druid's blood in his mouth, then he slammed Zak into the mud, pinning his arms.

Cold filled my hand.

Looming over the druid, Izverg licked his blood-smeared lips. *Remember this, Zaharia?*

Baring his teeth, Zak snarled, *"Ori lux te arceat!"*

A crystal around his neck flashed brightly, the flare of light repelling Izverg with a sudden stench of burning fur. Izverg reared up with a roar—and I flung an ice spear into the back of his head. As it exploded against his skull, Zak rolled away. Creating a crystalline sword, I swung it into Izverg's knee. It sliced into flesh and muscle, then burst, tearing the wound open.

Izverg spun. I darted backward, hands flying up. Ice whooshed out from my right hand into the shape of a shield an instant before Izverg's poisoned claws hit it. I let it go as it shattered into a jagged lump around his thick fingers.

I dove sideways, rolled across the spongy ground, and shot up again, another ice weapon forming. Izverg turned, following my movement, and he lunged for me.

His foot broke through the moss into stagnant water. In the instant where the beast faltered, off balance and distracted, Zak's sword arched upward, slicing through Izverg's elbow. His flesh parted, and his gauntleted forearm thudded to the ground. Blood gushed from the stump of his elbow, and Izverg wrenched his foot out of the muck, lurching away.

I held up an ice sword, the blade smooth and sharp, and beside me, Zak raised his shadow blade. Side by side, we faced Izverg.

His blood-red eyes blazed, and his lips peeled back. Up close, I could see more wounds than just the dismembered arm and damage to the lower abdomen. Zak had landed half a dozen hits, and blood shone on the beast's ragged fur.

Izverg glanced at his bleeding elbow, then threw his head back in a fit of cackling laughter. The stench of rot in the bog thickened, the air still and heavy. Power roiled through the earth, and I remembered Zak's warning—that injuring Izverg only made him stronger.

Still laughing, the beast unleashed a wave of death.

The dark magic rushed out of him, turning the mossy ground black. It was so fast and so powerful that I didn't have a chance to think, let alone defend against it. The life-sucking miasma swept over me, and weakness flooded my limbs. My knees hit the ground. The earth died, its energy consumed and extinguished. My heart pattered in a weak, wild beat, and every nerve in my body burned with desperation.

A hand squeezed my arm, and a flood of cool, familiar energy rolled over me. Zak's aura. My blurred vision focused.

Zak was on his knees beside me, one hand holding my arm. The other gripped his sword, the blade pointed at Izverg as he poured everything he had into an aura sphere—but it wasn't enough to stave off the death magic.

I threw my remaining energy outward.

My aura sphere merged with Zak's, and the horrific grip of death on my body lessened. All around us, the ground bubbled with toxic rot, the decaying moss beds reduced to murky sludge. I panted, sucking in the reeking air, fighting to hold back Izverg's power—but it pushed toward us, inexorably overtaking our druidic energy.

Izverg grinned, magic spilling out of him in an endless flood of death. The bog was dying. Everything was dying, and we were next.

I gripped Zak's wrist, holding on desperately. It was one thing to risk death. It was another to feel death creeping through you, stealing the life from your body.

"Saber," Zak panted. "I'll hold him off. Run."

My fingers tightened around his wrist. Moments before Izverg had ambushed us, I'd wondered if I could live a life with Zak in it. He'd inflicted so much pain on me. He represented so many terrible memories. He caused me so much conflict and uncertainty.

But his presence in my life had shaped me. Knowing him had changed me. Being with him challenged me. We'd collided over and over again, and no one else in the world was so deeply connected to me.

"Together," I gasped as a deep, empty ache burned in my chest. "Or not at all."

I was almost out of energy. I'd given too much to Marzanna. My aura sphere would fail any second, and Izverg's power would overwhelm Zak's. His fingers dug into my arm.

A wintry chill hit my back. The rush of cold swept past us, and the bubbling slurry of decomposition frosted over, then froze solid. As a blanket of ice spread across the bog, my endurance ran out. My arm fell to my side, my chest heaving for air and dizziness spinning in my skull.

Footsteps crunched across the frosted ground. A white cloak appeared beside me, and I looked up.

Ríkr's eyes glowed faintly. Shining ice armor covered his shoulders and chest, but it hadn't protected him from all injuries. Blood stained his arms and had splattered his cloak, but he showed no sign of pain as he faced Izverg.

With softer footfalls, Lallakai halted beside Zak. Phantom wings arched off her back, and the Undying pattern shimmered on her skin. Shadows spiraled around her fingers. Zak hastily shoved to his feet, and I clambered up a second after him, my knees quivering with fatigue.

Izverg's blood-red eyes moved from Ríkr to Lallakai, then he raised his head, scanning the bog. The sounds of battle and magic continued, but they were growing distant.

"My loyal courtiers are driving yours away."

Marzanna's voice floated through the wintry quiet. I looked over my shoulder. Sitting astride Artear, as regal as any queen, she watched Izverg from a safe distance.

"Those malicious fools will soon perish." She was far enough away that her quiet, breathy tones shouldn't have been audible, but I heard her clearly. "As will you."

Marzanna, Izverg growled softly, delightedly. *How kind of you to return. I had feared you would die in your pathetic hole and I would be unable to devour you.*

"My power will never be yours, beast."

If you wait a few moments, I'll show you how wrong you are. His burning gaze swung to us. *It seems I have no more time to play.*

"What a coincidence." Lallakai's voice was a malevolent hiss. "Neither do I. My vengeance has waited too long already."

The shadows around her fingers solidified into two black swords identical to the one she'd gifted to Zak, and she launched at Izverg. He grinned, blood dripping from his severed arm.

She charged him with a furious scream, and he sidestepped one blade. The other cut deep into his shoulder—but he didn't react to the injury. He slashed with his claws, and she twirled in midair, evading the strike.

Wings flaring, she darted around him, blows flashing between them. With a crack, his fist caught her chest. He rammed her into the ground and his muzzle shot downward, tearing out her throat.

Lallakai's blood gushed across the frozen moss. Her limbs twitched and spasmed, her black blades dissolving.

Izverg straightened, licking his chops in satisfaction. *Disappointing, Lady of Shadow, after so many years of—*

Dark green light flared across the Undying pattern. The markings blazed, and her ruined throat glowed. She raised her hand, fingers pointed.

A bolt of black magic shot from her fingertips and tore through the center of Izverg's chest, just missing his heart. He staggered backward, growling. Lallakai lunged to her feet, breathing hard. The glow faded from her neck, revealing her unblemished throat.

"Your foul ambitions cost me my status, my reputation, and my dignity," she snarled. "I will have vengeance."

She flung her arms out, magic shooting for him—and Ríkr raised his hand. An azure circle flared under Izverg's feet. Ice cascaded over his lower legs, freezing them to the ground.

Izverg roared. Dark power exploded off him, dissolving Lallakai's shadow attack and crumbling Ríkr's ice.

"Druids," Ríkr murmured as a smooth, eight-foot-long ice spear formed in his hand. "Suppress his power once again."

It wasn't a request, and my exhaustion didn't matter. I stretched out my hand and Zak grasped it. Together, we unleashed our combined aura sphere, and as our energy suffused the frosted earth, Ríkr launched into the battle.

Shattering ice. Rippling shadows. Slashes of darkness and waves of death. The three fae tore into each other with merciless savagery. My chest ached, hollow weakness spreading through my torso, but I didn't relent.

Wings beating, Lallakai attacked Izverg's upper body, and darting on agile feet, Ríkr struck relentlessly at his lower body. Izverg's blood splattered the ground—but it wasn't enough. He roared, slashing with his remaining arm, death rolling off him in stronger waves.

Holding the aura sphere with everything I had, I summoned an ice spear into my hand—four feet long, shiny, and aerodynamic. "Zak."

I didn't need to say anything more. As Izverg whirled, throwing Lallakai off him and forcing Ríkr to leap clear of his claws, Zak thrust his sword out. A roiling cascade of shadow burst from the blade and blasted toward Izverg.

As it rushed at the beast, I hurled my spear with all my strength. Izverg turned at the last moment, caught off guard. The shadow attack hit him full in the chest—and as it blasted him, my spear pierced his belly and exploded into jagged shards.

Ríkr thrust out his hand. The starburst of ice from my spear flashed blue and exploded, ripping Izverg's torso open.

Plunging out of the sky with black swords in her hands, Lallakai rammed them both into Izverg's chest.

And this time, she didn't miss his heart.

His jaw gaped open, shock rippling over his canine face. She tore her blades out and dropped to the ground. He staggered, the bloody ice jutting from his torso. Blood dripped from his open mouth.

A quiet chuff. Another, louder. Slowly, with growing volume, Izverg began to laugh. Darkness swirled around him. It boiled across his wounds, dissolving the ice, and gathered at the stump of his elbow. It stretched into the shape of his missing forearm and hand, then turned from darkness to dripping, quivering black sludge. His makeshift hand flexed as rotting goo dribbled down his chest from his wounds.

He raised his head. His red eyes had paled to milky white.

Did you think death would stop me? His voice scraped painfully across my mind. *I am beyond death.*

Magic spilled off his oozing, animated corpse, and a dark cloud of death boiled out from him, spreading fast.

Ríkr retreated toward me. Lallakai copied him, her wings flaring as though she were about to take flight. I stumbled backward, reaching for Zak's arm.

My fingers brushed across his wrist, then he stepped away from me—*toward* Izverg.

He walked into the deathly miasma like it wasn't even there. Izverg's milky eyes watched the druid come, his lips peeled back to display his fangs. As Zak drew closer, the undead beast snarled. He wasn't laughing anymore.

Zak raised his arm. Something small dangled from his fingers—a talisman made from red and white yarn. The one he'd taken off Bane's door. The dark miasma boiled away from it, clearing the air around the druid.

"Do you know what this is, Izverg?"

Izverg recoiled. The talisman swayed gently.

"Bane had these everywhere to ward off Marzanna and Marzaniok. They didn't affect you—not until you consumed Marzaniok." He raised the talisman a little higher. "But this isn't just a ward."

He lifted his other hand, a scrap of paper between two fingers. A single rune had been drawn on it in black marker, and he slapped the talisman and the sigil together.

"*Igniaris.*"

A tongue of orange fire flared between his hands. He dropped the burning talisman, and as it fell, Izverg burst into flame.

28

IZVERG'S HIGH-PITCHED ROAR rang across the bog. Fire engulfed his body, and he clawed at his face and chest. The talisman fluttered to the ground, still burning. Bellowing, Izverg staggered toward a pool of foul water. He splashed into it and dropped to his knees, but the fire didn't extinguish. It burned under the water, steam rising in waves.

"My brother's greatest weakness." Marzanna's quiet voice sounded in my ear, and I started, surprised to find her standing only a few feet away. "And mine."

Izverg writhed in the pool of water, his cries weakening.

"What's happening to him?" I muttered.

"He used the power he stole from Marzaniok to cheat death." Zak studied his blistered hands. "Once he did that, he became vulnerable to the effigy of the undead."

An effigy … so that's what those talismans were. Effigies were common in certain traditions and folklore, but I hadn't known they could be used against fae—or that burning one was more than symbolic.

Izverg let out a final, desperate roar. Marzanna watched as the creature that had killed and eaten her twin brother collapsed to the ground, his blackened hands scrabbling at the mud. The flames flickered and shrank, and as the undead beast slumped lifelessly, the fire snuffed out.

Lallakai shot forward.

Rushing at Izverg, she plunged her sword into his charred back. Dark magic erupted in a violent whirlwind, sucking into her blade and rushing up her arm. His power raced into her, and she let her head fall back, spine arched and limbs stiff.

I gripped a handful of Ríkr's cloak, fury and fear twisting through me.

The surge of power trailed off, and Lallakai relaxed. Her black sword rippled as she pulled it from the corpse. Izverg's body had shrunk in on itself, desiccated and crumbling into black dust.

With a gloating smile, Lallakai turned. Her emerald eyes were a shade darker than before, and red specks glittered in their depths.

An arctic chill rolled off Ríkr. "You broke your promise, Lady of Shadow."

Her smile widened.

"Your word is worthless," he continued, his voice dangerously flat, "and the courtesies of barter no longer protect you."

She turned her wrist, rotating her blade and causing the early morning sun to sparkle across the Undying pattern on her arm. "I need no protection now, Lord of Winter. You think I would so easily give up Marzaniok's power? Or so easily let *you* claim it?"

"My brother's power should have been mine to hold," Marzanna whispered. Several members of her court hovered nearby, keeping close to their returned queen.

My grip on Ríkr's cloak tightened. Halfway between Lallakai and us, Zak stood very still, his stare locked on his mistress.

"You thought me naïve," Lallakai mocked, "but I knew you only gifted me The Undying for a chance at the King of Death's magic. And I knew that once you had it, you would kill me and reclaim the Undying gift."

Ríkr canted his head. "How very clever, Lady of Shadow. But are you so confident you can slay me before I wrest both the Undying gift and the King of Death's power from your corpse?"

Lallakai lowered her eyelids, watching Ríkr through her lashes. "Shall we call a truce, Lord of Winter?"

My breath hissed through my clenched teeth.

"You see," she added, "there is something else I have much desired to do."

She swung her sword away from Ríkr. The blade arced forty-five degrees until it was pointed at a spot a few feet to my right.

Directly at Marzanna.

The sword extended, as fast as a bolt from a crossbow, and slammed into Marzanna's chest. The piercing blade burst out of her back in a splatter of blood.

For a shocked heartbeat, no one reacted. Then the Shadow Court fae charged toward their queen with furious shouts, but darkness exploded off Lallakai in a spiral of shadow blades and death magic.

Clamping his arm around me, Ríkr leaped away, the world blurring with his speed.

"Zak!" I screamed, but I couldn't see him in the black maelstrom.

The courtiers reeled back, hurling magic at the impenetrable wall of darkness, but they were no match for Lallakai's, Izverg's, and Marzaniok's power combined into a single unstoppable force.

The maelstrom flared, then dispersed in a gust of stale wind. Lallakai reappeared, her face tilted toward the sky and arms spread as though embracing the morning sunlight. At her feet, a crumbling corpse turned to black dust, the rotting filth of the bog soaking into Marzanna's silk garments.

"Ah," Lallakai sighed. "I hadn't dared hope I would get to pay her back for turning against me."

She lowered her head, and when she faced me and Ríkr, I sucked in a breath. The whites of her eyes had darkened to murky gray, her deep emerald irises shimmering in contrast.

"Was that part of your plan too, Lord of Winter?" she asked coyly. "Absorb Marzaniok's power from Izverg, then double it with Marzanna's?"

The Undying markings on her arm had darkened too, the green tint gone. The Shadow Court fae watched her warily, but they didn't attack—and they wouldn't, not unless they wanted to die.

"And now, Arawn of Annwn ..." She sauntered toward us. "I will take what remains of your power."

Panic flared through my chest.

"Lallakai."

Zak walked across the soggy, rotting moss, his shoulder where Izverg had bitten him wet with blood. Slices and scratches marred his body. His potion belt was almost empty; he must've downed a cocktail of healing potions to stay on his feet with those injuries.

"This is your choice?" he rasped. "Power over everything else?"

Lallakai's terrifying eyes drifted across him. "That has always been my choice. Until recently, it was yours as well. We were of one mind."

"And I was miserable." His jaw tightened. "You promised you'd try to change."

"I did, and I am." Smiling sweetly, she spread her hands. "You can have everything you want *and* power, my druid."

"I don't want power on your terms. I don't want to live on your terms."

He turned, walking away from Lallakai and toward me and Ríkr. His green eyes met mine, his face haggard with pain, resignation, and an edge of fear.

My hand rose, reaching for him.

"Zakariya."

He stopped, my fingertips inches from his chest, and looked back.

Her stare bored into him. "How dare you walk away from me."

"We're done, Lallakai."

"I created you." Shadows flickered over her right hand. "I own you."

He stepped between me and Ríkr, then pivoted to face his fae mistress, his feet set. Trembling with dread and exhaustion, I gathered the last of my strength.

Lifting her arm, Lallakai curled her hand into a fist, shadows flickering over her skin. "I thought it might come to this."

She snapped her fingers open.

I expected a bolt of lethal shadows or a wave of unstoppable death. But with the sharp motion, the dark magic flickering over her fingers merely flared like a flame in a gust of wind.

Zak jolted like he'd been struck.

I spun to him. The ebony rune on the back of his right hand had appeared—and shadows spilled out of it. Lines of darkness raced up his arm like sickly veins, snaking along his neck and over the side of his face. The inky power bled across his wide eyes, turning them black.

As his shadow blade swirled out from his palm and solidified, his expression shifted from shock to a strange blankness. His fingers clenched around the hilt.

Then he slashed it across my stomach.

The cold edge cut through my sweater, grazing my skin— and Zak jerked backward, yanked away by Ríkr before the blade could tear my belly wide open.

Ríkr threw Zak aside, then lunged for me. He caught me around the middle, tossed me over his shoulder, and leaped into the air. Ice formed beneath him, taking the form of a huge serpent, and he landed on its head in a crouch. The serpent surged across the bog, its undulating body leaving a trail of jagged ice in its wake.

My mouth hung open, no air in my lungs. As we sped away, Zak stood eerily still, his black blade in his hand and dark magic veining his right arm. His black eyes stared after me, his face empty of emotion. With a graceful sway of her hips and a smile flitting over her full lips, Lallakai joined her consort as she watched us flee.

No, not Lallakai. That name no longer encompassed what she'd become.

She was the Queen of Shadow and Death, and no fae or druid could stand against her.

ABOUT THE AUTHOR

ANNETTE MARIE is the best-selling author of The Guild Codex, an expansive collection of interwoven urban fantasy series ranging from thrilling adventure to hilarious hijinks to heartrending romance. Her other works include YA urban fantasy series Steel & Stone, its prequel trilogy Spell Weaver, and romantic fantasy trilogy Red Winter.

Her first love is fantasy, but fast-paced adventures, bold heroines, and tantalizing forbidden romances are her guilty pleasures. She proudly admits she has a thing for dragons and aspires to include them in every book.

Annette lives in the frozen winter wasteland of Alberta, Canada (okay, it's not quite that bad) and shares her life with her husband and their furry minion of darkness—sorry, cat—Caesar. When not writing, she can be found elbow-deep in one art project or another while blissfully ignoring all adult responsibilities.

www.annettemarie.ca

SPECIAL THANKS

My thanks to Erich Merkel for sharing your exceptional expertise in Latin and Ancient Greek.

Any errors are mine.

THE
GUILD CODEX
UNVEILED

A vigilante witch with a murder conviction, a switchblade for a best friend, and a dangerous lack of restraint. A notorious druid mired in secrets, shadowed by deadly fae, and haunted by his past.

They might be exactly what the other needs—if they don't destroy each other first.

THE
GUILD CODEX
SPELLBOUND

Meet Tori. She's feisty. She's broke. She has a bit of an issue with running her mouth off. And she just landed a job at the local magic guild. Problem is, she's also 100% human. Oops.

Welcome to the Crow and Hammer.

THE GUILD CODEX
DEMONIZED

Robin Page: outcast sorceress, mythic history buff, unapologetic bookworm, and the last person you'd expect to command the rarest demon in the long history of summoning. Though she holds his leash, this demon can't be controlled.

But can he be tamed?

THE
GUILD CODEX
WARPED

The MPD has three roles: keep magic hidden, keep mythics under control, and don't screw up the first two.

Kit Morris is the wrong guy for the job on all counts—but for better or worse, this mind-warping psychic is the MPD's newest and most unlikely agent.

DISCOVER MORE BOOKS AT
www.guildcodex.ca

STEEL & STONE

When everyone wants you dead, good help is hard to find.

The first rule for an apprentice Consul is *don't trust daemons*. But when Piper is framed for the theft of the deadly Sahar Stone, she ends up with two troublesome daemons as her only allies: Lyre, a hotter-than-hell incubus who isn't as harmless as he seems, and Ash, a draconian mercenary with a seriously bad reputation. Trusting them might be her biggest mistake yet.

GET THE COMPLETE SERIES
www.annettemarie.ca/steelandstone

A destiny written by the gods. A fate forged by lies.

If Emi is sure of anything, it's that *kami*—the gods—are good, and *yokai*—the earth spirits—are evil. But when she saves the life of a fox shapeshifter, the truths of her world start to crumble. And the treachery of the gods runs deep.

This stunning trilogy features 30 full-page illustrations.

GET THE COMPLETE TRILOGY
www.annettemarie.ca/redwinter

CPSIA information can be obtained
at www.ICGtesting.com
Printed in the USA
LVHW111938180922
728695LV00002B/223